The Second Key of Kalijor

Paul Lell

The Second Key of Kalijor by: Paul Lell

© 2009 Paul Lell

Cover art by: David Magoun (Full Spectrum Arts & Services)

© 2009 David Magoun

Editing/Proofreading: Christina Lell, Paul Lell, Tiffany Tolar, David Magoun, and Ali Christensen

ISBN 978-0-578-03264-1

For more information,

 See the author's website at

www.kalijor.com

or the artist's website at

www.fullspectrumarts.com

Dedicated to anyone who has ever loved a great story. Without you, where would we be?

Special Thanks: To my wife, for her love and support, and my children for their daily inspiration. To my parents for their encouragement in following my dreams. To my friends for letting me test out my stories on them around the gaming table these past 25 years.

The warm afternoon air streamed through Riana's dark purple hair as she moved swiftly across the Plain of Serenity. Her hair had grown quite a bit in the months that she had been searching. It now fell nearly to her waist in a ragged pony tail, a contrast to the neat arrangement that used to hold her shoulder-length locks. Her long elven ears were perked up, listening for any signs of danger as her violet eyes scanned the horizon with an intense scrutiny. She quickly covered the distance to what she hoped would at last be her final destination.

Fine features reflected her time in the wilds of Kalijor, being wind lashed as she roamed from place to place searching, always searching. The soft black leather top and breechcloth, enchanted to ease friction against her newly tattooed skin so long ago, looked as if she had only purchased them yesterday. The mystical tattoos themselves had long since healed, ceasing to be a constant source of discomfort to her, although her skin was still slightly more sensitive than it used to be. In the months of her searching, many of the mystical markings that had previously been faded and dulled due to her lack of power and skill, had since come into sharp focus, reflecting her strengthening will and skills.

Xanthe sped along the grassy plain with a smooth, constant gait that far outstripped the pace of even the strongest horses in the realm. His sinewy, scaled body looked like shimmering white crystals flowing in the daylight as his four powerful legs propelled them along close to the ground. His long neck and tail swayed hypnotically as he moved, his long horns hugging his neck as they arced gracefully away from his serene dragon-like face.

Together they had been searching Kalijor for more than six months for any sign, any indication of where her sister had been taken. Katrina had gone to give Malice the crystal key in Kalijor, while Riana was to retrieve Solidarity Online's prototype processor from the mercenary, Gregory Shantal, at the same time on Mars Station. Both meetings had turned out to be traps. Riana had barely escaped from her exchange with her life, and had seen a vision of her sister being beat, nearly to death, by Malice in Rathalon. She was forced to watch helplessly as, after the beating, Katrina had been dragged into a magical portal and vanished. So Riana had dedicated herself to finding her sister, wherever she was, and freeing her of whatever bonds were keeping her in peril. In the meantime, her body remained in its game pod on the Tyconderoga, with IV's feeding her body essential nutrients and piezoelectric stimulators working to keep her idle muscles from deteriorating.

The search had begun in the Crossed Swords tavern in Rathalon, the unofficial capital city of Kalijor. Despite the fact that she had seen many of the patrons there in a vision, none of them had been forthcoming with any information. They all remembered the fight, but none of them had any idea where the pair had vanished to or how. They had simply disappeared into thin air.

Gornin, at the Cohai Observatory, had not been of much use either. The mysterious old troll had only said that there were many places in Kalijor that were beyond the reach of the gods. These places were accessible only to those who knew how to get to them, and almost anyone who knew such things, would never reveal their secrets. At least, not without some hefty persuasion.

Now she was trying to track down any tale of places so difficult to find and enter that no one knew anyone who had actually been there. It had been a daunting task when she first began six months ago, and was no less so now, although she had been able to put to rest several rumors. One such rumor had suggested that there was an old hollow tree in the vast Forest of Brume, and if one rapped on its gnarly outer surface in such a way, a portal would open to a secret dungeon beneath it. After researching every conceivable approach to the tree and combing through the forest for a month, following each set of instructions to the letter, she had never encountered such a hollow tree.

Another rumor suggested that there was a secret chamber beneath the Burning Expanse that could be accessed by the wielder of the enigmatic Master Sword. The Master Sword was a weapon of such beauty that it enchanted those that laid eyes on it, forcing them to stand and stare at its magnificence. Of course no one knew anything about how or where to acquire the sword. However, the records in the Magic Academy's extensive library seemed to support that the weapon existed, or at least had existed at some point in the past. That trail ran cold there though, with no leads as to where the sword might be.

Currently, she was chasing down a rumor about an ancient tower that sat in the middle of The Bramble. The story went that the defender of the tower could allow access to a secret chamber if he was bested in combat. This particular tale required a person to acquire the key to the tower from the leader of a tribe of goblins inhabiting The Bramble. So, she and Xanthe had ridden hard through the night, having left Rathalon at first light the day before. They had just sighted the edge of The Bramble, a tangled and gnarly forest with thin, spindly trees that seemed to grow in every direction but skyward. The entire forest, hundreds of acres in size, seemed more like a giant shrub or bush than an actual forest. Long since overrun by the strange, twisted trees that grew from nowhere with the speed and voracity of a bed of thistles, it had once been the site of a large human city.

Xanthe's powerful strides drew them toward the dark spot on the horizon. From her perch on his back, Riana spied a prone form on the ground ahead of them. It was small, faintly green, and partially hidden among the knee high grass. Drawing the great half-dragon to a halt, she slid off his back and patted him reassuringly on the neck as she cautiously stepped towards the body to investigate.

Tentatively, she prodded the diminutive form with her booted toe. When it failed to respond, she rolled it over onto its back so she could see it more clearly. The creature would have been about three feet tall had it been standing upright. The greenish tint to its skin faded into a pale yellow color on its stomach and the insides of its arms and legs. Its head was a little too large for its body and bore a long, crooked nose beneath sharp, protruding eyebrow ridges. Solid black eyes stared up at the sky lifelessly and its clawed hands still clutched at a short bow and a handful of arrows. Apparently it had never even managed to get one of the projectiles knocked before its life was cut short.

Four long, deep gashes across the creature's chest, running from its left shoulder down to its right hip were clearly the cause of the creature's demise.

"Goblin." Riana said aloud, causing Xanthe to look down at her curiously, blinking his large blue eyes. "Dead, and without much of a fight. Someone caught it completely by surprise."

Passing several more dead goblins as they continued toward The Bramble, Riana realized that they were not the only ones heading into the thicket. The only question she had was, were these 'others' going to be a problem for her?

As they drew even with the edge of the 'trees', they could hear the faint sounds of combat emanating from within the forest. The occasional clash of metal on metal and the high pitched squeals and grunts of goblins. Looking up and down the tree line, Riana could see no way for Xanthe to get into the forest with her, so she dismounted and patted him affectionately on the neck. "Looks like you'll have to stay here and cover our retreat friend."

Xanthe bowed his head in understanding and then pushed her towards the trees with his nose, urging her on. He seemed as anxious to find Katrina as Riana was.

Drawing Elkorine with her right hand, she examined the short sword as the light played off of its matte grey finish, the elven runes on its blade soaking up the light. A memory of that morning in the cellar of the Cohai Observatory as Gornin and Dorin had given her and Katrina the magical weapons played through her mind. Master Gornin had told her that the the magical sword had been a part of every major event in Kalijor's known history, and that it would serve her well for as long as she needed it. She felt a sudden pang of guilt for not being there with her sister in order to defend her against Malice. She had protested Xavier's chosen course at some great length, but in the end, he had forced the issue, and they had separated. Shaking the memories off with a shudder, she pressed into the thickly matted trees of The Bramble, heading toward the sounds of conflict.

The trees grew close together, at extreme and strange angles to one another, creating a thickly woven mass of branches and trunks that made it difficult to navigate. Pressing through the mass as quickly as she could, Riana felt the brambles scratching her skin and grabbing at her clothes. Catching her foot in a protruding root, she fell, bruising her knees and shins. By the time she got close enough to see what was causing the noise, she had scratches and bruises from head to toe thanks to her hasty journey through the impossible tangle.

In a large clearing, several crumbling buildings—the remains of the former human city—offered a dozen or so goblins an easy advantage over a single man. A full mane of blonde hair fell to the middle of his back and his thin, muscular frame was adorned with a simple brown leather belt supporting a breechcloth. A series of leather straps across his chest supported two empty scabbards on his back. He wore brown leather boots and plain metal bracers. Wielding a sword-staff similar to those of the Rathalon Defenders, although shorter, the man moved in a graceful dance around the circle of goblins. After watching him twirl the weapon this way and that, Riana realized that the goblins had no advantage here. Each time the weapon moved, at least one goblin fell to the ground, clutching its head, neck, or body in pain. She was considering helping him when a goblin with a bow in hand made its way to the top of a dilapidated building. Drawing a bead on the lone man his arm pulled back, ready to let fly a wicked looking hooked arrow. Without a second thought, Riana stepped into the clearing. With the briefest moment of concentration, one of the tattoos on her body glowed brightly in chorus with her violet eyes, and she threw her left hand forward. She pointed at the goblin archer and an arc of lightning leapt from her finger tips.

The goblin yelped in surprise and pain as the bolt of lightning struck, enveloping it in electricity. A moment later, it fell to the ground, a smoking heap. Some of the other goblins immediately broke off from their attack on the man and headed toward her with weapons drawn. Again, she concentrated and her eyes flashed. This time, with her fingers spread wide, a fan of electricity leapt from her to the onrushing goblins. Jumping back and forth from goblin to goblin, it lit up the clearing with flashing, blue light. Half a dozen of the goblins dropped lifelessly to the ground. From nowhere, more appeared to climb over the charred bodies.

In a flash, Riana summoned a freezing cold whirlwind. Surrounding her in a fury of driving ice and snow, the squall swirled around her briefly before abruptly blowing itself out. A protective layer of ice armor now covered her body. Without hesitation, she waded into the group of goblins swinging Elkorine. The magical sword cut the creatures down as easily as it would stalks of grass. The goblins' various assaults chipped at the magical armor as she made her way toward the blonde man. He continued his assault on the flood of goblins, seemingly taking no notice of her own battle on his behalf.

Before she saw it, she felt the strands of magical ether coalescing around one of the creatures. Turning to face the goblin shaman, she heard the last words of the spell and felt the forest floor came alive with roots and vines that wrapped themselves around her legs with the strength of a vise. Her eyes flashed again as she hurled a tongue of flame at the shaman. Enveloped in a ball of fire, the creature fell to the ground screaming in pain. It had managed to call out another incantation before it fell, however. A sphere of blue energy surrounded Riana, collapsed in on her, and caused the icy armor to crumble into frost at her entangled feet.

Goblins surrounded her as her protective enclosure dissipated. She eyed the advancing horde and knew she was in trouble. Her eyes flashed and a large fireball formed in her left hand. Throwing the ball of flame at her feet, her eyes flashed again. With a faint popping noise, she disappeared from her bondage, popping back into the clearing on the far side a second later. Staring in astonishment at the spot where Riana had been an instant before, the goblins confusion turned to determination. As they began to look around, the fireball exploded into a torrent of heat and light, engulfing everything within twenty feet of where she had been rooted to the ground. Wails of shock and pain echoed from the giant fireball before it receded into nothingness, leaving only blackened ground and desiccated goblin bodies.

"Nice moves." The soothing tenor voice rolled across her sensitive ears, causing them to perk up.

Turning to find the source of the voice, Riana saw the blonde man standing a dozen feet away holding his sword-staff in one hand and grinning mischievously at her. His deep cobalt eyes twinkled as he looked at her.

"You have some experience fighting goblins?"

She blushed a bit. "Never such large groups of them…" As she realized he could see more or less her entire body, she blushed crimson from head to toe, suddenly more self conscious than she had ever been before. Trying to look anywhere else in the large clearing, but somehow always coming back to his deep blue eyes, she knew he was sizing her up.

He grinned again. A show of playful exuberance revealed his white teeth that may have been just a little bit too sharp.

Reflexively, Riana's eyes rolled over his athletic body. Well toned and muscular, but not overly so, he was thin for an average human, and tall. Clean shaven, there were a series of thin braids running through his mane of blonde hair which was secured into a loose pony tail behind his neck. She wasn't sure, but she thought she could detect hints of slightly darker spots in his hair.

The man grinned again at her roving eyes, causing her to blush a deeper red. "Well you handled yourself admir…"

He stopped short. A faint sound, the sound of a sinew bow string being drawn, nearly escaped Riana's sharp elven hearing. Spinning around to find the source of the sound, she saw the miniscule goblin archer just as he loosed his arrow. Her eyes flashed and a bolt of lightning leapt from her fingertips, singeing the arrow as it sailed directly toward her head, but not stopping it. A flash of panic flowed through her as she watched the arrow. She didn't have time to take another shot. *Not like this, not now. I still haven't found my sister.*' She thought as the whole world slowed down to a crawl.

Entering her line of vision, moving faster than the arrow by a good margin, the man's hand plucked the arrow out of the air while the tip was mere inches from her forehead.

He handed her the arrow and took a small metal object from his belt. In a flash of speed and a blur of motion, he spun around and flung the small metal blade, striking the confused goblin archer between the eyes and knocking him bodily from his perch.

Turning back to Riana, still standing inches apart, he grinned broadly. "So. Come here often?"

Riana turned away from him as her skin flushed and unfamiliar feelings rushed through her body, pretending to check the clearing for any more signs of trouble. "I... um..."

"First time uh?" She felt as much as heard him move away. Stealing a glance over her shoulder, she saw him prodding a charred goblin with his right foot curiously.

"Yeah." She managed a whole word somehow this time.

"Are you here for a particular reason? Or just for the company?" His tone was light, as if everything going on were a mere game.

Riana looked down at the arrow still clutched tightly in her hand and snapped its wooden shaft, tossing the splintered pieces to the ground at her feet. "Definitely not for the company."

"I thought not." His soothing voice slid over her like silk, but now it was coming from in front of her. Looking up, she saw that he was now poking and prodding though some of the fallen goblins packs and pouches looking for valuables.

"How did you...?" Riana looked over her shoulder at where he had been a moment before.

"How did I what?" He looked up at her. "Get over here so quickly?"

"Uh..." Riana looked down at the ground. "Not that I am ungrateful or anything, I just... have never seen anyone move so quickly before. Not without a spell of some kind." She hadn't felt the build-up of magic energy that normally preceded the casting of a spell.

"I get that a lot." He stopped his rummaging for a moment, a thoughtful look on his face as he considered her words. Finally, he grinned again. Cobalt eyes sparkled in the motley forest light as he said half-jokingly "I'm part cheetah."

Riana gaped at him for a moment, then grinned. "My name is Riana. I'm looking for the Goblin Chieftain. He supposedly has a key…"

"To the tower on the southern edge of The Bramble. Yeah, me too." He stood up and ambled back toward her. Shifting his sword-staff to his left hand, he came to a stop in front of her. Confidently, he offered his right hand to her in greeting, "My name is Jumah. Jumah Wataru."

Riana sheathed Elkorine and then took the proffered hand. "It's nice to meet you m'lord. Thank you for the assistance."

"You're very welcome Riana. And please, call me Jumah. I am no lord."

She flushed again but launched back into the conversation, hoping he wouldn't see. "So, what are you seeking in the tower, Jumah?"

He looked at her for a moment. It was as though he was looking right into her mind and soul searching for something. His light-hearted demeanor renewed itself as he released her hand, looking back toward the dead goblins. "Nothing really. I've just never been there before."

She gaped at him, trying to figure out what this man was thinking. "You mean to tell me, you are single handedly moving through this tribe of goblins, to get the key from their chieftain in order to enter a heavily defended, likely trap ridden tower simply because you have never been there before?"

"That pretty much sums it up, yeah."

"I think you may be totally deranged."

"I've been called much worse."

"Oddly enough, I believe you." Now she was grinning from ear to ear herself.

"That's the spirit. So, you want some company?"

"I told you I didn't come here for the company." Riana chided him playfully.

"Oh. Right. Well then let's just say that we are moving in the same direction at the same time through happenstance." Jumah took his weapon in both hands and twisted the handle in the middle. It pulled cleanly apart into two separate swords which he then slid home in the crossed sheaths on his back. Bowing low before her, he swept his arms to the side indicating which direction they were headed.

Riana shook her head with a quirky grin on her lips and headed off in the indicated direction, her new companion moving up beside her as they made their way toward where the goblin chieftain's hut was rumored to be.

-2-

Riana ducked to the side as the wild boar leapt past her. One of its wicked tusks gouged her upper arm as it passed. Gritting her teeth against the pain, her eyes flashed bright violet as she countered the noxious cloud of vapor spewing forth from the goblin chief's fingers.

Thinking that this would be as easy as the other goblins had proved to be, turned out to be a foolish mistake. There was a very good reason this fellow was their leader. The creature was tall for a goblin, somewhere around five feet, but looked exactly like his brethren in all other respects. The same long, pointy nose and protruding eyebrows, gaunt, angular features, and cold black eyes made up his visage. He turned out to be an accomplished mage, conjuring up wild boars and lightning bolts as soon as he had seen the pair approaching.

It had also turned out that Jumah was quite adept at dealing with magical attacks. His weapon seemed to absorb most of the attacks and his speed allowed him to block even lightning bolts with it.

Averting her gaze when he flashed a winning smile while dodging a fireball without looking, the rustling of leaves and branches drew her attention. The return of the conjured boar reminded her that she had to deal with it herself, while Jumah was keeping the goblin occupied. Her ears splayed out and she focused on the sounds behind her. Keying in on the animal's snorting, ragged breath as it charged her, she waited until she heard its feet leave the ground as it leapt, then cast a stop-time spell.

The world around her turned grey and bleak, everything in it frozen in place. An eerie silence caved in on her ears like an explosion in the sudden absence of the sounds of battle. She pivoted on her heel, spinning around to face the boar. The creature was suspended mid air with a foul look in its eyes. Positioning herself to one side, she placed her hand on Elkorine's handle and prepared to draw the weapon knowing that she would get only one chance.

She pulled in a deep breath of bestilled air and glanced toward Jumah just as she pulled the magical weapon from its sheath.

'What the...?' She thought to herself as the world suddenly sprang into full motion again. A cacophony of sounds smashed in on her sensitive ears like a tsunami breaking over a high cliff. Her focus snapped forward just in time to complete the graceful arc of her short sword as it swung out of its scabbard upward toward the startled looking boar. The boar ricocheted off Riana, knocking her to the ground. In a flash of electrical light the boar's lifeless body collided full force with the chief's head, stunning him. Jumah took the opportunity to land a killing blow with his swift blades.

Rolling to a sitting position Riana scanned the clearing to make sure they were safe. *That's not possible… time was frozen. He couldn't have…'* She replayed the scene in her mind once more and she was sure of it. Just as she had glanced in his direction… *'He winked at me!'*

-3-

"Well, if you say I did, then I must have. But, I thought it was impossible." Jumah said with a shining smile.

Riana pushed a branch out of her way as she stepped over a gnarly tangle of roots and sighed. "It IS impossible. That spell slows time in the immediate area down to a fraction of its normal pace. I mean the only way someone could possibly still move is if they were somehow immune…"

"Which I assure you I am not."

"…or…" she tossed him a sidelong glance, then winced in pain as a protruding branch dug into the freshly dressed wound on her shoulder.

"Or…" Jumah prompted her, after she had taken a few deep breaths to stem the pain.

"Or…" She continued, "If the person in question could move so fast that they could get to that state under their own power."

Jumah contemplated this comment for a moment as he bent a particularly thick branch out of the way and held it for her as she passed. "You mean the person in question would have to be able to move so fast that they could slow down time around them?"

"Not slow down time per se, just move so fast that it would appear to everyone else that they had simply vanished, or teleported."

"Wow. That sounds pretty fast. I don't think I can move quite that quickly, personally." His tenor voice called out from behind her as they forged on into the forest.

"I don't see how you could. I mean there's only one species…" Riana now held a branch back for Jumah. As he passed in front of her, she confirmed that his long golden locks had the faintest dark splotches speckled throughout.

"Thank you m'lady." He flashed her another grin as he ducked under the branch and moved ahead to the next obstacle. "So, what species is this that could move that fast?"

Riana shook her head, trying to clear her thoughts. "Were-Cheetah." She watched his face for a reaction before continuing. "But no one has seen any of their kind in decades, possibly a century or more. Most of the were-creatures were hunted to extinction after the great wars. Nobody trusted them to not spread their lycanthropy like a plague."

"I see." Jumah's voice was a bit less jovial as he held back a series of branches for her to get past. "So what do you think?"

"About what?" She turned to look at him and walked sidelong into a thick branch. Her foot caught in a clump of roots and she knew she was going to break something in the fall as she keeled over. Closing her eyes and clenching her jaw in preparation for the pain, she gasped as strong arms wrapped around her, stopping her mid-fall.

Opening her eyes tentatively and looking up she was met by Jumah's crystal clear blue eyes and his mischievous grin. "About these supposedly plague-bearing were-beasts." He used his free hand to delicately chase a few locks of hair out of her eyes.

Her skin turned hot and a deep blush suffused her cheeks. Finally she managed to turn her head away from his gaze. His hand pressed against her side and she was suddenly aware of the strength behind those fingers. His fingers were rough, but gentle as he helped her stand up.

She turned her back to him for a moment, pretending to adjust her belt and pouches as she tried to force her body back under her control.

Jumah watched as she shuffled and adjusted, patiently waiting and leaning against the tree he had rescued her from. When she turned back to face him, he stared into her deep, violet eyes.

Forcing herself to look at his chin or his shoulder, anywhere but those pools of crystal blue that heated her skin and made her heart thump in her chest like a goblin war drum. "Well, canine lycanthropes were the ones able to transfer their condition via bites, but the feline lycanthropes could only pass their abilities to their offspring. Or so I've read." She adjusted her sword awkwardly.

"I see." Jumah said as he stood up and pushed a series of branches aside, holding them for her.

She nodded a thank you as she passed him, trying not to think about his muscular body sliding past hers.

Taking a few strides, he was again in front of her, his hand reaching out toward the next thicket of branches. As he reached out to grab the branches, he paused just as her hand snatched his wrist. Turning to look at her with raised eyebrows, he saw her staring at his chest with a blank expression and her long elven ears perked up and splayed out in concentrated effort. "You hear it too?" He whispered to her.

"More goblins. Just there." She whispered back in a barely audible voice and pointed through the branches he was about to move, reluctantly releasing his arm in the process.

Quietly, they both crept forward and peeled away some of the smaller branches and leaves. Peering through them, they saw what they were up against.

A large clearing with a dilapidated stone tower standing in the center was just beyond their hiding place. The tower looked to be about five stories high with a disintegrating tile roof, no visible windows, and a single door around which huddled a mass of goblins. The creatures mulled about nervously as though they expected to be set upon at any moment by a monster.

"That must be our tower then." Jumah whispered.

"You think?" Riana whispered back with a grin on her face. "What gave it away? I mean, aside from the horde of goblins at the door?"

"Obviously it's the state of the thing. I mean, look at those roof tiles. I haven't seen craftsmanship of that quality in years." He grinned back at her.

With some effort Riana stifled a laugh. Forcing herself back to the matter at hand, she took stock of the situation. It was getting late in the day, with darkness due any moment. There were twenty goblins guarding the single door to the tower, and they stood in the center of a clearing that would guarantee anyone approaching the tower would be seen, unless...

"How much do you like me?" She hissed at Jumah who responded by sitting up so quickly that he hit his head on a branch and then was slapped in the face by the twigs he had let go of in surprise at the bluntness of the question.

"M'lady I... I'm sure you... ah..."

She turned and looked at him with an amused smile on her face. *'At least it's not just me.'*

She leaned in close to him and brought up her left forearm, pointing to a glyph there she explained, "I don't know an invisibility enchantment strong enough for multiple people yet. But the one I do know will affect myself and whatever is in my very immediate vicinity."

"Ah. How immediate are we talking about here?"

She grinned at him. For the first time since she had met him that morning she realized that this man was not imperturbable. "Physical contact close."

"You don't mean just holding hands, right?" His eyes darted from left to right as though he was half expecting her parents to break in on them.

She took the opportunity to play with him a bit, taking advantage of his apparent gentlemanly nature. Offering him a wry smile that he instantly took to daydreaming about. "I think we may have to get rather more… intimate, than that." She pressed on, relishing the rosy color of his cheeks. "Unless you want to fight the lot of them?" She jerked her thumb over her shoulder toward the clearing and the goblins therein by way of explanation.

"Not especially, no."

"Nor do I." She stated flatly. "So."

He looked around for a moment.

"Ok then. How about this? You invis yourself and head over there with the key. You open the door and I'll meet you inside. Just hold it open for a second before you close it."

Riana looked at him with a look of amusement on her face. "You're going to run from here to there in a second? And without alarming the goblins?" She raised her eyebrows skeptically at him.

"Yes. I am going to run that distance in a second, and no I won't alert the goblins. You'll already have done that."

"I'll already have done that… Why exactly?"

"Do you think they won't see the door opening by itself?" He smirked at her.

"Oh. I hadn't thought of that." She chided herself inwardly.

"Don't worry about it. This way, my movement will distract them from the door and we'll have a better chance of locking it behind us without a bunch of them spilling in first."

"Are you sure about this? If we do it my way it ensures we'll both get there at once."

"Because,"he paused, "we'll have to disentangle from one another before we can deal with the goblins. I think this will work better."

Suddenly the sky darkened. In a matter of seconds it transitioned from daylight to night, much like somebody turning down a dimmer switch on an electric light.

Jumah pointed toward the clearing and said, "Go now. While their eyes are adjusting to the darkness."

"Alright, but I want it noted that I think this is a bad idea." Riana whispered as her eyes glowed and then vanished from sight along with the rest of her.

A moment later, she pushed her way slowly through the foliage with a soft rustling sound and then quietly padded toward the ominous door at the base of the tower.

Holding the handle of Elkorine, to keep it from swinging on her belt and touching a goblin, or making some unexpected noise. Riana picked her way through the goblin guard detail, clenching Elkorine tightly in case something unexpected happened and she needed to defend herself. Moving as quickly as she dared, more than once she ended up face to face with one of the little green creatures. Eventually she reached the tower and squeezed herself behind a particularly burly looking, armor clad, goblin warrior, bearing a large—for him—axe. She gently slotted the old skeleton key into the door's lock and slid it home.

The key bottomed out in the lock and clanked against the back plate ever so slightly. Riana held her breath as the goblin perked its ears up and began to look around. After a moment it settled down again and Riana slowly let out her breath and drew in another deep draught of fresh air. Glancing briefly over her shoulder to where she knew Jumah should be watching from, she nodded in his direction, forgetting that she was invisible. Looking back to the door, she placed a hand on its rough surface and paused for an instant to prepare.

'Here we go. This is where we both get shot up by goblin archers.' With all the courage and speed she could muster, she twisted the key in the lock cringing when it echoed with a loud clanking noise. Wrenching the key back out of the lock, she pushed. The door swung in on its hinges and groaned so loud that she thought it must have alerted the Obscuri in their caves halfway across Kalijor.

She felt the activity before she heard it. The goblins realizing that someone was opening the door behind them. The slow and painful process that went in to that epiphany was almost comical, while their reaction was anything but. A sudden tidal wave of noise came up behind her as the goblins began yelling and screaming, raising their weapons in anger and foul intent.

Riana was already pushing the door aside with her body, pivoting around its open edge and bracing her shoulder against the inside of the wooden barrier, preparing to push it closed again. The goblins' confusion focused on the open space and the empty doorway. Several crooked arrows embedded themselves in the door near her head and she looked up to see the armor-clad axe-wielding goblin swinging his weapon in a wide arc in a blind attempt at the blood of the intruder.

She smiled at the goblin as an arc of lightning issued forth from her right hand, dispelling her invisibility enchantment. Before they could do much more than register her sudden appearance, the blast of electricity arced back and forth through the assembled mass of goblins, scaring some, stunning others, and outright killing a few.

'He's had his second and I need to get through this, with or without him.' She thought as she pushed with her legs, driving the wooden door closed with all her strength. The heavy door closed against the stone with a resounding thud. Jamming the rusty key into the lock on the inside, she twisted it home with a reassuring clank.

"Well that was fun!"

Riana jumped at the sound, whirling around to put her back to the door and her hand on her sword. "What the?!"

"Calm down m'lady. It's just me." Jumah smiled reassuringly at her in the wan light of the tower's interior.

"How did you... I mean, I just... And you weren't..."

His smile turned to a knowing, mischievous grin. "It's a trade secret. I could tell you but…"

"But what? You'd have to kill me?" She looked at him sarcastically.

"No. I just think it's more fun to make you keep guessing."

Riana stared at the blonde man with a look somewhere between amazement and incredulity. She had no idea why she liked him. He was arrogant and over-confident. He behaved like a child playing a game, and yet he was still somehow serious enough to make it seem as though he was here for all the right reasons. He smiled at her impishly as she stared at him.

"Look…" She said, releasing her grip on her sword's handle and moving to examine the small, dark, stone room they found themselves in.

"Is this where you tell me you don't like handsome, capable, eligible bachelors?" His grin widened. "Would it change things if I told you I cook too?"

She turned her violet eyes back toward him and gave him a look that instantly withered his mood. His back straightened and his muscles tensed. He was ready for instant action and the levity was gone.

"I am looking for my sister. She was beaten nearly to death and then dragged away by a man named Malice. I don't know where he has taken her, but I have been able to find out that it is a place where GM's cannot see, or go."

Jumah nodded solemnly, taking this new information in stride, he did not appear in any way surprised by what she had said. "How long has she been stuck in the system?"

It was a month ago in real time, when events had transpired that had separated the pair in order to make the exchange. The Mercenary, Gregory Shantal was to meet Riana on Mars Station and give her a prototype processor. At the same time, a meeting had been set up in Kalijor between Katrina and Malice, another mercenary. He was supposed to take a magical key from her, in exchange for the processor.

Riana had fought tooth and nail against the plan. She had a horrible feeling that something was going to go very wrong, but in the end Xavier had forced his will and they had separated. She remembered vividly the last conversation she and Willhelmina had shared before events turned against them.

"This isn't right Kat. He shouldn't be doing this to us."

"Calm down Ree. He knows what he's doing." Willhelmina's voice soothed over the comm. Her mouth was smiling, but her eyes betrayed her concern.

"Keep yourself safe Kat. I've got a bad feeling about this."

"I know Ree. It'll be OK though. Just remember what we've been through. No matter what happens, we'll always be there for one another."

The comm had gone silent with an ominous click that added a note of finality to the conversation Riana could never remember having heard before. Things had only gotten worse from there.

Her feeling had turned out to be dead on. When she arrived at her meeting with Gregory Shantal, she found herself surrounded by a dozen armed mercenaries. Her conversation with Gregory had been enraging and right in the middle of it, she was touched with an extremely realistic vision of Katrina being beaten nearly to death in the fighting pit in the Crossed Swords tavern of Rathalon. It seemed that she had been given a fake artifact to offer the mercenary, and he was not taking the offense well. Despite all her efforts to intervene, she could not help as she watched her sister's bloody body dragged through a magic portal before snapping back to the hangar full of armed soldiers.

The fight hadn't gone in her favor. She had let her anger cloud her judgement, and she had severely underestimated Gregory Shantal's capabilities. She'd lost one of her hands, and the other had been crushed. Barely escaping with her life, the processor had been left behind and her trip back to their shuttle, *The Kestrel*, had been made in a dream-like state. The trip from Mars back to *Tyconderoga* was the longest two days of her life, and she had arrived to receive the verbal beating of her life from Xavier.

He had chided her not only for the loss of the processor prototype, but also her hand, which he claimed was a very expensive piece of cybernetic technology.

She had endured his berating and bit back with a few words of her own, especially when she learned that Willhelmina had fallen into a catatonic state. It seemed that when her avatar, Katrina, was hauled through that portal in Kalijor, her mind had been taken to some unknown corner of the game server where the GM's and technicians could not find her. Riana had asked them to just disconnect her, but they had explained that to do so would be to permanently disconnect her body from her mind, which would result in her death, in both worlds.

Xavier maintained that his people would be able to locate her and get her out of the system, but weeks had gone by with no sign of progress, so Riana had determined to go in and get her sister personally. The image of her friend and sister, plugged in to her egg-like game pod, with the Encephalographic Induction Harness on her head and a bevy of nutrient lines and electrical muscle stimulators attached to her body burned into her mind as she plugged the ODN cable into the port in her wrist.

And now, here she was with a mysterious man in a stone tower. How long had Katrina been gone?

-5-

Riana's eyes misted over with tears as she thought about it. Looking at the man standing across from her, and his willingness to take this all in stride made her heart ache for Katrina. Only she had been more accepting of the strange things in her life.

"Nearly six months. Game Time." She looked at the floor as she spoke.

"Six months?! Who is this Malice person?" His eyes smoldered as he spoke. His voice was carefully controlled, but he could not hide the fact that he was angry.

"All I know about him is that he has some dealings with my employer, Xavier Quinn, and that he is either working with or for a mercenary named Gregory Shantal." Tears flowed freely now, something that could not occur with her cybernetic body in the real world. It seemed as though crying was all she could do whenever she took a break from her search.

"Have they made any demands? What do they want?"

"I can't say exactly. It's an artifact." She drew in a ragged breath. "Xavier isn't going to give in to them. Ever. So I am left to try and find her myself."

"I see. Well, you aren't working by yourself anymore."

She looked up at him and his gaze had turned to tempered steel. She could see that he had no intention of letting her go on alone, nor was he about to do anything foolish to cause her to fail in her search.

"I just wanted you to know why I am here. How important this is to me." She stared into his eyes, her ears pointing straight back as she pleaded with him through her gaze. Pleaded with him to not turn away, for some other soul to support her after months of searching alone.

"You're going to have a hell of a time getting rid of me. Now, what is it you hope to find in this tower?" He turned away from her to start examining their surroundings, while she wiped at the tears on her cheeks.

"Master Gornin told me that there are places that only people who know how can enter." She quickly recounted Master Gornin's information regarding her search. That GM's can't go there unless they know how. "Since we can't scan Kalijor for her presence from the server room, Katrina has to be sequestered away in such a place. My inquiries have led me to believe that one entrance to such a place is here in this tower."

"Alright. Do you know where to start looking?" He had made a complete circuit of the small room and was looking at her again.

"I'm not even sure it's here. It's just the best lead I have and it's been so long since I've seen her…" She looked away from his face, trying to hide the welling tears.

"Riana. Listen to me. We'll find her. We'll do whatever it takes. You are not alone anymore." He gently touched her cheek with his hand and pulled her around to look into her eyes again. "We'll find her."

She sprung forward and embraced him, sobbing into his chest. "I don't even know you. Thank you."

He let her cry for a few minutes before breaking the embrace and holding her by her shoulders. "Don't worry about it. Right now we need to try and figure out this tower." At that he released her, turning to the only other door in the room.

Gently he set his hand on the black iron of the knob. Jerking his hand back he exhaled sharply. "Wow!"

"What is it?!" Riana jumped at his reaction.

"It's hot. Stand away from the door while I open it." He used one arm to herd her behind him as he reached out and grabbed the knob again. With a quick twist and tug he flung the door open flooding the room with a bright orange glow. A wave of heat rolled into the room, washing over them.

When nothing else came through, the pair peeked around the door into the next room. Riana's mouth came open. "Oh my…"

"That pretty much sums it up." Jumah added, his own eyes wide with amazement.

The next chamber was very large, easily several hundred feet square with narrow walkways on their side and the opposite wall. In the center of the room, a river of molten lava streamed in from one wall and out the opposite with a low rumble. Spanning the river directly ahead of them, from one walk way to the opposite, was a wide stone bridge that looked as though it was ready to collapse under its own weight at any moment.

"Where the hell does a river of lava come from on the ground floor of a building in the middle of a forest?!" She blurted out.

"Hey. This is a video game. No one ever said it had to make sense. The danger is real enough." His smirk was back for a moment but turned serious as he rounded the door and stepped tentatively into the chamber.

Riana followed him through, nearly falling over when her first breath inside the chamber scorched her lungs. She gasped and wheezed, clutching Jumah's arm as her body violently rejected the stifling, igneous air.

"Take smaller breaths. Use your nose."

Following his advice, she found that while her nasal passages felt as if they were on fire, she was able to get some useable air into her lungs.

"I guess we use that other door." He pointed to a wooden door on the far side of the bridge. Slowly, he moved to take a step onto the bridge.

As he was about to set his foot on the stone walkway, Riana let out a yelp and pulled him bodily backwards causing him to nearly lose his balance. "Wait!"

"What?!" He spun around, hands instantly on the handles of his swords, ready for action.

Riana held her hands at waist level, eyes turned toward the ceiling. She cast a quick look in front of them before rolling her head and eyes upward again.

"That bridge isn't real. It's an illusion." She said as she slowly turned and again cast her eyes down to look out over the lava. Tears formed at the corners of her eyes as she squinted and thrust her head back up. All the while her hands seemed to be shielding her from something below.

"How do you know?"

"Because I can't see it."

"Of course you can't see it, you're staring at the ceiling." Jumah pointed at the decaying stone archway. "It's right there."

"I know it looks like that, but it isn't there." Tears were now rolling slowly down her cheeks as she repeated the movements, drying up in the oppressive heat before they reached her jaw. "There. The bridge is over there." She indicated the right side of the room with her chin, still shielding her eyes from the glow of the lava below.

"How can you tell?"

"I can see heat. And the bridge in front of us is not deflecting any of the heat coming off this lava. Over there is a thin arch that is."

"You're looking at the heat in the room? Isn't that a bit uncomfortable?"

"Exceedingly. So I would appreciate if we got out of here as quickly as possible." She said closing her eyes tightly for a moment.

Moving slowly down the narrow path to the end of the room, they stopped a dozen paces from the wall. Turning to face the lava, Riana gingerly raised her foot and extended it out over the lava. She cast her eyes down to her moving foot and, nearly closing her eyes again, prepared to set it onto the darkened spot in her vision.

"Riana. There is nothing there. Are you sure about this?" Jumah had his hand on her shoulder, ready to snatch her back.

"Yes. I'm sure. This is the way." Carefully she set her foot down. Picking up her other foot, she planted it in front of the first.

"Interesting." Jumah said, raising an eyebrow.

"Follow me closely. It isn't very wide." She said as she began making her way slowly across the invisible bridge.

By the time they made it to the other side, Riana's eyes were red and burning. A stabbing pain throughout the front of her head competed with the pain in her shoulder where Jumah had been squeezing while they navigated the invisible bridge. Finally, the door was behind them and the overwhelming heat of the lava closed off again.

"That was an adventure." Jumah quipped with a small grin on his lips.

"Oh. I think your adventure is just getting started here." Riana said with a level voice.

"What makes you say that?" He looked over at her to find that she was staring at the wall with a blank look on her face and instantly he knew the answer. "Riana!" In a flash he was encircling her with his arms, squeezing her to him. "Oh Riana…"

"It may not be permanent. I may be able to see again after I get some rest…" She wanted desperately to cry, but the tears would not come to her sightless eyes.

-6-

"How did you know to use your heat vision?" Jumah asked as he gently wrapped Riana's head with a bandage he had retrieved from her pouch of supplies.

"There was a glyph on the ceiling. It was Draconian for 'look through the heat.' So I figured it was sort of a double meaning."

"Clever, if stupid." He finished as he tied off the dressing carefully.

"Well, it kept you from going head first into a river of molten lava." She chided him.

"I suppose so…" His voice trailed off as he looked at her now covered eyes. "Riana, there's something I need to tell you, about me. I'm…" He cut himself off abruptly, unable to tell her.

"Jumah, save it. Whatever it is makes no difference. All I need to know is that you are genuinely interested in helping me find my sister." She groped through the air with her hand until she found his arm, then squeezed it reassuringly.

Jumah sighed heavily as he clasped her hand in his own. "You have my word on that. I won't leave you until we find her."

"Thank you Jumah. Now, where are we?" He helped her to her feet as she spoke.

"We're in a small room." He looked around as he described it. "It's similar to the entryway. Opposite the door is an archway and a set of stairs going up."

"Sounds like we are heading up." She said, hoping her voice sounded more confident than she felt.

Slowly, Jumah led her up the stairs. Letting her feel the outer wall of the spiral steps, she had to get her footing each time they ascended a stair.

At last they arrived at a landing, steadying her uncertain feet. Her sharp elven hearing picked up a small gasp from Jumah's lips.

"What is it?" She asked him in a worried tone.

"Doors." He said simply.

"Doors?" She repeated.

"Yes. Doors. We are in the middle of a hallway. It dead-ends in both directions. The entire wall opposite us is covered with doors of various types and styles. Some metal, some wood, some solid, some more like gates."

"Is there anything else?"

"There is a gate in front of us, and through it I can see a similar hallway, with more doors lining the opposite wall."

"Are there any symbols or markings anywhere? On the ceiling? Or the floor?"

"Just a moment." He responded, taking her hand and moving a little to inspect the walls and floor more thoroughly without letting go.

"Ok, the hall is maybe three paces wide, cleanly hewn stone, and well lit by a series of torches that are fitted into plain holes on the walls. On the floor in front of us is a circle with an arrow in it, pointing to the left. I don't see anything else that looks like it might be of use."

"Just a circle with an arrow in it? Pointing to the left?" Riana repeated.

"Correct. You think I should try one of these doors?"

"It seems likely that all but one would be trapped in some way." Riana sat down on the stone floor and disengaged herself from Jumah. Feeling around on the floor until her hands found the described circle, she then ran her fingers around the carving, feeling every inch of it, tracing its circumference multiple times.

"Jumah?"

"Yes?"

"How many doors are there?"

Suddenly, Riana's hair whirled around her head as a small gust of wind swirled around her. "Nine doors. Looks like nine in the next hallway as well although I don't have a clear view of the entire corridor."

"Nine doors… Circle… Left… Circle to the left… But it's a straight hallway…" Riana began speaking under her breath, trying to work out the puzzle.

"Jumah?" She said after a moment, her arms spreading out and feeling through open air to find her friend.

Instantly Jumah had her hand in his, kneeling by her side, "Yes?"

"Is there anything else? Anything that looks significant?"

"Nothing that I can see. Aside from the different types of construction, the doors all look plain."

With a sigh she dropped her hands back to the circle inscribed on the floor. After a moment of tracing her fingers around the image her ears perked up in excitement. "Jumah, this arrow doesn't fill the circle, it feels like it starts in the center?"

Jumah moved a bit to get a better view of the inscription around Riana's form. "Yes, it begins in the center, then extends to the left edge."

"Is it the center of the circle? Or just close to the center?"

Jumah paused for a moment then drew a short knife from his belt and used its blade to measure the length of the arrow and compare it to the opposite side of the circle. "It seems to be the center of the circle. Why?"

"It's the rest of the clue! Pi!" Riana exclaimed, silently thanking the Magic Academy for the years of studying math and science in addition to spell casting and theory. She remembered at one point she had even gone so far as to call all of those studies useless. Ha!

"Pi?"

"Yes Pi! It's a value that can be used to describe the geometric properties of a circle by using its radius."

"Ok. How does that figure in here?" Jumah sounded less than convinced.

"Look, the radius of a circle is the distance from its center to its edge. Just like our arrow here. The fact that it is an arrow pointing to the left may indicate our starting point."

"Starting point for what?

"Look, the value of Pi is roughly 3.1415957, and since there are only nine doors to choose from and they are all whole, we can assume that we use the whole value, so the third door from the left is the one we want."

There was a long silence before Jumah finally replied. "That seems like a pretty large assumption Riana. Are you sure you want to bet your sister's life on it?"

"Jumah, it's all we have to go on. Do you have any other ideas?"

"Yeah. You stay here and I'll go open all of the doors, I'm sure I can dodge whatever traps are sprung."

Riana waited a moment for him to say he was joking. When the comment never came, her ears drooped down low and she replied, "That's the stupidest thing I have ever heard before. There could be gas traps, fire balls, and who knows what else. I doubt that even with as fast as you are, you could dodge all of it."

Jumah shuffled his feet as he mulled things over in his head. "Alright. The third from the left. But you are staying here while I go open it."

Letting off her own sigh, Riana acquiesced. "Fine. But…" She stopped short, unable to continue her line of thought.

"But what?"

"Just… Be careful."

"Yes ma'am." He replied quickly with a hint of the mischievous grin creeping into his voice.

She heard his footsteps off to her left. A moment of silence fell before he cleared his throat and announced, "Here we go. Door number three."

There was a loud clanking noise as the door's latching mechanism slid away and then the groan of the wrought iron hinges as the door swung open. Another moment of silence. She held her breath. Then without hearing him approach, Jumah's hand was on her shoulder.

Jumping with a start she hollered, "Hey!"

"My apologies Riana. It seems you were right about the door."

Gently, he helped her to her feet and led her through the open door into the next aisle. There were no markings on the floor here. Instead, over each of the doors was a mark. Jumah described each one to her. A wavy line, an arrow pointing left, and another pointing right, one each pointing up and down. As he continued, she smiled to herself when he said, "The sixth door has just a dot." She directed him to the door marked with the dot. Again there was a long silence surrounding the groaning hinges of the door, and again his hand on her shoulder.

"Keep it up. We'll be out of here in no time."

"Next is door one." She replied as they moved into the third aisle.

They passed through the next three walls without incident and their confidence was increasing in Riana's solution. In the sixth aisle, Jumah didn't think twice before opening the indicated seventh door with Riana on his elbow.

Suddenly there was a loud clanging noise and Riana was roughly shoved aside, colliding with the wall behind her so hard that it knocked the wind from her lungs. As she gasped for breath, she heard Jumah inhale sharply.

"Jumah?!" She rasped as best she could over her pained gasps for air. Her arms went out in front of her searching for him and found instead a piece of cold steel sticking out of the floor. Feeling around the object she discovered that it was flat with two sharp edges—a blade.

With a sickening grinding noise the blade moved down, slicing her finger and thumb open as it retracted into the floor. When the noise stopped, her ears were met with a sickening thump.

"Jumah!" She gasped. She felt her way across the floor to where his body lay crumpled against the base of the door. "Jumah no! Jumah… I'm so sorry…" Her voice cracked as the sobs wracked her body, but still, tears did not come to her eyes.

"Three point one four one five nine TWO six. Not seven, *two*! He died because I…" Dry sobs still wracked her body as she felt her way along the stone wall, ascending another spiral stair case in darkness.

As she groped her way up the steps, she became aware of a heavy, rasping, breathing coming from nearby. Shortly after, she detected the smell of decayed, rotting flesh. It took all of her willpower to keep from retching as the smell grew stronger, filling her nostrils with the pungent stench of death. She continued to grope her way forward resolutely.

Finally, her probing hands reached a door and after a moment located the catch. She released the catch, realizing that she was poorly prepared to deal with any opponents or traps without her sight. Pushing the door open, she stood on the threshold waiting and listening for any signs of activity or danger. The ragged breathing was louder here and judging by the volume of the breaths, she imagined that whatever it was, was very large. The stench grew worse, more intense, and her hands involuntarily clamped themselves around her nose and mouth.

After she stood for a moment in the doorway, the breathing changed timbre and her ears perked up. It sounded as if some great, clawed beast were shifting its weight around in an open space in front of her. She had a sudden urge to turn and throw herself down the stairs, to scream for help or hide in a shadowed corner, but her legs would not move and her voice was caught in her throat. She stood motionless in the open doorway for an eternity before she heard it speak.

The voice was low, almost below her range of hearing. It rolled over and through her like an earthquake, reverberating through her body. "Close the door."

She jumped at the sound, taking in a sharp breath and immediately regretting it as the pungent taste and smell of decayed flesh washed through her again. She staggered to the side, launching her arms out in random directions to try and steady herself. Roughly she collided with the door frame, knocking her head against the stone arch. Finally coming to a stop, she stood motionless for a moment as if trying to decide if she really had heard the voice.

"Well?" The voice rumbled again.

Dumbly, she turned and felt around her for the door, managing to locate its edge and push it closed. The catch fell home with a resounding, terminal 'snick' that cut through Riana like a sword. Unable to think straight, she stood there, leaning against the wall near the door. Staring blankly into her world of darkness, she waited for something to happen.

After a few long moments the creature shifted its weight around the stone room again and spoke once more, this time causing a wash of putrid, hot air to envelope her.

"Welcome to my home little elf." The voice rolled through her lazily. "How can I be of service to you?"

Splaying her arms out on the wall behind her for support, she dug her finger tips into the mortar between the roughly hewn stones and managed to force her voice out of hiding. "I… I'm looking for my sister…" she croaked, barely audible even to her keen hearing.

"And what fool led you to believe you would find her here, alive?" There was a hint of humor in the voice now.

"Rumors. Urban legends. She has been taken from me and I want her back." She forced back another attempt by her body to vomit as she finished speaking.

"If I had her. What makes you think I would release her?"

"I…" She stopped mid-sentence. She had no idea what she was going to do. She had no idea what she was up against. She collected herself, steeling herself with the thought of Jumah, dead below, and Katrina locked away somewhere. "I was told there might be a doorway here. A gate to somewhere else."

There was a long, low, rumbling that filled the room then, it sounded very much like the agitated growling Xanthe made when he sensed trouble. "There is such a doorway here."

Riana's heart leapt with joy and she stood up straighter, releasing her white-knuckled grasp on the wall behind her. "Where is this door?"

"It is here. In front of you." The voice rumbled. "But you can not enter."

Instinctively, Riana's hand dropped to the handle of her sword and she stepped into a fighting stance. "I will enter. You can't stop me."

The laughter was a tidal wave of low vibrations that rolled around the room and vibrated through Riana's body harshly. "You amuse me little one. But no, you shall not enter the doorway."

"You can not stop me from finding her. I will fight you. Kill you!" Harshly, she drew Elkorine from its scabbard and held the sword in front of her menacingly. Glaring at the darkness in front of her, trying to focus on the sound of the omni-directional voice.

Now the laughter became a deep, echoing spasm that shook the walls and caused a shower of dust to rain down from the ancient ceiling. "My little elf. I like you. I have not laughed so hard in centuries."

"Stop laughing at me! I will not be stopped until I find her! Not by you, or anyone else!" She yelled, her voice finding strength again in her anger.

"I can see this, but your sister is not here. What lay behind this door is not for you, little one."

With that single statement ringing in her ears, Riana's knees buckled beneath her and she slumped to the ground. Again, dry sobs shook her body as the immensity of her quest settled in on her.

"Be calm little elf. You will see her again." The voice rumbled through her.

"I don't think I can go on. I've lost so much already. It's been six months now. I don't even know if she is still alive." She hugged herself tightly.

"She lives yet, and you will be reunited, but you will pay much more before that day arrives."

Sniffling pitifully, Riana lifted her head, searching out the source of the mysterious voice. "Who are you?"

"I am the guardian of the key." The voice responded, once again defying her attempts to locate its origin. "Your time here is finished little elf. I have enjoyed our talk but I must caution you not to return. If we meet again it will be as guardian and aggressor."

"Done? I… I don't think I can get out of here… The lava… Jumah… I can't…"

"Do not fear. Seek out the Obscuri. It is with them that you will find your answers. Now, rest little elf. Rest and then you and your companion may continue your journey."

Her head grew heavy and a thick blanket of drowsiness settled in on her. She tried to fight against it, but in the end the feeling won out. She slid gently to the floor, unconscious.

-8-

Riana came around slowly, stretching languidly in the soft sheets of the bed. She felt relaxed and rested and her head was clear. The stench of death and decay was gone; in its place was the smell of sweet, fresh air and growing things. The musky scent of freshly cut wood filled her nostrils as she inhaled deeply and stretched again.

Focusing her senses she could hear the sound of children playing in water near by, their laughter bringing a smile to her lips. A dream. It had all been a dream. Slowly she opened her eyes. Her world remained dark. "No!" She screamed out, jolting upright and throwing her hands out in front of her.

As the reality of her situation settled in on her, she folded herself over in the bed and began crying. "Katrina. I can't do this. I've lost my sight. I've killed Jumah. I don't know where I am, and a strange voice has told me to do something no one has ever done before in recorded history. There is no hope left to me."

"Well it isn't *quite* as bad as you make it sound." A familiar voice said calmly from near by.

Her jaw dropped open. It couldn't be. "Jumah?!"

Her arms switched awkwardly between holding the bed-sheets to her body and moving around in the direction of his calm voice. Almost instantly she found an outstretched hand. Wrapping her fingers up in his she pulled him to her and embraced him. "I thought you were dead. I heard the trap and felt the blades. I heard you fall to the floor. You were dead. I know it!"

There was a pause as the embrace continued. Finally, he spoke. "Riana, I..."

"Tell me this is real Jumah. I don't care. Tell me this isn't a dream." She sobbed into his bare shoulder.

"This is real and I am indeed alive." He seemed relieved by the change of conversation.

"What happened? Where are we?"

"We are in Pandoria with the druids. As to what happened? I am not at all sure. I woke up here three days ago and have been here with you since then."

"With me...? You stayed by my side? For three days?"

"I did. I wanted to know you were safe, and I knew you would need a familiar voice near by when you came around. Riana, the druids say they can't fix your sight. They say nothing is wrong physically…"

"It's OK. I've grown used to their kind of help." She said sourly. "The important thing now is that you aren't dead. I am so sorry Jumah, about the door. For getting you hurt…"

"You can't be expected to know everything all of the time. I'm fine and, now, so are you."

When they finally broke apart, Jumah asked her what had happened after the trap had been sprung. Slowly, Riana detailed what had happened to her. When she told him about the stench and the low, rumbling noise his hand tightened on hers and continued to grow tighter and tighter as she described the conversation she had had with… whatever it was. She told him what the voice had told her to do finishing with waking up there, in Pandoria.

When she sat silent, exhausted from her retelling, Jumah embraced her again. "I am so glad you made it. Those creatures are some of the worst. You must have caught it on a really good day."

Riana broke the embrace and, fumbling, pushed him off to arms length. Trying to look him in the face despite the personal, eternal darkness that clouded her vision.

"What creatures?" She asked sternly.

She flinched as a tender finger touched her cheek and relocated a wisp of her hair, brushing it behind her ear. The contact with her sensitive ear sent shivers down her spine. "You are beautiful, Riana Thorindal."

"Don't change the subject Jumah! What kind of creature was that? What is it you think I was facing in there?" She tried to glare at him, unsure of where her useless eyes were pointing.

Jumah paused a moment before speaking in a measured voice. "Riana, there is only one creature in Kalijor that smells as you described and is capable of speech. That creature is a Death Dragon."

"A Death..." Riana repeated, her voice trailing off.

"Yes. A Death Dragon. They are horrible creatures Riana. Totally self-serving and rank with the smell of death and decay. It is said that they are precognitive, that they can see the future. They do not share the gift of foresight lightly. Most people who approach one die instantly at the sight of them. "

"People die from looking at them?"

"Yes, although the reasons why are uncertain. Some say it is simply because you can see so much death in their eyes that they just, drag you in. Others say it is some magical power the beasts possess. Either way, most do not survive the experience."

"So these powers they have. They can see the future? Really?"

"So it is said. The extent of their abilities is not known to any but them, but it is known that every recorded prediction made by a Death

Dragon has come to pass exactly as they have detailed. However, they are very seldom amenable to sharing such information."

"So when he said that I would see Kat again…" Riana suddenly stood up and began groping around under the bed.

"Riana? What are you…"

"Jumah?" She stopped rummaging through the drawers under her bed and lay her forehead against the bed frame, ears drooping low.

"Yes?" He said, his voice sounding like it was coming from the other side of the room.

"I don't know how to ask this…" Her voice trailed off.

"Riana, you can ask me anything at all. Just ask." He sounded nearer now.

"It's just that… I don't know how I am going to do this without help. Not being able to see…

"Riana, I told you once before that I would help you find your sister. Nothing has changed. I am with you until the end of this adventure."

Slowly, she withdrew a piece of clothing from the drawer. She played with it idly, feeling its edges as though she was trying to figure out where it went. "Thank you Jumah. I can't even begin to repay you for your kindness."

There was a moment of silence before he spoke again. "Please. Think nothing of it m'lady. I will be just outside if you need me."

She heard his footsteps move away and a door close behind her. She allowed herself a moment to sob before forcing herself to pull on her clothing. Feeling each piece to discover what it was, then orient it properly and pull it on or attach it appropriately. She could not remember it ever taking this long to get dressed and she secretly longed for the moment when she could go back to the Tyconderoga and use her eyes again.

Carefully, she found her way across the room and located the door. Opening it slowly she called out. "Jumah?"

"Here." Came his tenor voice from her right side. Gently, he wrapped his hand around hers. "You look ravishing."

She felt a heat run through her body. She had no idea how long it had taken her to get dressed, but she was fairly certain everything was in its proper place. She had just given up on doing anything with her hair, brushing it out.

"Thank you." She said quietly. Jumah's hands brushed along her shoulders as he gathered her hair and bound it at the nape of her neck, before speaking.

"So. The Obscuri eh? What's our plan of attack?" He changed the subject suddenly, his hands moving away.

She smiled the tiniest of smiles then before saying, "I'm not sure. All I know is they live somewhere in the mountains, up at the top of the world."

"That's about all I have heard. Well, that and the fact that anyone going up there never comes back again." He chuckled briefly. "Not that a little thing like that will stop us. Seriously, though, maybe we should ask around and see if anyone knows how best to approach this."

"We should talk to Master Gornin then." She said simply. "Can you lead me to the portal chamber?"

"Of course m'lady." He grasped her hand and led her forward. "What of your curious friend though?"

"What friend?" Her ears splayed out curiously.

"This large silver fellow playing with the children in the lake here." Jumah said as a wash of fresh air rolled over her senses.

"Large silver..." she paused before it struck her, "Xanthe!!"

Suddenly, some children shouted out in laughter and there was a large splash followed by a heavy galloping sound as the animal approached them. There was a rush of air and debris as Xanthe skidded to a halt in front of her then nuzzled her affectionately with his nose. She returned the affections, her hands finding a spot to scratch as she cooed at him, wishing she could see the light play across his sleek silver scales.

"So our friend sent you along with us did he?"

Xanthe bumped her with his head in affirmation.

"Would you mind waiting here for a while? Jumah and I need to go speak with Master Gornin. We should be back soon unless something happens."

Another nudge of affirmation and an affectionate nuzzling followed. She hugged his neck lovingly and sighed.

"Thank you friend. We will be back. And you be nice to those children!" She chided him playfully.

-9-

"Riana Thorindal." The troll's voice was reassuring to Riana as she turned toward its familiar sound and smiled weakly.

"Master Gornin, this is my friend Jumah…"

"Jumah Wataru. Yes we have met before. How have you been Jumah?"

"I have been well Master Gornin. Thank You." Jumah's voice issued from Riana's left side. He had taken to standing there so she would know where he was. Tentatively, she reached out and grabbed his shoulder.

"I take it things are not going well Riana?" The troll's voice took on a tone of concern as he spoke.

"Master Gornin, I've lost my sight."

"And you came to see if I could help you see again?" His voice turned to one of near disgust and she heard his body twist as he turned away from them.

"No, Master Gornin. I was told by the guardian of the tower that I needed to go and see the Obscuri. We came to see if you knew anything about how to contact them."

His movement stopped abruptly as he considered her words. Then he turned around again and moved towards the pair. "You spoke with the guardian of the Goblin's tower?"

"Yes." She nodded in acknowledgement.

"And he told you to seek out the Obscuri?"

"Yes." She nodded again.

"And you intend to go and see the Obscuri, without the use of your eyes, in the company of someone you have known for… less than a week?"

"Yes, Master Gornin. Please, if there is anything you can tell us that will help us safely contact the Obscuri, I would be forever indebted to you."

"I do not want your indentured servitude, Riana. I want you to be successful in your endeavors. You have learned much in your travels. Including the will to go on in the face of your sightlessness."

"Well, I had some help there Master. Jumah has been very understanding, and I have had some troll's voice echoing around in my head telling me to not give up." She smiled to herself as much as to Gornin.

"It sounds as though this troll knows what he is speaking of. I am proud Riana. Proud of what you are becoming. I must tell you, however, that there is no safe way to approach the Obscuri. The road is treacherous and their hospitality is not much to speak of. But if that is where the Tower Guardian has sent you, then that is where you must go. I do not know his reasons for sharing this information with you, but to ignore it would be utter folly."

"Thank you, Master Gornin. What can you tell us about the Obscuri?"

Gornin let loose a long, slow breath. Riana got the impression that he was about to tell them something rarely spoken.

"The Obscuri. There is not much to be said about them really. Be aware that they do not feel, not as we do. They do not care for our morals or principles. They see us as petty, vengeful creatures, and they are not often wrong. They are in touch with a force that most people can not even begin to comprehend. They live it and breathe it."

"How do we get to them?"

"You must first go to Avian. In the northern-most corner of the top-most tier of the city there is a gap in the railing. Through that gap lay the road to a treacherous pass, at the other end of which lay the gates to their city, Onoba."

"From the top tier of Avian?" Riana repeated with disbelief.

"Yes Riana. The only way to make it is to make a leap of faith. The road is there. You have but to follow it. If you doubt it is there, then it will not be there."

"But Master Gornin, there is nothing connecting to Avian except the tree."

"You must believe it Riana. Nothing else will do."

"Alright. I will try Master Gornin. Thank…"

"No!" Gornin's emphatic comment broke over Riana like a heavy stick. "You can not try. You MUST believe it will work. If you do not believe it, then you will die."

Riana thought for a moment about all of the things she had seen in recent months. All of the new, impossible things she had discovered. What could be so terrible about this? "Very well. We will follow the path into the pass. Do we need to know anything else?"

There was a long moment of silence in which Riana could feel the troll's gaze drilling into her, sizing her up. Finally, he broke the silence. "When they approach you, you must behave as though you belong there. Give them no indication that you are in any way uncomfortable or out of place. Tell them that the Tower Guardian sent you to them."

Riana nodded slowly. "Thank you Master Gornin." She bowed in the direction of his voice and then reached out to grab Jumah's shoulder again. Finding it quickly with his help, she latched onto it with her left hand.

"You are welcome Riana. Before you leave I have something for you. Something to help you."

"Master Gornin, you've done so much already. I couldn't possibly…"

"It is precisely because you have not asked that I offer. Here. Take this."

She felt the troll's rough hands press a large leather pouch into her free hand. Squeezing the pouch gently to try and discern its contents, it squished under the pressure, conforming to the shape of her hand, its contents shifting and moving to accommodate the change in shape. It felt like, "Beans?"

Gornin chuckled slightly, a sound like handfuls of gravel being smashed together. "Close Riana. They are Brume Tree seeds."

"T-Thank you master. But I don't know…" She was cut off again by his low voice.

"I have always enjoyed the sound of a falling Brume Tree seed. Haven't you Jumah?"

At that Jumah chuckled heartily. "Yes Master, Gornin. Always." Drawing out the last word with what sounded distinctly like sarcasm.

"Travel safely my friends. The road to Avian is long."

"Thank you Master Gornin." Jumah and Riana replied in unison, both of them bowing low again.

After heading back to Pandoria and spending the rest of the day preparing, the pair set out into the Forest of Brume, heading south with Riana perched atop Xanthe leaning bodily into his neck, clinging to him with a vice-like grip. He carried a few bags and packs on his back as well, containing their provisions.

Making their way through the forest as quickly as they could. Xanthe was certainly intelligent enough to handle the trip with his blind friend, but his size made traversing the forest more difficult, especially with him trying not to dislodge Riana from his back. For her part, Riana was doing everything she could to not cry constantly. She clung to her friend for dear life, her ears splayed out, attempting to pick up every single sound in the forest and make sense of them, when Jumah stopped suddenly.

"What's the matter?" She asked quietly, more than half expecting some danger to appear.

"Nothing. It's just getting late. We should make camp for the night.

"Late?" She hadn't realized it before, but her legs were sore from clinging to Xanthe's back. Now that they had stopped, the weariness made itself known to her muscles.

Helping in any way she could, they managed to cobble together a fire and get some food cooking. She was slowly stirring the thin stew as Jumah set about building a lean-to to cover them while they slept, in case of rain.

"Jumah?" She called out softly after a long silence.

"Yes?" He replied from next to her with a smile in his voice.

"What are you doing?"

"Just watching you." He said simply.

Riana's body went hot and her ears drooped in embarrassment. She knew she was crimson from head to toe. "Can I ask you something?"

"Of course. Anything."

"What are the seeds for?"

His melodic tenor voice rang out in laughter at the mention of the seeds. He laughed for several long moments before she vented her frustration. "You don't have to laugh at me! Is it my fault I don't know what they're for? I can't even SEE the damn things! What the heck am –I-supposed to do with them?!" Her temper boiled and her ears projected straight back as she yelled in his direction.

"Riana, I'm sorry. I wasn't laughing at you. Please... Put the spoon back in the pot." He was still chuckling under his breath as he spoke.

She hadn't even realized that she had been pointing the spoon menacingly at his voice, brandishing it as though it were a weapon with which she could make him stop laughing. Dejectedly, she turned back toward the fire and tried to locate the stew pot. After a few moments she reached out with her free hand and yelped in pain when it found the hot container. "Dammit!" She hollered as she tossed the spoon roughly into the pot and jammed her wounded fingers into her mouth.

Suddenly, she felt his presence near her again. His voice rolling softly over her as he spoke. "Calm down. I am truly sorry. I did not mean to upset you."

She tipped her head into her hands, trying once again to make the tears come, but they wouldn't. "I just feel so..."

"Helpless?" He quietly finished her sentence as his arm curled around her shoulders. With a far off sound in his voice, he continued. "As if the world just got a lot larger and you have to find your way though it all over again..."

"Yes." She conceded, turning her face and bumping against his warm chest. She tensed, but when he only held her closer, she relaxed into his embrace. "You sound like you've felt this way before."

"I know those feelings. Yes." He still sounded miles away, lost in thought.

"When I was young, some friends and I tried to kill a basilisk. They were all killed," He sounded troubled as he spoke. "I escaped with some pretty bad injuries, including the loss of my sight." She realized he was more upset because of the loss of his friends than his own troubles. "We were so foolish."

"But you can see now, can't you?" Riana lifted her head and pushed herself upright, facing his voice.

"Aye, I regained my sight, but not until years later. In the mean time, I sought a way to cope. It was Master Gornin who finally offered help."

"What did he do? Some form of ancient healing technique?" Hope sprung into her spirit, quite unbidden.

"No. He taught me to use my blindness to my advantage. How to see with my other senses. Force them all to compensate."

"How did he do that?"

"With these." Jumah said simply. He took her hand in his and pressed the pouch of Brume Tree seeds into it.

She frowned, frustration pressing forward again. "Jumah I don't know what to do with these. And I swear if you laugh at me again I'll..."

"Wait. Calm down." He cut her off. "Listen to me."

She forced herself to calm down with some great effort. After a few moments of silence, she finally spoke again. "Are you going to say something?"

"No." He replied from the other side of the fire. "Just keep listening."

"Fine, I'm listening." Again, she fought against frustration and listened.

Everything was quiet. The crackling of the fire and the bubbling of the stew in its small pot sounded loud in the silence.

Slowly, she began to hear other things. Xanthe breathing across the way. The fabric of the lean-to flapping in the subtle breeze. The rustle of some loose leaves and foliage around the forest floor. As she forced herself to focus on the sounds around her, she thought for an instant that she could hear Jumah's breathing. A moment later she heard a small whooshing noise and was suddenly struck in the forehead with something small and hard.

"Ouch! Dammit!" She burst out and was hit in the forehead again. "Jumah!"

"You make too much noise." He said from behind her as she was hit in the head again.

She spun around and up to her knees, lashing out with a balled up fist that passed through empty air. "Jumah!"

"You'll never get it like this." He said, his voice coming from behind her again. Another small object hit her in the head.

"Get what? What is going on here?!" She spun around, splaying her hands out in front of her, searching for him.

"You have to listen. Use your other senses. You can feel my presence when I am close to you can't you?" He was behind her again, she *could* feel it. A tingle ran down her spine.

"Yes." She blushed as she turned her head.

"Then why can't you feel my presence when I am further away?"

Now he was at least ten feet in front of her. She turned her head back and focused her senses, trying to feel his presence. Another sharp pain as she was hit in the head once more, "I can't."

"Why?" Behind her again.

"I don't know. I just can't." She said in frustration as another seed bounced off of her head.

"That is half your problem right there. As long as you think you can't, you won't be able to. Stop it."

"Stop what?!" Her voice began to crack as her emotions tried to take control of her again when yet another seed careened into her head.

"Stop defeating yourself before the battle begins." Now he was on the other side of the fire.

"I don't know how!" she cried. "I want to. I just don't know how…" Finally she crumpled forward, her body racked with dry sobs. And then, he was there again, his arms enveloping her in a comforting embrace.

"It's OK, Riana. We'll get there, together. "His voice was soothing. "We will make it happen. It takes a while to change your paradigm, to begin to see in the darkness, but it can be done."

It was the longest night she could ever remember. After she had calmed down enough to eat the meager stew, she spent the rest of the evening being pelted in the head with Brume tree seeds until she couldn't stand. With Jumah's help she crawled under the lean-to and fell into a restless sleep, dreaming of Katrina being beaten by Malice while the entire city of Rathalon cheered him on.

-11-

It took them nearly two weeks to make it through the Forest of Brume and the Southern Plane of Tranquility. By the time they rounded the southern end of the Uraval Mountains and began heading toward the base of Avian, Riana was catching eight out of ten of the Brume Tree seeds that Jumah threw at her.

Her senses had sharpened and she could almost picture her surroundings at any given time. She could sense the location of anything around her that was moving, especially if it was an animal. She could smell new scents on the air and feel the presence of living things around her. She was beginning to see the world again, but in an entirely new light. Or lack of light. She had even stopped clutching Jumah's arm as they walked, although she still stayed very close to him.

Jumah kept repeating how amazed he was that she had developed her other senses so quickly. It had taken him months to start hearing the little seeds as they zipped toward his head, and more than a year before he had developed an ability to picture his surroundings accurately in his mind. The weeks saw the two of them getting closer, Riana finding Jumah's presence comforting in her darkened world. Despite her growing ability to picture her surroundings in her mind, there was still a loneliness associated with her blindness that made her feel better in close proximity to him. She wasn't sure if it was her condition, or something else that made her heart race when he touched her. She tried to convince herself that it was the sudden contact in the darkness causing her heart to jump, but there was a lingering suspicion that the feelings were coming from somewhere much deeper than that. Her sharpening senses made every contact seem electric and before long, she was having trouble convincing herself that it could be anything but developing feelings.

However, none of her senses could adequately describe the scene as they cleared the final bend in the mountains and were presented with the base of Avian.

"Now that is truly something." Jumah said with awe in his voice.

"What is it?" She asked calmly.

"Have you ever seen Avian?" He asked. turning his head to look at her.

"No."

"I'm not sure I can do it justice." He smiled, shifting his gaze back to the city. "It's a huge, stone tree. Wider at the base than any of the great trees in Pandoria. It stretches up out of sight, beyond the clouds. There are branches spiraling around it, like a stair case. They start at near ground level and continue up, also out of sight."

"Is there anyone here? Mom always said there were griffon riders at the base that would carry people and goods to the top."

"There is no one here but us."

"That's strange. How are they getting their supplies?"

"I don't know. But it looks like we'll have to climb it."

"That's going to take days, Jumah."

"I know. Something must be going on up there."

"Alright. Let's get to it. If we have to climb it, we aren't getting any higher off the ground standing here talking about it."

-12-

The climb was not just long, it was torturously long. Riana's legs ached, and the vast open air at the edges of the stairs threw off her senses during much of their journey. It took them more than three days ascending the giant stone branches before Jumah reported sighting the lower tier of the city. They slept for scant hours during the night and took frequent rest breaks after ascending several branches. Each branch was nearly ten feet tall and tossing a grappling hook, then pulling themselves up the rope was the best way they could find to climb up.

Xanthe managed to scramble his way up from branch to branch on his own. After a while, Riana convinced him to take the rope up with him and hook it on usable anchor points which sped things up a bit, but it was still time consuming. As they rose higher and higher above the Southern Plain of Serenity, the temperature began to drop, especially at night. But they discovered that the closer they stayed to the trunk of the great tree the warmer it was, despite its having been made of stone.

Jumah tried to describe the view numerous times for Riana. The Forest of Brume's dark shadow dividing the Northern and Southern Plains of Serenity to the West. The Burning Expanse fell away to the southwest, its arid, parched sands looking lifeless and desolate. The Uraval Mountains swept northward from under the base of the great tree, rising up like an angry wall of broken rock and running out of sight. East was the bleak, monochromatic wasteland of the Plain of Sorrow. And far to the northeast, he was certain he could make out the acrid black cloud of smoke that hung over the city of Bête Noire.

He described the deceptively beautiful, mirror-like surface of the Sea of Death to her with the eyes of a poet, but Riana already knew what lay there. It had not been a year since she had lain her mother and her mother's best friend to rest on the shores of that same sea with her own hands.

"How much longer do you think it will take?" She asked Jumah as she pulled her cloak around her shivering body and leaned in closer to his still bare, but very warm chest.

"Before mid day tomorrow I think." He responded casually.

Her ears perked up instantly, detecting his attempt to conceal his concern about something. "What's the matter?" she cocked her head up towards his as she spoke.

"What makes you think something is the matter?" He tried to change the subject.

"You have been teaching me how to pay attention to the details, now don't get all wishy-washy when I start putting your hard taught lessons to use." She playfully punched his shoulder as she chided him.

"Fair enough." He sighed in resignation, all playfulness draining from him in that one breath. "It just seems odd that we have not seen or heard anything from anyone since we arrived at the base of Avian. There should have been somebody around."

Riana grew serious as well, pushing her head further into him, trying to drive off the chill she felt in her bones. She was now sure it had nothing to do with the air temperature. "I know. Mom said this place was always crawling with people, and birds! We haven't seen any birds up here!"

She fell silent an instant later when Jumah made a funny noise, and then cocked her head up at him again when she realized that he was chuckling quietly. "What is that about?"

"Nothing." He said, his voice smiling again.

"Nothing my left foot! What are you laughing about?" She felt his humor picking at the edges of her own mood, but fought to keep some measure of annoyance in her voice in order to keep up appearances.

"It's just nice to hear you say the word 'see'."

"Well I wouldn't be using it if it weren't for you. You and Master Gornin. It is a totally different sensation I have to admit, but it is better than being scared and alone in total darkness." She paused. "I know I have a lot to learn still, but just what you have given me already is so much better than where I was two weeks ago. Thank you Jumah." Snuggling up beside him, she put her cheek back against his chest and wrapped her arms around him.

"I am glad to be of service." He said quietly as he felt her breathing change to a pattern of sleep.

-13-

By mid-day the following day they cleared the last branch and set foot on the lower tier of Avian only to be met with the sound of swords being drawn and angry voices shouting at them.

"Halt! You are not allowed here!" A winged soldier growled. Riana could hear the rustle of feathered wings as the soldiers moved around them to position themselves for the best possible angle of attack.

"Just a moment. We mean no harm." Jumah said calmly. "We're just passing through."

"This is not the sort of place one just passes though." The other guard said gruffly. "Go back the way you came."

"Look, I don't mean to be rude but we just spent four days climbing up here and we really will be here just as long as it takes to get to the third tier and then we will be gone again."

"The third tier! Ha! Now we know you're up to no good. No one goes to the third tier but the royal family. Who are you?"

Riana felt Jumah's body move as the guard jabbed him with the blunt side of some weapon and seized his hand quickly, as she heard him grunt in pain.

"My name is Jumah. This is my friend Riana and her companion Xanthe." He paused and she could feel him tense slightly before continuing. "We are on our way to see the Obscuri, not to cause any trouble here. Please, let us pass."

"No one enters or leaves Avian until the source of the corruption is found. Especially not fools who say they are here to see Obscuri." The guard's tone changed as he made a decision. "You will go nowhere until the king says so."

"Excuse me." Riana said calmly, "You said there was some corruption here. What is going on?"

"As if you didn't know! All of Kalijor knows by now!"

Riana sensed more guards arriving as the man spoke. She counted six of them moving in and surrounding them, weapons drawn and at the ready.

"Now you will be taken into custody until such time as the king sees fit to release you."

"The hell we will!" Jumah said, finally losing his cool and reaching for his swords.

He stopped abruptly when Riana grabbed him by the shoulders and spoke softly, "Jumah we can not fight the whole city."

"Then we will go back down. Find another way to Onoba." He hissed, taking his hands off of his weapons angrily.

"No. I think we should stay here and figure out what is going on. I have a feeling it is related to our quest somehow."

"I don't like this Riana. There is no guarantee we will ever get out of their prison."

"Nor is there any guarantee that we would wake up in the morning on any other day." She said softly with a smile on her face. "Please. Trust me."

He looked around at the array of guards and sharp implements waiting for them to make a threatening move. Finally, with a sigh of resignation he removed his belt and harness, letting his weapons fall into his hand which he held out to his side in compliance. "Very well. But I still don't like it."

"I know." She replied as she unbuckled her own belt and held it out to her side as well.

"That's more like it." The gruff guard's voice sneered as he removed Riana's belt from her hand and reached for Jumah's.

"If you touch those swords they will kill you." Jumah said out loud, causing the guard to stop suddenly and the entire group to take half a step backwards.

"You presume to threaten me?" The guard snarled at Jumah.

"No. I am telling you. The weapons are magical and attuned to me. If you or anyone else touches them they will kill you. Please, for your own safety, only handle the leather."

Tentatively the guard reached out and took the weapons from Jumah, careful to touch only the leather of the scabbards and harness, but sneering at Jumah the entire time.

"Take them away." He ordered the rest of the group.

In an instant, a wall of flesh, armor and feathers closed in around them and they were roughly hauled away into the heart of the city.

-14-

The small room's stone walls and floor were cold to the touch and the tiny window, set high in the wall, let in a continuous, cold draft that washed through the cell, seemingly touching every part of it on its way through. Riana sat on the tiny bed that was attached to the wall. She had pulled her cloak around her body and was holding it closed from the inside with her chilled fingers, trying to keep the cold wind off of her exposed skin.

"Well this is nice." Jumah's voice rolled around the corner sarcastically. "It's been a long time since I've been in prison."

Riana smiled slightly to herself, imagining Jumah pacing back and forth in his tiny cell, throwing his arms up in exasperation. "Thank you Jumah." She said as sweetly as she could.

"Don't get all sappy on me. I am here for you already. You don't need to do any more convincing."

At the very least he sounded sincere. "I appreciate it Jumah. Do you mind if I ask you why?"

"Why? Why what?"

"Why you are suddenly my shadow. Why you are so willing to drop everything else and help a poor, blind elf find her lost sister. Not that I am ungrateful mind you."

"Why... Well I don't really have anything else to do. I'm ah... not exactly what you would call a home owner. I just roam around looking for..." his voice trailed off suddenly as though he didn't want to say what almost escaped his lips.

"Looking for what?"

"...for something to do." He finally managed.

"So I'm the flavor of the week then? As good a project as any?" She admonished him playfully, a wide grin on her face.

"No! It isn't like that Riana. I just... Well I've never been one to settle down anywhere. Never really had cause to. I've enjoyed our time together."

"But when we're done and I have my happily ever after... You'll just move on to the next damsel in distress..." Her own voice trailed off now, why was she talking about this? What was she trying to say?

Now the familiar smile was back in his voice, "Why Riana Thorindal. Whatever are you worried about?"

"Er... Nothing. I just... I was just a little..."

"Riana Thorindal?" A different man's voice cut into their conversation from outside her cell.

There was a long moment of silence before Riana answered the new voice. "Yes." She said tentatively.

"I see. So you are the one all this fuss is about. I must admit that you are not what I had expected." The voice was silky smooth, but carried with it a sharp quality that Riana could imagine commanding armies.

"I'm sorry sir but... what fuss are you talking about?" Riana asked, confused as she had ever been.

"Come now, surely you must know that there is a price on your head."

"A price?!" Jumah and Riana exclaimed at once.

"What have I done?" Her mood shifted almost instantly to indignant denial.

"I do not know." The voice replied coolly. "But I do know that you are the solution to the problems here in my kingdom."

"Sir. I don't even know what is going on here, let alone how to fix it." She stopped, trying to think. "I don't know why there would be a price on my head, or even who would be after me. I'm searching for my sister and I was told that the Obscuri could help me. We only came here to get to Onoba."

"I believe you. However this does not change the fact that the fate of my city lay with you."

Before Riana could say anything more, Jumah interjected. "What is going on here? Why were there no griffon riders at the base of the tree?"

The voice was silent for a moment before responding. "The city of Avian has always been under the influence of a spell that has created warm updrafts and winds to surround it. These winds have kept our city comfortable, our crops growing, and our people functional. Recently those winds have inexplicably grown cold. Our crops are dying and our people have begun to stay inside as they are not well acclimated to the cold."

"How do I have anything to do with that?" Riana made no attempt to conceal her sarcasm.

"Straight to the point I see. Very well, I can respect that. Recently a man appeared before me and told me that he was responsible for the change. That he had altered the spell that kept the winds warm and life promoting. He told me that at some point you would be making your way through my city and that when you did, I was to detain you and notify him. He swore that once he had you in custody, that he would return our city to its prosperity."

Riana sat and worked her jaw. She had no idea why someone would do such a thing. To threaten an entire city full of people just to get to her? Such a thing was barbaric! But if anyone she had ever met would be capable of such a thing it would have to be, "Malice."

"Ah. So you DO know someone who would do such a thing. Now, the question at hand is, why?"

"I don't know! He kidnapped my sister. He beat her. Nearly to death! Then he hauled her off. I've been looking for her for months now."

"So you say. But WHY did he take your sister?"

Riana grew silent. She knew why. Malice had taken Katrina because Xavier had cheated him. She was supposed to have been delivering the key to one of Kalijor's most powerful artifacts, but instead Xavier had given her a fake and Malice had responded by beating her to within an inch of her life. This was all a byproduct of what had happened on that day some six months ago and while she did not believe Malice would have stopped coming after her—or more specifically the key—she never imagined the possibility of him destroying an entire city to get to her.

"You know his reasons don't you?" the voice guessed her line of thought.

"I... I know what he wants... But I don't have it." She conceded.

"But can you get it for him?"

That was a good question. Could she get it? Could she convince Xavier to give it to her? Or even steal it from him? Somehow she imagined that he would not make any of the possibilities attractive, if they were even possible. "I don't think so." She finally replied.

"I see. And what is it exactly that he is after with such vehemence?"

Riana paused for another moment. Should she tell him? What harm could there be in his knowing? Gornin said that the keys were merely the first steps in obtaining the artifacts. Finally she decided that honesty was the best course of action. "One of the five keys." She breathed, barely audible.

"One of... Ah I see. This explains much. And how is it that you came to know its location?"

"I ah…" Suddenly she had a flashback to the vision she had seen of her mother, laying dead in the Burning Expanse with the key in her hand. "My mother found it. In the Burning Expanse."

"I see. And she then gave it to you?"

"No. I think she was working for someone else and they ended up with it. But they traded it with my employer for something else. Some piece of information. Kat and I made the exchange with Malice in Rathalon."

"So Malice already had the key?"

"Apparently. But why would he give it up if he wanted it so badly unless…"

"Unless the information he was given was of substantial value." The man finished her thought for her.

"Damn it! Why am I always the last person to figure these things out?"

"Because Riana. You are passionate. You react on emotion and do not think until after the action settles." Jumah's voice came around the corner again with a hint of amusement.

"That was a rhetorical question Jumah, but thanks for your vote of confidence." She sighed at him.

"Your companion may be right. But the important thing is that now you know more about what is going on." The man broke in to their exchange.

"I'm afraid I don't know much more than when I got here. Except for the fact that I am being used by more than just my boss. And anyway, it isn't as though any of this information does me any good while I am in here." She said, raising her arms to indicate her cell.

"I may be able to help you with that last issue." The voice responded, adding, "I have some pull with the local constabulary here."

Riana thought she could hear Jumah stifle a laugh, but it was quickly overshadowed by the sound of the door to her cell opening. Looking in the direction of the door she waited a moment, not wanting to get her hopes up.

"If you do not act soon our window of opportunity will be lost." The voice urged her into action.

She stood up and felt her way around the tiny cell to the door where the man was standing. "Why are you doing this?"

"Because I believe that you are on the right path, and that in following that path, you will save my people. But you must be quick. Our best estimates say that we have no more than a month before our crops are irreparably damaged and the air becomes too cold for my people to stay here. Here are your things."

Riana reached out and her belt was placed in her open hand. Feeling its way around her waist she buckled it down as the man moved around a corner and opened another door.

"Thank you." Jumah said in earnest. "We will move with all haste."

"I know you will. Now follow me please. I will take you to the third tier of the city. From there you are on your own, I can not be seen letting you go or there will be a revolt. Sir. Your things."

"Thank you very much your majesty." Jumah said as he swung his harness and belt into place and fastened them to his body.

"You are quite welcome. Now if you will please follow me."

The man led them down a hallway and through a door into an even colder area. Closing the door behind them with the sound of stone grating on stone, he then led them through a winding route that eventually turned into a wide spiral stair heading upwards.

"This is not a regular passageway." Riana said to Jumah quietly as they dashed after the man. "It feels different somehow."

"No it isn't." Jumah replied knowingly. "There has always been a rumor about a series of secret tunnels within the great tree of Avian. It is said that you can get to almost any point in the city through these tunnels."

"While they are not as extensive as the rumors suggest," the man replied from ahead of them without slowing his pace, "these are the same tunnels referred to in the rumors. Of course, if you reveal anything about their existence or location, I shall have to have you both put to death." Riana couldn't tell if he was serious or trying to make a joke. "Here we are. Your stop. From here you need to head north, no more than a hundred yards. What you seek is behind a building there. Go quickly and remember my people's time here is limited unless this madman is stopped."

Riana faced the opening in the tunnel, a cool breeze sliding over her like a cold hand on her bare skin. Suddenly she turned to the man with a start, "What about Xanthe?!"

"Your animal will be taken care of. I assure you he will come to no harm and when this is all settled you can come and get him. Until then there is simply no time, the stables are on the first tier."

"Thank you sir. I am in your debt." Riana curtsied as she spoke.

Jumah then ushered her out the opening and the sound of stone grinding on stone could be heard again as the passage sealed itself behind them.

Riana could smell plant life around her and the rustling of dried leaves rattling together in trees told her they were standing in some kind of garden or park. The cold wind embraced her like an unwanted caress, chilling her to the bone. Barely keeping her teeth from chattering, she spoke to Jumah quietly as she pulled her cloak around her tighter. "What are we up against?"

Jumah's voice rumbled around in his chest a moment before he whispered back, "It doesn't look too bad considering this is the palace level of the city. A few guards wandering around. There is the building he spoke of, about ninety yards north of us. Unfortunately, there are about forty yards of dried leaves on the ground between us and the building."

"Can we get around them somehow?" Riana asked as she focused her hearing on the surrounding area. Everywhere she turned she heard the sound of the wind passing over the desiccated foliage.

"I don't think so. We need something else."

"Jumah?"

"Yes?"

"How fast can you run? Can you cover the distance in say, five seconds?"

"Easily."

"Could you do it while… Carrying me?"

He turned around and looked at her a moment. "I've never… I… I don't know if that's…"

"It's OK Jumah, I know. I don't care if you are a lycanthrope. You have more than proven your worth. Right now there are more important things."

Jumah was quiet for a long moment before he even breathed again. "How long have you known?"

"I don't know. I've suspected since we met and you caught that arrow. I think it was the trap though. I know you suffered more than a flesh wound."

"So you don't believe the stories? About Lycanthropes?"

Riana looked toward him, trying to put on a sympathetic face but unsure how it was coming off because her face was feeling the effects of the cold wind. "I've never been one to believe stories about others Jumah. Besides. Like I said, you've proven yourself more than once. I trust you."

He seemed to grow more confident as she spoke, finally he swept her off her feet, holding her against his bare chest. "I am ready when you are m'lady."

Briefly Riana concentrated and she felt the familiar heat run through her body as the magic went to work, freezing time around them. The wind stopped for an instant and then came back with a vengeance, easily three or four times faster than it had been. She was about to question whether her spell had worked properly when she realized they were moving. She could feel Jumah's body working, his muscles carrying them across the distance in huge, quick steps.

A moment later the wind calmed down, resuming its familiar strength, and Jumah was setting her back on the ground. "Thank you." She said as he made sure she had her balance before letting go of her. "How much further do we have to go?"

"We are here." He said with that smile in his voice.

"You ran over ninety yards in five seconds while carrying me?" Riana sounded amazed. "How fast are you when you aren't carrying someone?"

"Don't know. Never timed myself or anything. Here is the break in the hand rail that Master Gornin told us about. It opens up to empty air Riana." There was a break as he moved around a bit then, "It looks like it drops straight down to the mountains below us. I don't see any way down."

Riana felt her way to the gap in the railing and passed her hands through the empty air on the other side of it a few times as if to confirm that there was indeed nothing there. "But he said there would be something here." She hissed.

"I know he did. I was there. But I see nothing here, save for the break in the railing."

"What else did he say?"

"He said you had to believe it would work." He replied.

"No. He didn't say you had to believe it would *work*, he said you had to believe it was *there*. Stand here a moment." She pulled Jumah to her and they stood silently in place for a moment.

Finally, Jumah chuckled. "There is warm air blowing at us."

"Exactly." Riana beamed. "I think we just need to… go." She motioned towards the edge of the city with a pushing motion.

"You intend to just walk off the edge? It took us four DAYS to climb up here. Do you have any idea how high up we are?!"

"No. None at all." She said matter-of-factly. "But I don't believe Master Gornin would try to kill us."

"Well. If you go over the edge, I am following you. But you know I can survive the fall. Even if it *will* hurt like hell for a while."

"Well. I honestly don't see what choice we…"

"Hey! You there! What are you doing back here?" An angry voice shouted from Riana's left. Metal-shod foot steps closed in on them quickly, surprise entering the soldier's voice as recognition struck him. "You two are supposed to be in prison! How did you get up here?!"

"Well it seems we have no choice now, do we?" Jumah's voice seemed at once joking and concerned.

"No. It seems we don't." Riana said as she stepped off the stone platform into open air.

-15-

The feeling was amazing. As Riana was... falling? She wasn't sure. There was a strong wind surrounding her, tingling her skin, caressing every part of her body. The sound of the rushing air made her feel totally blind once more, taking away the benefit of her sharpening senses so recently developed by the loss of her vision.

Yet, she was not worried. She felt at peace as she was surrounded by the vortex of warm air. It swirled around her, underneath her, supporting her without any physical contact. She felt as if she were in the zero-gravity training classes she had taken part in on the Tyconderoga more than a year ago.

After floating in the stream of air for what seemed all too short a time, her feet suddenly touched solid ground and as she found her balance again as the wind seemed to blow itself out around her. Taking a moment to shake off the disconcerting change in environment, she focused her senses. The sounds of rocks falling echoed back and forth between what seemed to be sheer vertical walls on either side of her. With a few steps and a quick scrape of her hand along the ground, she determined that she was in a rocky canyon, perhaps two hundred feet wide.. Listening for any signs of life, she quickly came to the conclusion that she was not alone, but whatever it was, was not Jumah. Further down the canyon, someone or something was moving around. By the sound of the footfalls, it was very large, and heavy.

A sudden gust of air whipped up around her, obscuring her senses once more, but an instant later it was gone, and the comfortable presence of Jumah was once again near by.

"That was a hell of a thing." Jumah's voice enthused. "Remind me to do that again sometime."

Riana smiled slightly at his good humor. "Welcome to… our own little box canyon?" She said, phrasing her words somewhere between a question and a statement of fact.

"It would seem so, yes. Nice thing about that though, is we don't need to put too much thought into which direction to go from here." His voice carried its usual humor as he looked around the place for himself.

Riana chuckled slightly. She didn't understand his motivations, but she was suddenly very glad to have Jumah along on her journey.

"So what do you think?" He continued in his jovial tone, "Should we head in to the canyon there? Or should we head *into* the canyon there?"

Riana screwed her face up in mock concentration, putting her hand to her chin and pretending to think extremely hard. "Well I don't very much care for the idea of going into that canyon, what with the sounds of very large *somethings* moving around in there. So instead I say we take option two and head into the canyon instead."

Now Jumah was chuckling. "You should be careful Riana. If you don't look out you may end up having some fun along the way here."

Riana turned around to face him, placing her hands on his bare chest. "I know I'm pretty serious Jumah. I'm sorry, it's just that…"

"Hey." He stopped her, "Don't worry about it. I understand the stakes. Just know that even when the stakes are high, *especially* in fact, there is a need to keep the spirit up."

Moving in closer, Riana pressed against him, pressing her face to his skin, her eyes still refusing to shed the tears that she so badly needed to rid herself of. "Thank you Jumah. Whatever your reasons are for being here, I don't care. Thank you for coming."

Embracing her in a comforting hug, he spoke with a tone of seriousness, "You are very welcome. I am yours to command."

Returning the hug, Riana sighed heavily. She felt comfortable in his arms, almost at home with them wrapped around her. Suddenly, a flash of Katrina being dragged through the portal, bleeding and broken, filled her mind and she pushed away from Jumah almost violently, turning away from him. "We should get moving."

Jumah sighed quietly, but still acquiesced. "You're right. Standing here is only going to attract one of those giants."

"Giants?" Riana breathed with a sudden bout of fear.

"Yeah. They're the only creatures I have ever heard that make sounds like these."

Riana shuddered. She had read descriptions of giants before, heard people talk of them, but she never imagined she would actually encounter one. They had been described as great humans, standing twenty or more feet tall and weighing several thousand pounds. But their great size seemed to be limited to body and did not, apparently, extend into the mind. As such they were extremely strong, but not terribly intelligent, creatures that tended to be very territorial and suddenly violent.

"Ok. Giants." She breathed deeply; trying to steel herself for what she was sure was going to be a long trip across the canyon floor.

"So." Jumah began as they started to move into the canyon, "This is where we start the next phase of your training."

"Here? In this canyon full of giants?!" She replied incredulously.

"Yes. Here. In this canyon that is, as you say, full of giants." He said with his normal amused undertone.

"I fail to see how that is a good idea."

"You'll get it before too long, don't worry. Here's the deal. We have been working on you sensing things moving, and things coming toward you. Now we work on things moving away from you."

"Alright. What's the drill this time?"

"That depends. What is your most powerful spell that produces a missile of some kind? Fireball? Lightning bolts?"

Riana thought for a moment before responding, taking a mental inventory of what she was able to do. "Probably the Sphere of Annihilation. It's pretty serious stuff."

"Can you cast it repeatedly?"

"Um… For a while I suppose. Too much casting all at once physically tires me out. I am still testing the limits of these things." She gestured towards the glyphs covering her body by way of explanation.

"Ok. We'll work with what we have and see what happens. Here's the deal. When we get attacked, I will draw their attention and when the time is right for a spell ball I will throw a coin at them. You cast the spell at the sound of the coin strike. Think you can handle that?"

"I think so. But what if I miss? I don't want to endanger you by not striking the mark. Or worse yet, actually hit you by mistake! Even lycanthropes are affected by magic. Jumah I could kill you by mistake!!"

"Well. Don't miss and we won't have a problem." He said with a smile in his voice.

"Thanks for that. It was a real confidence booster."

Suddenly Jumah had her by the shoulders, his forehead pressed to hers. He spoke quietly, the levity gone from his voice. "Riana, I know you can do this. Don't let doubt shake your confidence. Just let your body react without your mind getting in the way and we'll be fine."

Turning her face away from him, she took a moment to breathe deeply and calm her nerves. "Alright but when you get blasted to bits, don't you blame me for it! This is *your* crazy plan!"

"Fair enough. Let's get a move on."

-16-

They had been walking for more than an hour before they encountered their first giant. They were rounding an outcrop of stone and nearly walked into the creature's overly-large leg. Riana knew they were in trouble when Jumah inhaled sharply and spread his feet out into a fighting stance.

"Here it comes." He said in a harsh whisper as he roughly yanked her into a crouching position. "Get down!"

She felt a rush of air wash over her. The great club sang as it passed through the air where she had just been standing. A thunderous crash sounded through the valley as it collided with the rock wall, causing her to flinch. Tiny fragments of debris and rock, freshly dislodged from the stone face, rained down on their heads. Riana howled as the explosion echoed in her newly-sensitive ears, trying not to lose her focus on the engagement.

Riana's heart skipped a beat as she heard Jumah draw his swords from their scabbards and roll away from her, leaving her alone in the darkness with only her developing sense of hearing to keep her out of harm's way. Focusing, she could tell that the giant was now eagerly trying to crush Jumah with the rough club as he dodged and rolled around the stony valley floor.

She tried as hard as she could to keep track of where he was in relation to the giant but he moved so quickly that sometimes he actually appeared to be in two or three places at once. Finally, the moment of truth arrived. The distinct sound of a metallic report signaled a coin bouncing off the creature's thick, stone-like hide. Without hesitation, she conjured up one of her most powerful magical assaults, the sphere of energy forming in her hand like a sea of roiling lightning waiting to be unleashed, and launched it with all of her might toward the sound of the impact.

It was difficult at best for her to picture what was happening using only her sense of hearing, but what she could make out told her that something living had been struck by the deadly spell-ball. Her ears were met by a sickening explosion of crackling energy and the acrid smell of burning flesh as the spell instantly vaporized a large portion of either Jumah or the giant, she wasn't sure which.

There was a deep booming yell of surprise and… pain? Then the giant seemed to stagger backwards into the cliff, causing another shower of stone and debris to pelt the area. Another rush of air swirled around her and for an instant she thought the giant had swung its club at her again. But before panic had a chance to set in, she heard Jumah next to her, his breath steady despite the exertion of the fight.

"You weren't kidding when you said that was a powerful spell were you?" His soothing voice washed over her, relieving her anxiety about having blasted him into oblivion.

"Jumah! I thought I had hit you!" She fell into him, hugging him with all of her might.

He chuckled a bit as he wrapped an arm around her shoulders and gave her a comforting squeeze. "You'll have to try harder than that to get rid of me. Nice shot by the way, he never knew what hit him."

"Do you think we can actually do this? How many of these are we going to have to fight?" Her voice was low, barely audible, as she leaned against him.

"Of course we can." He replied matter-of-factly, as though it was the most obvious conclusion in the world. "But if we don't keep moving, I fear all this noise may attract some of this guy's friends." At that, he released her from his arms and as soon as she nodded her agreement they set off again, heading deeper into the valley.

-17-

It took nearly two days for the pair to navigate the canyon floor to its far end. They had several more encounters with giants, all ending in similar fashion to their first. There had been a couple of close calls for Jumah as Kiana had thrown one or two wild spell balls, but all in all they had pulled through with little permanent damage. The hair on the right side of Jumah's head was almost back to its previous length already, having been singed away by one of her wilder throws. He simply shrugged it off, but she still couldn't help cringing in guilt as she ran her fingers through the rapidly-regenerating locks at the side of the fire on their last evening under the night sky in the canyon.

As they closed in on the far side of the canyon, the presence of giants had diminished significantly and for the past few hours they had neither seen, nor heard, any sign of the creatures.

Finally, they had come across a set of large stone doors set into the North wall of the canyon floor. They seemed to be wholly unremarkable in every regard, if one were to disregard their presence in a canyon wall on top of the Uraval mountains.

"Describe them again for me?" Riana asked quietly.

"There isn't much to describe really," Jumah spoke from a few feet in front of her. "The doors are set flush into the wall. They appear to be made of the same dark grey-black stone as the wall around them. There are no markings of any kind on them that I can see. The only features that I can discern are the hinges and the pulls, all of which are some kind of black metal that looks like iron but feels a little different to me."

"And this whole cavern wall is black?" She asked again. Her ears could make out the shape of the area, but colors of the materials were obviously beyond her without help.

"Yes, just the end wall of the canyon, it looks like it may be a vein of some other type of rock. Although whatever this material is, it stretches up out of sight along with the other canyon walls."

"I suppose we should go inside." She said with little conviction.

"So it would seem." He grunted as he exerted himself pulling on one of the doors.

There was a loud groaning noise as the hinges complained about the movement of the heavy stone door, followed by a hissing rush of air as the seal on the door was broken. Riana winced at the shrill sound, realizing how much she had come to focus on her hearing and how sensitive it was becoming.

118

"Well if there is anyone in there, that racket should have pretty well tipped them off to us." Jumah said with a neutral tone, seemingly unsure if that was a good thing or a bad thing.

"In for a copper..." Riana said as she reached out her hand and clasped it around Jumah's upper arm.

"In for a pound..." he finished the saying as they both stepped forward through the opening into the depths of the Uraval Mountains.

-18-

Riana could tell immediately that they had moved inside. The sounds of their foot falls echoed off the smooth stone walls, reverberating back and forth, fouling her ability to form an image of their surroundings in her mind based on what she could hear. Suddenly scared again, she clutched tightly to Jumah's arm, leaning heavily into him as they inched forward into the depths of the mountain.

"What does it look like?" She whispered to him. "The echoes are messing with my ears."

"Mine too." He replied quietly, "I have no idea what it looks like. It's completely black except for the light coming in from behind us."

"Black? You mean its dark?"

"Well that, and it's black as well. The walls, the floor, the ceiling, they are all carved from the same black rock of the cliff face outside. That vein seems to run deep."

His statement was punctuated by the loud thud of the door closing behind them. Jumah whirled around, almost tossing Riana to the floor before she managed to let go of his arm.

"Damn! Amateurish. Irresponsible. What was I thinking?"

She could hear his hands sliding across the smooth stone surface of the door as he searched for some way to open it again. The sounds continued to reflect off the smooth stone walls causing a cacophony of noise and confusing images to form in her head. Groping in the darkness, Riana found a wall and leaned against it heavily as she waved her arms round in front of her, trying to find Jumah in the inky blackness that her world had become once more. The silence that crashed down on her as they both stopped moving around was even more frightening than the jumble of noise.

"Jumah?!" Her voice was panicked.

"I'm here." His calm reply came as her hand touched his body. He stepped in close to her and wrapped an arm around her back, almost instantly calming her mind.

"Can you see anything at all?" She asked, wincing at the flood of sound and images her voice caused.

"Nothing. It's completely black."

"You don't have a light? A torch? Anything?"

She could feel him shake his head, "No, I've never needed anything like that before. I've never seen a darkness so complete. What about you? Can you cast some sort of spell to create light?"

She hadn't even thought about it until just then. Silently cursing her thoughtlessness, she focused her thoughts on a spell to create a sphere of light. The energy flowed through her body, but as the ball of light was forming at her fingertips, the energy of the spell surged back through her body. In the force of the backlash she was thrown against the wall, dazing her momentarily.

"Ugh." Was all she could manage as the air was forced from her lungs by the physical blow.

"Are you alright?!" Jumah half-yelled as he wrapped himself around her, supporting her body to keep her upright.

"I... I think so... I've never felt anything like that before..." She panted back.

"What caused it?"

"I tried to cast a light spell and it... exploded. Didn't you see it?"

"No. I saw nothing happen at all."

"So it either never manifested, but I could feel it forming in my hand so that can't be it." She reasoned. "Or there is some sort of powerful enchantment on this place that both kept you from seeing it and caused it to backfire on me."

"Well considering we are almost certainly in the lair of the Obscuri, that seems a likely possibility." He confirmed.

"What do we do? Jumah, I'm scared."

"So am I, but we have to push on right? For your sister?"

At the mention of Katrina, Riana stood up straighter, squaring her shoulders and perking her ears up. Her fear dissolved into determination. "You're right. We have to move on." She hoped her voice did not betray her feeling of foreboding.

"That's the spirit." He replied with his usual smiling voice. "Now all that remains is to decide which wall we are going to follow, the left or the right?"

"Let's use whichever this one is that I'm leaning against."

"Fair enough. Here, keep hold of my hand." He offered her a hand which she eagerly took and squeezed.

Slowly they made their way along the mirror-smooth surface of the wall, heading into the unknown, magical darkness of the Obscuri world.

-19-

It was impossible to tell how long they had been in the magical blackness of Onoba. Even their touch seemed dulled after sliding along the wall that served as their guide. Constant contact with each other and soft, small conversations reassured them that they were not standing alone in the impossibly deep void that was their surroundings.

They had not stopped moving once since they had started, although in the darkness it was impossible to tell how much ground they had covered. Several times, they had come to several sharp corners and once the wall arced out into a gentle curve that sloped downhill for they knew not how long.

All at once Riana saw a dim, purple outline of something moving ahead of them. Gasping loudly, she came to a halt and was almost pulled off her feet by Jumah as he continued on, unaware for a moment that she had stopped.

"Riana? What's the matter?"

She was so absorbed in watching the faint purple outline of a humanoid form moving slowly toward them that she almost didn't hear the question.

"Huh?" She finally managed.

"What's the matter?" He hissed at her.

"I… I see something…" She whispered back, barely audible.

There was a long pause as Jumah absorbed her words. "You see something?"

"Yes…" She said tentatively, as though if she vocalized what was happening, it might break whatever spell had made it happen.

"What do you see?" He asked quietly.

She looked at the purple outline moving ever closer to them, carefully placing one foot in front of the other in small, measured, acutely controlled steps. "It's a person. They're moving toward us."

She felt Jumah's body shift as he reached over his shoulder and grabbed hold of one of his swords.

"Wait." She stopped him. Then whispered, "Oh my…"

She could see the outlines of the glyphs and runes that were scattered across her arm. They glowed faintly with the same purple light and as she looked down, she noticed that she could see all of the magic tattoos on her body, even the ones on her back.

"What?" Jumah twisted around and put his hand on her shoulder to make sure she was alright.

"My tattoos…" She stammered.

"What about them?"

"I can see them."

"You can see them?" His usual levity seemed to have been replaced with a mixture of shock and concern.

"Just them, I still can't see the rest of me, or you, or... wait a minute… I can see your swords now." She looked toward Jumah's voice and saw his sheathed swords, crossing in mid-air, moving slightly as he breathed. "I can't see anything else except whoever is coming up on us. Jumah what's going on with me?"

At the reminder of the other figure, Jumah's grip tightened on his sword handle and his muscles tensed in preparation. "I don't know, but we need to deal with this person before we spend any real time thinking about it."

"Maybe we should try to talk to them first? We are in their home after all."

"Yes," he said curtly. "Their home where they leave the door open and let you come in only to slam it closed and lock it behind you. Forgive me if I am not feeling terribly social."

"All the same, can we at least try and communicate with them before we resort to cutting them to ribbons?"

"Alright, but now you have to be in the lead as you're the only one that can see them, or anything else for that matter."

"Alright." She said, mustering her courage as she slipped around Jumah, careful to keep a hand on him. As she stood there watching the figure move slowly toward them, she was amazed to see various mystical glyphs slowly fade into view, lining what she assumed to be the walls. The floor stretched away in consuming night and she could make out where it met the walls and where the walls met the ceiling.

The glowing outline moved closer still, nearly within shouting distance. Almost all at once, more figures appeared in her vision, all simple shapes in various shades of purple. She looked around in amazement, craning her neck and looking behind them, above them and below.

They were everywhere, hundreds of them. Some were walking. Some were sitting. Some were laying down. She could make out figures that were apparently standing face to face having conversations. She could make out all of the edges of the walls and floors, and the mystical symbols were everywhere, apparently lining the walls of the subterranean city. It was almost to much for her to process, suddenly she was seeing through walls when only moments before, and for weeks previously she had seen nothing but darkness. As the details of halls, rooms, and people started to create an overlapping matte of nonsensical light in her vision, she squeezed her eyes closed tightly, trying to block out the glowing jumble. A brief spike of pain surged through her head, but was gone before she could even wince. when she opened her eyes again, the glowing, purple lines had almost all gone away, revealing only an outline of their immediate area, and their mysterious friend.

Turning her attention back to the approaching figure she slowly raised a hand in as friendly a gesture as she could and spoke, trying with all of her might to keep her voice calm and level.

"Greetings. My name is Riana Thorindal. This is my companion Jumah. We have come seeking the location of my sister and to find a way to restore Avian to normal."

The voice that issued forth from the figure was hollow, almost as if it was coming through a long tube before reaching their ears.

"We know who you are, child of Reyals. We have been expecting you since the dawn of our time in Kalijor."

-20-

"What do you mean?" Riana blinked, not even realizing that she could see the person through her closed eyelids as easily as she could through her open eyes.

"We mean that you are in our home according to the design. Come with us, we will take you where you need to be."

The figure turned around and started making its way slowly away from them. After a moment of standing there watching dumbly, Riana squeezed Jumah's hand and then headed off after the figure with him in tow.

They were led through a maze of hallways and chambers. Now that Riana could see more or less where they were going, they moved at a much quicker pace. It was still slightly disorienting to be able to see again, even in such a strange way, but she found that if she focused on the person in front of her it wasn't too bad. Jumah put his hand on her shoulder, placing his trust in her, and was able to keep up with surprising ease.

Eventually they came to a stop in what looked to be a large chamber of some kind. In the center of the chamber, a brightly glowing, purple silhouette of a female form was suspended in mid air. Riana gazed at the image in awe for a few moments before realizing that there were other people in the room.

"Who is she?" Riana almost whispered.

"Who is who?" Jumah asked from behind her and she remembered that he couldn't see anything at all.

"There is a woman floating in the middle of the room." She responded before one of the other figures in the room began to speak.

"She is someone very close to us. And to you as well."

"I know her?" She asked, focusing her attention on the floating figure again. Her arms were stretched out wide on either side of her body as she floated there. Her legs were pressed together and her toes pointed toward the floor. Riana could see a mane of sparkling purple hair cascading down the woman's back and the long, thin, pointed ears that were the tell tale sign of elven heritage. But with her eyes working in this strange new way, she could not make out any specific features to try and discern who the person was. "Who is she?"

"She has asked us not to tell you until your task is complete." A figure to her right responded.

132

Her eyes lingered on the floating elf a moment longer before she finally tore her gaze away and focused on the closest figure to her. "So you know why we are here?"

"We know everything. It is all according to the design." Another figure spoke out, voice as hollow and echoing as the others.

"What design?"

"The design of all things, past, present, and yet to be." Another voice replied.

"You mean you can see the future?"

"That is probably the easiest explanation for you to accept at the moment." The figure opposite them, nearly obscured by the light from the floating woman, spoke.

"Master Gornin said you would know how to find my sister. And the people of Avian are suffering at the hands of some lunatic. Apparently their home will be restored if we offer up one of the keys." she tried not to sound indignant when she replied, but she was growing tired of people treating her like a child.

"We know this, and your Master is correct. It is in the design for us to assist you." The Obscuri seemed to respond in turn, forcing Riana to turn and face a new voice each time they spoke.

Riana glared at the figure in front of her. She wasn't sure if she wanted to slap them, or thank them. In the end, Master Gornin's words rolled through her head, '...*they do not feel emotions, at least not in a way that we understand them...*'

"Alright. What do we do?" She finally said, deciding it was best to accept whatever help they offered and move on, rather than make an issue out of it.

"We will send you back to the trade city, Rathalon. There you will seek out the door that belongs to this key." Once again, a new voice echoed out. While it spoke, the figure that had guided them into the chamber produced a faintly glowing key, dangling from a string, and held it out for her to take.

She reached out to take the key and quickly found out that it was difficult to grasp, not being able to see her hand. She could tell where her arm was because of the tattoos, but her hand remained invisible. After a few attempts, she was able to get a hold of the key and tuck it into one of her belt pouches.

"Where in Rathalon is this door?" Jumah asked from behind Riana.

"The design places the door near the place of Katrina's abduction. She will know the door when she sees it." An eighth voice issued forth.

"And this door will lead us to my sister?" Riana asked hopefully.

"It is according to the design." The next voice responded, raising Riana's ire.

"What about Avian?" She replied.

"We think you will find that your two problems are inexorably linked together. However, the people of Avian will continue to suffer according to the design after your sister is freed." Again, the voice had changed position and timbre, but the strange hollow tone remained consistent no matter where the voice originated.

"How do we help them?" She couldn't help the anger in her voice. She was frustrated at their lack of a straight answer.

"You must do as they ask and bring them the second key. However, if those responsible for the suffering of so many possess the key, more than the people of Avian will suffer for it." The voices were circling the room again she realized.

Riana sighed in exasperation, "So what are we supposed to do?"

"Destroying the man who wove the enchantment will dispel his magics and save the people of Avian."

"So we need to get the key in order to see this person, and then kill him to end the enchantment rather than give him the key."

"It is according to the design." Anticipating the direction, she was staring across the room at the Obscuri who spoke.

Riana scoffed at the figure's outline. Treated like a child again. "What the heck is so important about these keys anyway? Why is everyone so willing to destroy lives over them?"

"It is not in the design for you to know these things. We have long ago sworn an oath to never again speak of these things past. To do so would unravel the design completely."

"So, whose design is this that you keep talking about? Who is in charge of crafting the future of the world? Is it you?"

"We merely view the design. It is not within our power to change it." The voice remained unperturbed despite Riana's temper.

Riana sighed deeply, the only thing keeping her temper in check at this point was Jumah's reassuring grip on her shoulder. "It's obviously pointless trying to get anything from you that you don't want to tell me. Where is the key?"

"You know the location of the second key. Now it is time for you to go back to Rathalon."

"I suppose that is according to 'the design' as well right? You know? You people are more than a little frustrating, and I've only been here for an afternoon."

"It matters not, everything is according to the design. Your portal is ready." The unperturbed voice replied, then the figure that had led them into the chamber moved to indicate a portal forming to their right with a sweeping gesture of their hand.

The portal was exactly as Riana remembered them to be, a series of concentric rings floating in mid-air, bobbing lazily up and down in a small column. They glowed purple in her new magical vision instead of the normal yellow or red color but she suspected that was due to her newly acquired vision rather than the portal actually looking that way. She seemed to be seeing anything magical in shades of purple and everything else was still invisible to her damaged eyes. Turning to look at Jumah she realized she could now make out the outline of his body as well, his swords still glowing brightly, crossed on his back.

"Ready to go Jumah?" She asked, placing her hand on his.

"And then some." He replied, his tone still light, and surprisingly confident.

Riana turned to the figure in front of her again. "So is there anything else you would like to confound us with before we go? Or is that it?"

"Your portal is ready." The first figure replied coolly.

"I figured as much." She snorted, then walked to the floating rings, and stepped into the center. There was a brilliant flash of purple light followed by the sounds of the Rathalon portal chamber.

"Sssssstop. Sssstate your name and the nature of your bussssinessssss." A voice said from in front of her, causing her to smile slightly at the familiar sounds of her home town.

-21-

It only took them a moment to get past the guards in the portal chamber and make their way through the cavernous space, out the great doors and into the streets of the trade capital of Kalijor. Riana quickly learned that her newly acquired vision was still with her, although fewer things seemed to register to her. It was strange being able to see only some things, and even those could only be seen as outlines of occasional people, odd creatures, or objects floating along in a pouch or on a belt. She had to focus her mind to try and fill in the gaps in her vision with her hearing. It was amazing to her how quickly she had reverted to relying on her eyes again in Onoba.

"So where are we headed?" Jumah said from beside her, his hand clasped around hers as she was lost in thought.

"Huh?" She replied, snapping back to attention and looking around for some sign of trouble.

"I said, where are we headed? Where was your sister abducted?" His voice was all grins as he spoke.

"Oh. She was taken from the Crossed Swords in the northwest corner of the city."

"I know the place." He replied, a note of disappointment in his voice.

Quickly, they made their way across the city and into the vicinity of the Crossed Swords. From where they stood on the street, they could hear the sound of clashing steel and the cheers and jeers of the crowd from within the establishment.

"How did it happen?" Jumah asked as they looked around the area.

"How did what happen?" Riana replied absently as she scanned the area for any signs of the door they were seeking.

"How was she taken? Why did she even go in there?"

Riana snorted derisively, "Our employer arranged an exchange of items with a man named Malice. The Crossed Swords was the venue chosen for the exchange. But our employer sent her with a fake item..." She sighed heavily, remembering her conversation with Xavier after she had returned from the Mars Station, wounded and beaten. "Malice dragged her into the arena and beat her nearly to death before hauling her off into what ever oubliette he had access to."

"So he beat her, then dragged her through the streets of Rathalon?" Jumah said with a note of disbelief in his voice.

"No. He used some kind of portal. It appeared right there in the ring, he stepped into it with her in tow." She slowly spun around, scanning the area, and gasped as she saw a bright purple rectangle several paces away from where they were standing. "I think I found our doorway."

As Jumah led her around the few people that Riana didn't realize she was looking straight through, he kept asking questions about the abduction.

"Your sister is a mage as well?"

"Aye. She's an elementalist, much like myself. Although she probably has a bit better command of her abilities to be honest. I always spent too much time practicing with a sword to be anything other than passable as a mage."

"You tell that to one of those giants." Jumah quipped, eliciting a giggle from Riana. "But seriously, what bothers me is that I have heard of this Malice person. He is a warrior, and a pretty good one too. But where does he get the ability to access an oubliette through a mobile portal? Last time I checked that ability was not in the fighter's bag of tricks."

Riana sighed as she clipped her shoulder on the edge of the house they were walking around. "So he's working with somebody. So what?"

"Well," Jumah continued as he grabbed her hand and yanked her harshly to the side, then steadied her before she fell over, "Sorry, there was a garden fence there you were about to walk into. Anyway, if he is working with some kind of magic user capable of porting directly to an area that is not part of the regular portal network, that is bad for us.

Jumah paused for a second as he thought. "If he is working with a mage powerful enough to enchant an item to give someone else that ability, it's *extremely* bad for us."

"Why?"

"You're sort of new to the whole concept of oubliettes aren't you?"

"Gee, am I that transparent?" She made what she hoped was a sarcastic face in his general direction. Guessing by his chuckle that she had gotten it correct, she continued. "Seriously though, what does that have to do with anything?"

"Here's the deal. An oubliette is a place that is so secret that most people have no idea they even exist. And more to the point, your average GM can't even get to most of them. So any person capable of getting to one though their own spell magic is someone to be feared. They are either so powerful they can bend this reality to meet their own wishes, or they are… ahem… hacking the system."

"I thought hacking this system was impossible." She remembered her lessons in ICE breaking and how they had talked about all of the countermeasures that were in place in the Kalijor systems.

"Nothing is impossible Riana. I mean, I heard a rumor the other day that some NPC a while back got too smart for the system, actually became sentient or something, so Solidarity pulled it out of the system and put it in a cyborg body just to see how it would get along in the real world."

Riana stopped short. Causing Jumah to yank on her arm as he kept walking, unawares. She bit her lip and looked toward the glowing doorway. "Is that the sort of thing that would bother you?"

"The only reason it bothers me is because it demonstrates a lack of control on SO's part. It means that there are definitely ways to maneuver in the system that they are unable to track."

"Ok, I'll give you that. So if we are up against a mage that can break the rules, how do we deal with him?"

"Well normally I would suggest calling a GM, but Malice seems to have a leg up on them, not to mention the game itself. And since your sister is sort of hanging in the balance, I think a more hands on approach is in order. I can handle quite a bit in the way of magic attacks, it's just a question of what Malice is really capable of doing."

"And of course the only way to figure that out..." Riana said.

"Is by facing him and finding out." He finished for her.

She sighed heavily as they drew to a stop in front of a normal sized door that, to her, was a brightly glowing purple rectangle.

"So this is it?" He asked idly.

"It would have to be. It's the only door in the area that is glowing brighter than a glowstone."

"Fair enough." He said as he reached around her and grasped the doorknob. "Ready?"

"Yes. Let's go get my sister."

There was a collective intake of breath as Jumah turned the knob and pushed the door open, his hand a dark spot in her vision as it closed around the knob. A moment of silence followed before Jumah spoke again.

"It's a shed." He said flatly.

"What do you mean, 'It's a shed'?"

"I mean." He gestured helplessly toward the door with his arms, the door still glowing in the otherwise blackness of her vision. "It-is-a-shed."

"It can't be a shed. The door is screaming to the world that it is magical. Who would put a magical door on their shed?! And then not even lock it!" Her ears laid back in frustration as she considered what was going on.

"Wait." Jumah said, sounding as if he had just had an epiphany. "Locked. That's it. The Obscuri gave you a key remember?"

"But the door isn't even locked!" She protested.

"I know, but what else do we have to go on here?"

144

"Fine." She gave in as she started rummaging through her pouch for the key the Obscuri had given her. "Here." She said as she withdrew the key by its string and handed it to him.

"OK. Here we go again." He said as he pulled the door closed then slowly slid the key into the lock and turned it. There was a definite clicking noise as the bolt moved and Riana gasped again as the door glowed even brighter for a second.

"Whatever you did, it had some kind of effect." She told him. "The whole thing just pulsed with energy."

"That's good... I think." He said as he turned the key back again, eliciting another clanking noise from the mechanism and another pulse of energy from the door.

"It pulsed again." She informed him.

"Ok, here we go again." He said as he kept one hand on the doorknob and one on the key, then gave the knob another twist and gently opened the door once more.

"Woah!" Was all Riana had to say. As the door opened she was met with a vivid, purple landscape. The floor, wall and ceiling that she could see through the partially opened door were solid panels of purple light. "That seems more like what we are after."

"Yes it does." He replied as he pushed the door slowly open the rest of the way.

-22-

The room made Riana's head ache. Every bit of it blazed purple in her strange new vision. It was like looking into the sun, but in this case throwing her hands up to her eyes to shield them didn't work, as she could see right through her hands. She could vaguely make out a few pieces of furniture, but it seemed as though everything in the room was either magical or had been there long enough to absorb some measure of magical energy.

Through the brightness, Riana determined that one of the furniture pieces was some kind of couch. A bed sat opposite the couch. Concentrating on the contents of the room instead of the purple haze, she was able to discern a table and small chairs stuffed away in a corner.

From the bed, a muffled sigh and some movement drew their attention. There on the bed Riana could make out the very faint outline of a person.

"Jumah. Is that...?"

"A young elf. About your height I would guess. With platinum hair and wearing something that looks like it may have been mage's robes at one time. Her hands are tied behind her back and she seems to be unconscious."

Riana almost dove onto the bed. Crossing the space between the door and the bed in a single step, she threw herself onto the figure's back. She lavished the woman with hugs as words just flowed from her.

"Kat! Wake up Kat! Oh Kat I missed you so much! I've been looking for you for months! Oh Kat, wake up!" She shook the woman vigorously a few times before finally getting some response from her.

Finally the woman seemed to come around, shaking her head groggily a few times before craning her neck to see who was laying on her back. After a long moment she started mewing and making strange noises that Riana could not decipher.

"Kat? What are you saying Kat? I can't understand you."

"Allow me please." Jumah said from the edge of the bed. Riana could feel him reaching in and fiddling with something for a moment and then there was a gasping breath from below her and her sister's voice rang out. She sounded weak, but overjoyed.

"Oh Ree! I thought you'd never find me! They've kept me in this little room all tied up and feeding me next to nothing. Oh, I missed you so much!"

Riana fumbled uselessly with the ropes holding her sister's wrists together for a few moments before giving up and moving away to let Jumah handle the knots. She let go of Katrina's hand, unwilling to let her go again as he set to work.

As soon as her arms were freed, Katrina jumped up and the sisters embraced one another for a long moment. They simply stood there and held each other.

-23-

"How long have I been gone?" Katrina asked the moment their embrace came to an end.

"Nearly two months real-time." Riana answered.

"How many people have been looking for me?" Her voice betrayed amazement at how long she had been held hostage.

"Just me."

"What?! Xavier didn't put together a task force or something?" She almost shouted.

"No, Kat. He did nothing at all, except take me off active duty so I could look for you." Riana tilted her head down as if she were trying to divine the floor's magical properties.

"He sent no one?" Katrina sounded perturbed, at best.

"Kat, he sent you to meet Malice with a fake key. That's why Malice did this to you."

"Fake? He sent me with a fake?" Disbelief echoed in her voice when she continued. "No. He wouldn't do that. Not to me. I'm like his daughter. He wouldn't throw me to the wolves like that."

"Kat I asked him point blank and he admitted it. He said he would never give up the key, no matter the cost." Riana could see the faint outline of her sister's head shaking back and forth in disbelief as she spoke.

"Well let's get out of here so I can log out and have a word with him." Katrina finally managed.

"We can't log out yet Kat. We have to deal with something else first."

"Like what? You know I've been cooped up in here for six months right?! I'm tired and filthy and hungry..."

"It's OK. We'll stop at home and take care of all of that but we have to go get the second key so we can save Avian."

"What's the matter with Avian?"

"It's a long story, we'll talk about it over food at home. By the way this is Jumah." Riana motioned to Jumah as the sisters got off the bed and prepared to depart.

"Happy to meet you Jumah. Thank you for helping my sister." Katrina curtsied to him.

"It was my pleasure." He replied. "However I think it best if we move on from here. I fear that if we linger too long we may encounter…"

"Resistance?" A voice called out from the other side of the room.

The group turned towards the sound. Riana saw a large sword floating in mid air, poised and ready to strike. The weapon glowed brightly, brighter than the walls and floor of the oubliette in point of fact. Even as a glowing, purple silhouette she recognized the sword immediately.

"Malice…" She hissed at him.

"Indeed. And I believe you are taking something that belongs to me. I am afraid that until I receive the item I was promised, there will be no leaving here for your pretty companion." He sneered at them.

In a flash, Riana had Elkorine in her hand, its blade glowing as brightly as his in the flaming purple of the room. A flurry of movement beside her told her that Jumah had drawn his swords as well. Katrina stood on the other side of Riana, the force of her anger fighting against her weakened body and lack of a spellbook.

"How adorable! You think you are going to fight your way past me!" His voice grated across Riana's nerves like fingernails on a smooth piece of slate.

"I'll tell you what Malice. You let us go peacefully and I won't have to hurt you. You put up a fight and I'll make it the worst decision you've ever made. Your choice." Riana smiled to herself as she heard Jumah chuckle.

"I'll take option two. Just so I can see what you think pain is…"

Riana didn't wait for him to finish his statement. Instead she felt the magical energy surge through her body as she called down a lightning bolt on him. An instant later Jumah was on top of him, twin swords flashing brightly in her vision as they criss-crossed through the air, deftly knocking aside Malice's attempts to strike him and pressing the attack on him with blinding speed.

Riana's body surged again as she cast a spell to make Jumah's skin as hard as diamond and another spell to increase his reflexes and strength beyond even his supernatural levels.

The fight between them raged on for long moments, neither one ever gaining a real advantage over the other. Despite Jumah's blinding speed, Malice seemed to be able to counter every one of his attacks.

Afraid to cast an offensive spell for fear of hitting Jumah, Riana merely watched the outline that was Jumah fighting against the sword that was the only magic Malice possessed, and yet it seemed enough to keep them at a stand-still.

"Kat. Remember the lake shore?" She hissed toward her sister.

"What lake sh…" You mean where you and Ambrai?!" Katrina sounded aghast at the thought of it.

"Exactly. Are you up for it?"

Without responding Katrina began chanting the words to a powerful spell. When she finished, the entire room seemed to come to a stand-still. Across the room Riana could see Jumah's form outlined, hanging in mid-air, swords still moving visibly despite the time slowing spell that Katrina had cast.

Riana's body surged with power again as she teleported across the room, appearing on the opposite side of Malice where she drove Elkorine toward his exposed side. As the time-lapse spell came to a halt Riana felt the tip of her sword bite into Malice's flesh, but just as it was diving deeper into his side a concussive force caught her in the chest and knocked her to the ground, coughing and sputtering from the blow.

Almost instantly, Malice was standing clear of Jumah, his back to the door a few paces away. Riana could hear his labored breathing.

"That was a rotten trick." He spat as Riana picked herself up from the floor and looked toward the sword, still held at the ready, pointing toward them.

"Well you're a rotten person, so I thought it only fitting." She scowled as she launched a sphere of annihilation at him.

The spell-ball careened across the short distance between them only to be met by Malice's sword. The resulting flash of magical energy almost knocked Riana out, but Jumah dove back into the fray without hesitation, pressing the attack again with his swords slicing in every direction at once.

The sound of metal on metal filled the room in a cacophony of sound that washed over Riana's sensitive ears like a tsunami. Forcing herself to concentrate she cast another spell, causing a dozen tendrils of magic to sprout from the floor and entangle themselves around Malice's legs and feet, securing him to the ground. The fight did not seem to slow even a bit however, as Malice seemed totally unconcerned with what had happened.

"Ree, the vines!" Katrina whispered to her sister as she moved closer.

"Vines?" She asked.

"The ones you just cast."

Of course they were vines, that was the spell. They just looked like something different to her now. "What about them?"

"Electrocute them." Katrina whispered to her.

"Gotcha." Riana grinned as the energy coursed through her body and leapt from her finger tips. The arc of electricity jumped across the room and struck the magic tendrils that held Malice's legs to the floor. In an instant he was enveloped in glowing blue arcs of electric fire, he screamed out in pain and dropped his guard long enough for Jumah to drive one of his blades home.

"You meddling little freak!" Malice screamed at Riana with a hint of a gurgle in his lungs.

"You've had it Malice, there's no way you can take all three of us with that wound in your lung." Jumah said. He was standing clear of Malice now, swords still at the ready.

Riana felt a surge of power coursing though her body as a sphere of destructive power formed in her hands. The same sphere of annihilation that she had used on the giants. It glowed menacingly as she prepared to hurl it at the man that had beaten her sister to within an inch of death.

"Ree, no." Katrina said as she stepped in front of her. A faint purple outline in her vision.

"Move Kat, he needs to be punished for what he did to you."

A faint chuckle issued from Malice, the gurgle of blood in his lungs still quite noticeable.

"Then you would be no better than him Ree. You can't do that."

Riana focused her attention on her sister's outline for a moment. "It may surprise you. What I'm capable of."

Looking back to where Malice still stood fast, in the grips of her spell, she offered him what she hoped was a look of pure hatred. The sphere of energy in her hand dissipated with an audible popping noise. Then she cancelled the spell that was holding him to the ground, the tendrils melting away into the ground again, allowing Malice to stagger back.

"Go away. Before I come back to my senses."

"This is a mistake. You know I won't let this stand." Malice gurgled. He was leaning equally against the wall and his sword, one hand clutching the wound in his chest. "I'll find a way to make you pay fo…"

He was cut off as Riana reconjured the spherical maelstrom of energy and hurled it at him full force. He dived toward the floor, narrowly avoiding the deadly projectile which instead collided with his sword. There was a blinding flash of light followed by an explosion that echoed throughout the room. Riana was knocked back, ears ringing and eyes seared from the magical blast. Katrina and Jumah seemed to fare little better.

When they all came back to their senses and took stock of the situation they found that Malice was gone. A trail of blood leading out the door told Jumah that he was wounded even more than he had been a mere moment before. There were broken shards of his sword scattered around the room that were slowly fading from Riana's sight as the magic drained from them. A sizable chunk of the floor had been turned into a blackened crater by the blast.

"Jeez Ree, you think you could have made a bigger mess?" Kat said weakly.

"You're the only family I have Kat. And I'll be damned if some pig like that is going to threaten you, let alone beat you and keep you from me for months."

"Thank you Ree… For coming for me."

Riana didn't respond, instead she embraced her sister again and squeezed her with all of her strength.

After a long moment, Jumah finally spoke up. "Ladies, I know what this moment means to you both, but I would really be much more comfortable holding this reunion some place a little safer."

The twins pulled apart and Riana smiled at her sister, her ears perking up in joy. "You're right Jumah. How about that bath, and some food then?"

"Now THAT sounds good." Katrina said.

"Lead the way." Jumah bowed to them both and indicated the door they had entered through.

-24-

The rest of the day could easily be described as lazy. They made their way across Rathalon to the girls' apartment where they proceeded to dust off most of the furniture, bathe, and get into clean clothes. Jumah went out to the market and returned with enough food for a week.

While he was gone, Riana scrubbed her leathers and set them out to dry. After some assistance from her sister, she was now lounging around the house in one of the silken outfits purchased during their last trip to the bazaar. It felt like it had been decades ago. Katrina sounded much better just being clean and putting on one of her robes, chosen from the closet-full she had treasured.

While Katrina began sorting through the mountain of food, Jumah cleaned himself up and returned to the kitchen wearing a thin cotton poet's shirt and loose pants, his long blonde locks tied back into a pony tail behind his neck. As Katrina watched from a stool near Riana, he proceeded to prepare nearly every shred of the food he had bought.

"That smells incredible!" Riana commented from her perch on the other side of the counter, mouth watering.

For a few moments they all ate in silence. None of them had realized how hungry they really were. Riana found that eating at the table was a bit of a challenge. She had a great deal of difficulty with the utensils and trying to get the food into her mouth without making a terrible mess. She had to force herself to eat very slowly. Using her fingers to find things on her plate, getting her fork into them, and then raising them to her mouth seemed to take an eternity. Her frustration was rising as she tried to stab a piece of food that kept rolling away, but she didn't want to spoil the evening for the others so she tried to keep her temper under control.

"Thank you for cooking." Riana said, her cheeks flushed a bit and her ears splayed out in embarrassment. Jumah seemed to have taken special care to prepare food that did not require forks and knives, but she still felt obligated to use them while at the table. Suddenly, she found herself actually longing for the dried meats and breads that were normal traveling fare.

"It was my pleasure. Rarely do I get to put my less martial skills to use, so I always look forward to the opportunity. Besides, it isn't every day that a person such as myself gets to dine with two beautiful elves."

"Well it was very gallant of you to help Ree come after me. I very much appreciate that."

"That was also my pleasure." His voice smiled as he spoke. "I am always willing to help."

"So Ree. You really can't see?" Now her voice was much more… motherly.

"Well I can see some things. I think just items and people that are infused with magic. I mean I can see you, more or less, and Jumah. But not much else in here, except the plumbing and the doors."

"I'm so sorry Ree."

"It isn't your fault Kat. I did it to myself. This is better than it was before anyway. I used to not be able to see anything at all."

"When did you start seeing magical stuff?"

"When we were in Onoba with the Obscuri."

"You SAW the Obscuri?!" Katrina squealed.

"Well… not really, no." Riana grinned. Jumah offered a chuckle.

"That isn't what I meant and you know it Ree!"

"Well then, yes, we met the Obscuri." Riana acquiesced.

"What were they like?"

"Surprisingly frustrating." Riana mused, "A lot like talking to Master Gornin actually."

Jumah laughed out loud at that comment.

After they took a few minutes to clear the table and start the dishes soaking in the sinks, the trio ensconced themselves in the comfortable chairs of the living room with glasses of elven wine and a warm fire on the hearth. "Ok, so down to business then." Katrina spoke first. "You said we need to go do something else before we can log out?"

"Yes." Riana said as she attempted to sip from her glass without spilling the wine on her silken garments. "Avian has been bespelled by someone. Their weather has been fouled and it is killing their food supplies and making the city uninhabitable. They said that the person responsible wants the second key. Only when they get the key will they return Avian to normal."

"Who is this person?" Katrina asked, "Do we know who they are?"

"No." Jumah replied, "But I have a suspicion that it may be the same person that enchanted Malice's sword. To be able to empower a weapon with the ability to create portals into that oubliette would take a lot of skill."

"So we aren't dealing with just one person here. It's some kind of group that is trying to collect the keys." Katrina thought out loud.

"Exactly." Jumah replied. "And I think it is reasonable to assume that whatever they have done to Avian is not normal magic, but something outside the system, like the oubliette portal. They are probably the only person that can undo it."

"So we are going to get the key?" Katrina's voice was edged with anger and fear. "And then give it to them?"

"No. We are going to get the key and use it to make them restore Avian." Riana replied. Turning first to Jumah, then to her sister, she continued. "The Obscuri were fairly blunt in regards to that key and how much suffering would befall the world if these people have it. We'll do whatever we have to in order to keep it from their control."

"It won't be easy." Jumah chimed in. "They aren't likely to cooperate unless they actually have the key in hand."

"I know." Riana said.

"Plus, we don't even know where the key is." Katrina added.

"I'm not so sure of that." Riana said hesitantly.

"You know where the key is?" Jumah and Katrina said in unison.

"I think so." Riana fidgeted slightly, feeling around the wine glass she had set down a moment ago. "The Obscuri said I already know. I can only think of one place that would qualify as an acceptable place to store and protect such a thing…"

"No." Jumah said flatly. "There is no way."

"I don't see where else it could be. And he did say the next time we met we would be enemies. I mean… they see the future don't they?"

"What's going on here?" Katrina interjected.

"There is no way we are going up against a *Death Dragon* Riana, I'm sorry." Jumah said matter-of-factly.

"A *what*?!" Katrina blurted out.

"Jumah can you think of any other place that it might be? I mean, why else would something like a death dragon be cooped up in the top of a rickety old tower like that?"

"Riana most people drop dead at the mere sight of those things. How are we supposed to fight it?"

"I've no idea. But we had better come up with something."

"Ree!"

"What Kat?" Riana sighed heavily as she turned to face her sister.

"You met a *Death Dragon*?!"

"Yes. I did."

"And you're still alive?"

Riana cast her best glare at her sister. "No. I've died and just not realized it yet."

"Ree that's amazing!"

"So I'm told, but that really doesn't help us out with the matter at hand."

"No. It really *does* help us out Ree."

"What are you talking about Kat?"

"One second, let me get the book." Then Katrina jumped up and bounded off toward her room where Jumah and Riana could hear her rummaging through parchments and scrolls in search of some treasure.

"Is she always like this?" Jumah grinned.

"Pretty much." Riana said as she fumbled with her wine glass some more.

In a flash Jumah was out of his seat and standing beside her, taking the glass from her hands. His voice was colored with concern. "Maybe we should finish this in the morning."

Riana shook her head in response. She could feel his presence, warm and comforting. Pulling her legs up and leaning against the arm that had snaked around her shoulder. "No, we need to figure this out."

Jumah tipped her head up and she could almost make out the expression on his face. "We will." His lips brushed hers and Riana quivered, the sound of their breathing seemed to echo in the room.

"Am I... interrupting something?" Katrina's voice shattered the moment, bringing them crashing back to reality.

"Not really." Jumah said without missing a beat, his arm still wrapped protectively around Riana's shoulders.

"Uh huh..." Katrina said skeptically. "Anyway, I found the book I was looking for." Riana could hear pages being turned and then a heavy tome was plopped gently into her lap. "Look, here it has a recounting of every known Death Dragon encounter where the persons in question survived."

"Ok. How does that help us?" Riana said, confused.

"Look here." Katrina said, tapping the page with her finger. She realized what she had done a moment too late. "Sorry Ree. It says here that in every documented case of death dragon survivors, the survivors themselves become completely immune to the effects of all death dragons!"

"Ok so I am likely immune." Riana was trying hard to focus, her mind still on the brief and unexpected kiss. "How does that help you two?"

"Well," Katrina responded, sounding excited about her discovery, "it goes on to say that anyone in the immediate vicinity of one of these survivors is also rendered immune to the dragon's aura."

"Well *that* certainly would help." Jumah chimed in. "Does it say why? Or how large that area is?"

"No to both questions. No one seems to know why although several theories exist, some say the survivor's aura is altered in such a way that it is able to wrap itself around others and protect them." Riana heard her sister tap on the book again. "This one thinks that it's something to do with an empathic link that is formed between the dragon and survivor. Basically no one knows why, but everyone agrees that it *does* happen."

"Ok, so if we stick close together you all are safe from the dragon's aura-of-death. How do we get the key? Do you think we need to actually kill it?"

"Well there is only one way to really find that out." Jumah replied.

"And it seems the people of Avian depend on our finding out." Katrina added.

Riana sat there, her brow furrowed as she waded through possibilities. Her arms folded across her chest. She said authoritatively. "Alright then, everyone get some rest. We'll head back to the tower in the morning."

-25-

The door loomed in front of them like an unsightly, scabbed-over wound. To Riana, it appeared as a collection of glowing lines surrounded by outlines of the surrounding masonry.

It seemed that the goblins that had been guarding the tower previously had redoubled their efforts to protect their precious door, and the trio had had to fight their way through the group to clear a path to the door. The little creatures had put up a valiant fight but in the end Jumah's swords, backed up by the twin's spells had overwhelmed them.

Remembering the tests within the tower, the group was able to circumnavigate the dangers with relative ease. Now, Riana's hand rested upon the door handle that would lead them to the chamber of the Death Dragon that guarded the second key of Kalijor with its immortal life.

"Are we sure about this?" She asked tentatively. Jumah and Katrina each stood at one of her shoulders, almost close enough that their bodies were touching.

"We have to Ree. We can't let Avian fall because of these monsters." Katrina said, managing to keep her voice calm and level despite her own trepidation.

"Agreed. We can help them, and we promised the king that we would return." Jumah said in a serious tone.

"Alright then, stay close to me." She pulled on the handle as she spoke and the door swung silently open, washing the group in the putrid smell of decaying flesh and death. "Let's see what we can do to help those people…"

Riana, even knowing what was coming, could not completely steel herself against the olfactory onslaught. The others started to gag and wheeze, choking back vomit as the stench washed over their senses like a solid wall. Riana grasped their hands and took quick, shallow breaths through her mouth, fighting her own reaction.

"Riana Thorindal…" Came a gravelly, rumbling voice that vibrated the stone walls with its basso tone. "I told you what would happen if we ever met again."

Riana grimaced at the reminder. She remembered what he had said all too clearly. "I know, and I am sorry, but the people of Avian are being made to suffer for the treasure you protect. I have sworn to their people that I will do whatever I can to save their home."

"The key must not be allowed into the hands of mortals. They can not be trusted with such powers."

"Please! Help us! We will bring the key back after we help Avian!" Katrina begged.

"I see you have found your sister Riana, and your lycanthrope friend still travels with you. You have done well for yourself. However, I also have an oath to uphold. Once the key is freed from my protection it can not be put back again."

"You're precognitive! Can't you see their suffering?!" Katrina pleaded, her voice sounding pinched and nasal. Riana spared a glance in her direction and saw her sister's form outlined against the magic-infused walls, its hand pinching its nostrils closed to avoid the stench of the beast.

"I see it. All the same, the key must not be removed. My oath demands as much. It is time for you to decide Riana. You must either turn around now, or we must pursue this course to its final destination. I give you one last chance."

Riana sighed heavily. Before she spoke, she could feel Jumah's hands flexing on the handles of his swords and Katrina snapped her spell book closed. They were preparing for the inevitable.

"I have to do what I have sworn, as must you. If you will not help us, then we must settle this as you have foreseen, I'm sorry."

"And so it shall be." Rumbled the voice. Riana watched the shimmering figure as the dragon rose up and unfurled its gigantic wings. The beast filled the cavernous chamber, blocking out the glow of the walls with its own radiant magical form, as it reared up on its hind legs and let loose a roar that rattled the walls and brought dust and debris showering down around them. "For what it is worth, I have enjoyed what time we have had to speak. It was a pleasure knowing you, Riana Thorindal."

Before Riana could even think to respond, she was shoved roughly to the side by Jumah as a blast of heat seared the air where she had been standing. The acrid stench of death and decay mingled with the sharp tang of sulfur and burning flesh as the air was instantly heated to nearly unbearable temperatures.

Riana yelped as she stumbled to her knees. Looking to the side, she saw Jumah's ghostly outline leaping at the massive form of the dragon, no hesitation evident at all in his movements.

It was time her resolve was as sure as his. With a sharp intake of the sour air, she forced herself to her feet and drew her sword from its sheath. Focusing her will and concentration, she called down an arc of lightning toward the dragon as she prepared to engage the beast with Elkorine.

The ceiling shattered as the electric arc ran to ground through the dragon's body. The putrid air became energized by the electric bolt and the dragon roared in pain from the deadly jolt.

"Nice shot Ree! That bolt was HUGE!" Katrina hollered from a few feet away as she threw a fire ball of her own making at the beast. The ball of flame struck the dragon's wing causing the flesh to singe and smoke.

The dragon bellowed at them. With a forceful flap of its wings it blasted them with a gust of wind that knocked them both to the ground. Riana's body surged with energy as she summoned a protective shield to cover herself and her sister just as another blast of putrid hot air seared across them. The magical shield hissed and popped under the assault of the forge-hot stream of air.

"Good thing he likes you Ree. Otherwise we might be in trouble here." Katrina said sarcastically as the shield flickered out of existence.

"Good thing." Riana repeated as she stood up. Watching as Jumah's magical blades cut a swath of destruction across the dragon's shoulders. Pushing aside the question leaving Katrina's lips, Riana willed another spell through her body and struck the dragon's mind with a stunning jolt. The invisible bolt hit hard, stunning the dragon long enough for her to call up a ball of pulsing black energy. Jumah, taking advantage of Riana's spell, took another swing, startling the beast out of its stunned stupor. The Death Dragon rocked back and Jumah went flying. Riana, taking a step forward, hurled the black, crackling sphere at its chest with all of her might.

The sphere of energy careened into the dragon's chest, causing it to roar painfully as the spell ate away the armored scales where it struck home. The dragon twisted its body violently and before Riana could react, its tail darted across the room and slammed into her body. She gasped as she hit the stone wall and the air was forced from her lungs, followed by a burning pain across her chest.

The white hot pain did not subside even as the air began to slowly return to her deflated lungs. Running her free hand across her chest she felt the slick wetness of her blood there, and in no small amount. She gasped and wheezed, trying to force herself to breathe.

"Ree!" Katrina shrieked from somewhere to Riana's left.

Riana's head spun a bit as she turned her head toward the sound of her sister's voice. She could make out Katrina's outline moving toward her but saw the dragon's glowing purple claw coming down on top of her head. She reacted instantly, taking a raspy breath and concentrating, she summoned a tornado-force wind that swirled up around her sister and pushed against the dragon's descending claw with enough force to topple a building. The dragon pushed against the wind, trying to force its hand down onto Katrina's head as she stood, stock still, in the center of the maelstrom.

The dragon turned its huge head to look at Riana with narrowed eyes. Without moving this time, it shot its tail across the room again, intent on finishing her—and thusly Katrina—off for good. As its tail approached, she deftly stepped aside, narrowly avoiding the sharpened spines on the end of its tail. The tail slammed into the wall behind Riana and broke off several large chunks of masonry.

Whirling around to her right, Riana stabbed downward with Elkorine, its blade finding its mark with uncanny accuracy and sliding through the flesh on the dragon's tail as easily as it would a normal person's. Putting all of her strength into the attack she drove the sword through the beast's tail and deep into the floor beneath it, effectively nailing it there.

The dragon bellowed loudly and pushed harder against the column of wind surrounding Katrina. Its claw moved a few feet closer and almost as if it was pushing on her directly, Riana dropped to her knees, trying with all of her willpower to maintain the spell.

"Jumah... Katrina..." She was barely able to speak between the effort of maintaining the spell and still trying to recover from the blow to her sternum. She hoped he could hear her over the noise in the chamber.

An instant later there was a streak of purple across her vision and then Jumah was in the air, standing on the dragon's outstretched arm, driving his swords into its scaly hide. Another bellow of pain rattled the walls as the dragon snatched its arm back away from Katrina. Jumah dislodged himself from the creature's arm and landed lightly on the ground at its feet before springing back into the air again and slashing repeatedly across the dragon's chest where Riana's spell ball had struck.

Freed from maintaining the wind storm to protect Katrina, Riana turned to her sword which still held the dragon's tail securely, and placed her hand on the handle. Channeling more magical energy through her body, she pushed it into Elkorine and the sword conducted it directly into the dragon's tail. The temperature in the room began to drop noticeably as her magic created ice crystals in the dragon's body. The beast roared in pain and thrashed its tail about wildly, trying to pull it free of the floor. It tried reaching for Riana several times but each time it was met with an attack of blinding flurry from Jumah, or a spell from Katrina.

With all of her energy, Riana continued to push the cold through her sword and into the dragon's body. Leaning heavily on the handle as her energy began to wane, she looked over at Katrina.

"Ree. Are you alright?" Katrina's voice was almost in her ear, concern very evident as she spoke.

"Fine. Get… fireball… ready." Riana coughed as she spoke, trying to focus on her own spell.

The dragon began thrashing wildly, gasping for air and clutching at its chest. Its tail barely moved now and Riana could feel the cold radiating from the thick appendage.

"Ree, you're not fine, you're bleeding... *a lot!*"

Pushing on the magic again with all her energy, Riana felt the cold spell dive further into the dragon's body and close in on its heart. She smiled faintly and looked up at her sister.

"Fireball... NOW!" She gasped as she pointed toward the dragon's chest. Keeping one hand on her sword as much to keep the cold flowing as to maintain her balance.

Katrina didn't hesitate. She conjured up a ball of intense flame and hurled it at the dragon's chest.

The ball of fire collided with the creature's body, causing a sickening cracking sound as its flesh split open in deep fissures like a glacier breaking apart under intense heat. There was a deep gasping sound from the dragon. It drew a final breath and then crumbled to the ground, pieces of its body breaking off from the frigid cold and mingling with the debris from the ceiling and walls.

"Well played... Riana Thorindal..." The dragon's voice was weak, no longer rumbling through the room and shaking the walls. Now it was almost a whisper, barely audible even to keen elven ears.

Riana let go of her sword and staggered toward the fading purple outline of the dragon's head. Dropping to her knees in front of its mouth, she touched its nose with her outstretched hands.

"I'm sorry." Her voice came in hoarse raspy gasps as well.

"Do not fret... my oath is fulfilled. Now... your turn to uphold... oath..."

"I wish..." She looked away and shut her eyes against the pain in her chest. "I wish it didn't have to be this way."

"Doesn't... matter... Riana listen..."

Riana looked back at the dragon, leaning in close so she could hear what it was saying.

"Mother... resonate... They know... who she is..."

"I don't understand." She could tell he was all but dead. His words made no sense.

"Warn her... She'll diiieeeeeeee......" Its final word came out as a hissing escape of breath and then the creature was gone, the purple form faded from her vision completely.

-26-

"So what do we do now that we have the key?" Katrina asked from the other side of the room.

Riana sat in a large fluffy chair in their living room, staring at the crystal. In her vision, she could see the tattoos on her out stretched arm and the crystal floating in the air beyond them. She still could not see even the faintest outline of her own hand or body. She knew the crystal was held firmly in her hand and yet all she could see was the dark purple outline of the object surrounding a brightly glowing elven glyph. This one representing "The power of knowledge." She rolled the thing over in her hand a couple of times absently, feeling its smooth, faceted surface and hefting its weight.

"I'm sorry, what was that?" Riana responded absently after realizing that her sister had spoken.

Jumah chuckled quietly as he pressed a glass of wine into Riana's free hand, resting a strong hand on her shoulder. She offered him what she hoped was a pleased smile as Katrina huffed from somewhere near the kitchen.

"I said, what do we do with it now that we have it?"

"A very good question." Jumah replied as he massaged Riana's shoulders. "Whomever is holding Avian for ransom wants the key. So we could either give it to them, which the Obscuri told us was a very bad idea. Or… We could find the lock, and use the key ourselves. Maybe we could use whatever it's protecting to help the people of Avian."

Katrina stared at the pair for a long moment before responding. Something flashed across her face that was a combination of contempt and jealousy. "Well I'm not sure how wise that is. Whatever these artifacts are, the Obscuri went to a lot of trouble to make sure they were sealed away well and good. I'm not sure we should be dragging this particular episode from Kalijor's past out into the light."

"You're probably right about that. But, what else is there for us at this point?" Jumah had both hands on Riana's shoulders now, working her muscles thoroughly until her head lolled to the side and she sighed happily. Her chest had been repaired by a healer shortly after they gated back to Rathalon, but her body was still recovering from the ordeal.

Katrina scowled at Jumah. Nodding toward her sister she spoke curtly, "Don't you think she should be a little more involved in this conversation?"

Jumah smiled impishly and nodded, removing his hands from Riana's shoulders, eliciting an immediate complaint from her. "Hey! Don't stop!"

"Your sister is right Riana."

"About what? What did she say?" Riana looked up at the faint purple outline of her sister, standing across the room with her hands on her hips.

"I rest my case." Katrina said sarcastically.

Riana leaned forward in the chair, wincing in pain from the stress the movement caused her freshly-healed abdomen. "Alright. So what are we talking about then?"

"What to do with that." Katrina said, pointing at the key in Riana's hand.

Riana looked back down to the crystal and chewed thoughtfully at her lower lip. Finally, she seemed to come to an abrupt decision and looked back up at her sister. "We need to go and get whatever is behind the door this unlocks."

The room went still. Riana could feel the other two exchanging looks as she stared intently at the outline of the crystal, framing the elven glyph in her invisible hand. She knew it was crazy to go after whatever it was, but she had no idea what else they could do. Master Gornin would never approve of them reopening the ancient vaults that had, for so many centuries, locked away whatever it was that the Obscuri had traded their humanity to protect. In fact, she was sure that no one in their right minds would approve of it. The fact remained that whatever secrets the key was protecting would be better off anywhere other than in the hands of someone capable of destroying an entire city to get what they wanted.

She sighed heavily as she looked up at the faint purple outlines of her sister and Jumah. The pair where standing there silently, looking at her as she struggled with her thoughts. "What other choice do we have? I am open to suggestions here."

Their silence spoke volumes. Neither of them had any ideas about what else they could do. Turning over the key to save Avian was tantamount to giving away the Obscuri's secret outright. The Obscuri had said that would be even worse for Kalijor than suffering the loss of a major city such as Avian. The fate of the entire world seemed to be hanging in the balance of their decision. She had even considered just logging out and leaving the people of Kalijor to fend for themselves, but something in her was saying the consequences of these matters would be felt far beyond the barriers of this virtual reality. Not to mention the fact that this was where she had grown up; lived most of her life. She owed this world more than that.

"Well. We need to know what we are up against." Katrina broke the silence finally. She was trying to inject a bit of good humor into her voice, but it sounded hollow, scared even.

Riana smiled at her. She could always count on Katrina to help her though the rough times. "Ok. Where do we start?"

Katrina ran to her room in a sudden burst of speed indicative of an epiphany. Her ideas usually came in flashes and caused a sudden change in her behavior. Things such as running from a room suddenly with no explanation were fairly common with her.

Turning her attention to Jumah, still standing stoically beside her, she smiled again. Feelings welled up inside her as she looked at his faintly glowing outline. Even in her new sight, she could see the definition of his body, trim, muscled, his stance radiated the quiet confidence of a reluctant warrior who had won more battles than he had ever cared to have fought.

"You don't have to do this Jumah." Her voice was quiet, more serious than she had ever been in her life. She wasn't sure why but the thought of him getting hurt made her stomach twist into knots.

"You know," He replied with a smirk in his voice as he crouched down next to the chair and moved his face a breath's distance from her ear. "If you keep trying to get rid of me like this, it may hurt my feelings."

His breath was hot against her sensitive ears, causing them to slope back in anticipation and burn bright scarlet in embarrassment. Reflexively, she twisted around in the chair to face him and barely managed to stifle the yelp of discomfort as the freshly healed wounds across her abdomen complained about the sudden movement. As the fire in her wounds receded, she refocused her attention on Jumah. He was standing again, on the other side of the room, apparently looking out the window into the streets of Rathalon.

She let out another heavy sigh. "I'm serious Jumah. This isn't your fight. And I don't think that I…" She stopped herself suddenly and turned her head away from his figure.

Jumah politely ignored her half-statement as she heard him turning around to face her again. "As I understand it, the fate of Kalijor pretty much hangs in the balance here. Now correct me if I am wrong, but if Kalijor is destroyed or in any other way made unlivable, that pretty much puts me out of house and home. Being that I live here and all."

He was still smiling as he spoke. She wasn't sure if he was even remotely capable of taking a situation seriously. Had it not been for his business-like attitude when dealing with the guardian of the key she would have already given up hope for him. "Right. But there is no sense in you dying over it."

In an instant, he was less than an inch from her again, his face so close she could feel his breath on her lips and cheeks as he spoke. "I would rather die on my feet fighting for right, than live on my knees under the heel of some tyrannical dictator. Besides, you know this is just a game right? Death isn't permanent here..."

Then his voice shifted back into his normal jovial tone and he added, "Besides, if I come with you I get to spend more time in the company of the most beautiful woman I have ever met." He kissed her almost imperceptibly on the lips and was gone again, standing on the other side of the room.

Riana's mind was lost in the kiss for a mere instant before the thud of the books sounded against the table. Her senses tingled from her toes to the tips of her ears. She felt a longing for something, a deep desire to open up to it and let it consume her world. She managed to refrain from a startled movement, save for a jerk of her head in Katrina's direction.

"What was going on in here?" She asked them, already knowing the answer.

"Nothing." Riana said in a rush, her cheeks and ears flushing red. "I was just telling Jumah that he doesn't really need to put himself in danger."

"Uh huh." Now Katrina's voice was betraying her own smile, it had to have been ear to ear by the sound of it. "Soooooo, anyway. I suddenly remembered an old myth I read a long time ago about an ancient treasure that had been secreted away in the Forest of Brume."

Riana looked toward her sister, curbing her embarrassment and quirking an eyebrow. "Why did this just suddenly come to you out of the blue?"

Katrina made some noises as she shuffled the books around on the table and then seemed to select one and begin thumbing through it. Finally, she stopped on a page and there was the sound of the book being turned around on the table to face the room. Jumah moved across the space, drawing near enough to the table that he could inspect the proffered page and then chuckled a bit.

"What is it?" Riana asked, suddenly more frustrated at the loss of her normal vision than she had been in a long time.

"It's the same glyph that is in the crystal in your hand." Jumah replied. "It seems to be inscribed on the lintel above a massive stone door at the base of some kind of pyramid that is overgrown with forest."

Riana processed the information for a long moment before finally speaking. "You know, the elven symbol for knowledge is not exactly an uncommon character. That could be anything. What makes you think it has anything to do with this?"

"Well, that's why I didn't bring it up at first. But then I remembered this recounting of an archeologist from the Magic Academy that had come across an ancient ziggurat in the Forest of Brume. His notes suggested that the growth of the forest around, and on, the structure meant that its construction could probably be traced back to the time just after the great war, but his magics were unable to determine the exact age of the thing. He went on to say that despite the forest growth, the structure itself seemed pristine, and that he was not able to find any way inside."

Riana listened intently. She had never heard of such a structure in the forest of Brume, but it was a very large and ancient forest and she was fairly certain that even a large structure could remain undiscovered for great lengths of time, but here they were talking about the span of more than a few centuries. What were the odds of something that strange going unnoticed for that long? "Why has no one else ever seen this thing?"

"Well that's just it. Obviously someone has seen it or there wouldn't be any myths about it now would there?" Katrina admonished her. "Anyway, the other reason there is little known probably has to do with its defenders. This archeologist says that after he had been poking around for about an hour he was suddenly set upon by some kind of creature that chased him off into the forest. Apparently he left in such a panic that he lost his way and it took him a month to find civilization again."

"Ok. It sounds plausible, but how do we know it is really worth pursuing?" Jumah interjected from a seat at the table. He had seated himself while Katrina spoke and was munching on a fresh apple from a bowl on the table..

"Because," Katrina paused for effect, "he came away with this as he ran for his life." She produced a piece of thin parchment that made crinkly noises as she unfolded it and set it gently on the table next to the book. "This is a rubbing he made of a mark that was carved above the only discernible entrance to the structure."

188

Jumah chuckled again as he swallowed a chunk of the apple. "If I never see that damn glyph again I think it may be too soon."

-27-

"So are we ready?" Jumah asked as they finished checking over their supplies and equipment the following morning.

It had taken Riana hours to get dressed and gather her things. She still ached and refused to accept any help, determined to get ready on her own. Her vision was growing more acute over time, making some things easier. Now, she could even see her leathers as they had been infused—so long ago it seemed—with magic by an enchanter in Rathalon to make them lighter and less painful for her to wear on her newly tattooed skin. However, it wasn't finding or getting into her clothing that was the issue, or even the pain from her sore abdomen. It was everything else. Here they were, getting ready to go retrieve some mysterious *thing* that had long ago been sealed away in order to protect the world from those that would misuse them. She still wasn't sure if even they were the right people to have such things. Of course they meant well but once certain doors had been opened they were next to impossible to close again.

Cinching her bedroll tightly against her back, she glanced toward the sound of Jumah's voice. His entire body was visible to her, glowing softly with a mild purple light. The brightly glowing swords crossed on his back. She smiled to herself. Since they had met she had learned so much, not the least of which was how to deal with her new condition.

Her smile quickly turned to a frown with the appearance of another glowing outline. It took her a moment to realize that the new figure was in the hallway outside their home rather than in their living room with them.

"What's the matter Riana?" Jumah asked suddenly, realizing Riana's demeanor had shifted.

A flutter of paper and fabric near the table signaled Katrina's interest in the sudden change in the room's mood.

"There's someone at the door." Riana nodded toward the closed portal. "A mage of some kind."

"How do you know?" Katrina asked, raising an eyebrow at her sister.

"I can see him. The same way I can see you two." Riana replied, cinching her sword belt around her waist and setting her feet toward the door.

"OK, but…" Katrina's voice trailed off as she turned to look at the door.

192

"But what?"

"Through the door?" Katrina asked.

"That's a new one on me." Riana shrugged as Jumah offered a quiet chuckle before turning his attention to the issue at hand.

He turned to look at the door, reaching cautiously over his right shoulder and placing a hand on the sword handle there. Slowly he approached it. Reaching out to touch the stone slab with his other hand, he watched as the door slid into an alcove in the wall revealing the person on the other side, hand poised to knock. A moment of absolute silence filled the room before a fluttering of robes and a gust of wind whisked past Riana, trailing bits of parchment and feather quills in its wake.

"EXODUS!!" Katrina gushed as she dove through the door and wrapped herself around the man.

After only a moment's surprise, the man seemed to recover adequately to reciprocate some of Katrina's emotions and returned her embrace enthusiastically. "Katrina! I'm glad you are alright! We hadn't heard that you had been found yet. This is a most pleasing discovery!"

"You mean you missed me?" She asked in mock innocence, still hugging him tightly.

"To say I missed you would be akin to saying that the flowers merely miss the touch of daylight. No I didn't miss you. I felt your absence like a longing in my heart every day."

Katrina stopped and disengaged herself from the man, looking into his steel grey eyes searchingly. "You really mean that?"

He put his hands on her shoulders and looked back into her eyes with confidence. "I would not have said it otherwise. I have been lonely ever since you left Cohai so many years ago. I finally took up the search for you myself when Riana told us that you were, in fact, captive somewhere. I am sorry it was not me who could have rescued you, but my heart is lightened by your presence. This is good news indeed!" He embraced her again as he finished speaking, holding her tightly to him and simply soaking in the moment.

Finally, Riana spoke. "Master Exodus. Pardon my intrusion but what is it you were seeking here?"

He looked up at Riana with a slightly confused expression on his face. When he failed to respond, Riana pressed him further. "You said you hadn't heard that we found her, and yet here you are at our door. Either you were looking here for her, or you had some other purpose in calling?"

His whole demeanor changed as he focused on business for a moment. "Ah yes… I bring word from Master Gornin."

Riana arched an eyebrow at him, folding her arms across her chest as she waited for the news.

"He said simply that you must follow this through. I'm afraid that was all. I have no idea what it means, but he said it was urgent that you hear that before you left this morning, so I rushed straight here from Cohai."

Riana sighed again. She had no idea how that old troll got his information, but that message could only mean that Gornin knew they had acquired the crystal key and were planning on unlocking the artifact that it protected. She nodded her head solemnly before relaxing her stance and giving her equipment one last check. Turning toward Jumah, she said, "Ok. I'm ready. Let's get going."

Jumah inclined his head toward her from the door and turned toward Katrina and Exodus, still standing in the hallway. "Are you ready Katrina?"

Katrina turned to face him, slowly breaking away from Exodus. Her movements were suddenly lethargic, reluctant. "I just need to grab my spell book, then I'm ready." Her voice was melancholy as she took her time crossing the room to where she had been scribing spells in her book earlier.

"Where are you going?" Exodus asked from the hallway.

"We're going to save Avian." Riana said, dismissing Exodus with a look at Jumah. Moving toward the door and placing a hand on Jumah's shoulder, she drew conviction from her contact with him. Somehow he seemed to give her the strength to do these things that would have seemed impossible to her before. Here they were again, embarking on a journey to further unravel this tangled web of events, or tie them up further for all she knew. But she did know that without Jumah, and now Katrina, she stood no chance of success.

"Do you need transportation? I can get you to most anywhere in Kalijor directly." Exodus said, suddenly cheerful. "I would be only too happy to help, especially since Master Gornin seems to approve of what you are doing."

Riana offered him a disparaging glare, her ears swept back in annoyance at his insinuation that they would need Gornin's approval. "Thanks, but I think we have it covered."

"Ree!" Katrina admonished from the doorway. "You know we could use the help. It's just the three of us against... we don't even know what!"

"Which means he'd be better off not joining us, we could all die tomorrow."

"All the more reason for him to come with us!" Katrina retorted. Blushing scarlet as her ears splayed out in embarrassment, she continued softly, "I don't want to die without having spent time with him..."

Riana let the the barely heard statement sink in. Finally, her ears perked up and she raised her hand as if to point at her sister. Opening her mouth to speak she suddenly stopped short as a strange melody suddenly started playing. It was a haunting tune that jarred her physically, causing her to drop her arms to her side and her ears to twitch as she tried to focus on the tune. It was a lullaby that their mother used to sing to them. The voice was high and lilting, and just on the edge of hearing, yet it settled around her like a blanket on a warm day, comforting, but slightly uncomfortable.

"Where is that music coming from?" She twisted her head to look over her shoulder, but she could not locate a direction it was actually originating from.

The others in the room just stopped and stared at her for a long moment before Katrina replied, "What music?"

"That music!" Riana said, raising her arm with her index finger extended as if she could point them towards the sound.

Katrina looked to Jumah who shrugged nonchalantly. Then she turned and looked at Exodus who was just staring at Riana with an arched eyebrow.

"I don't hear anything." She finally said as she turned back to Riana.

"Nor do I." Exodus added.

Riana looked around the room again, her sight showing stark purple outlines against the pitch black backdrop that had become her world. The haunting melody continued, still refusing to divulge its source to her. It was almost as if the music was in her head. "You don't hear that?"

Jumah, Katrina, and Exodus all shook their heads 'no' in unison.

"Fine. Whatever. Let's just get moving. Avian is running out of time." Riana said, frustrated.

Katrina grinned as she wrapped her hand around Exodus' and pulled him into the living room. "So where are we starting then?"

Riana shook her head as if the action might stop the song. When it had no effect, she simply turned to her sister and stared at her for a moment, trying to block it out and focus on the others, looking at her expectantly. "Well, we know the ziggurat is in the Forest of Brume somewhere so I guess we just head to Pandoria and begin our search from the portal. Unless anyone else has a better plan?"

"That seems as good a plan as any." Jumah said as he stepped up next to Riana and put his hand on her shoulder reassuringly. Riana smiled at the touch, leaning towards Jumah and reaching out to him, placing her own hand on his shoulder.

"Very well. Pandoria it is." Exodus intoned as he withdrew his spell book from a fold in his robes and opened it to the necessary page. "Does anyone need anything before we go?" After a moment of silence, he looked down at the book again then snapped it shut and returned it to his robes. Stepping into the space in the center of the group he began to chant a few words of power and form magical glyphs in the air with expert gestures. An instant later, there was a brilliant flash of light and they were suddenly standing in the Forest of Brume, its thick mist swirling around their ankles and the sounds of the forest filling their ears.

Riana scowled when she realized she could still hear the lullaby at the edge of her senses, hanging out there in space, just out of reach.

"What's the matter?" Jumah asked quietly.

At the sound of his voice, the music stopped, disappearing as quickly and unexpectedly as it had begun. She swiveled her head around, trying in vain to locate where the music had been coming from. Jumah grabbed her by both shoulders and looked into her eyes, she guessed with some concern, even though she could not make out his facial expression.

"Huh?" She stammered, focusing on him. "Oh. Nothing. I'm OK."

"Are you sure? You don't seem OK." There was a deep concern in his voice.

"Yes. I'm fine. Just…" She trailed off, her ears drooping low. She turned her face away from him and focused on a spot of blackness at his feet.

"Just what?" He said as he hooked his hand under her chin and gently turned her face back toward his.

She thought for a long moment about whether she could, or even if she should vocalize her feelings. She was so unsure about things recently. There had been so many changes in her life and she wasn't sure of herself or what she was capable of any more. All she knew was that nearly everyone that had ever had anything to do with her had met some bad end or other and she didn't want to be the cause of that for someone she… cared about.

"It's nothing. Ask me again after we get through this." She finally said as she broke away from him and focused her thoughts back on the task at hand. Raising her voice so they could all hear her, "Ok, Katrina, I think this is your show now."

Katrina gaped at her for a minute, trying to decide if she should take charge, or look for a hole to hide in. Finally, her sense of duty seemed to win out and she cleared her throat. "Ahem. OK, the mage's notes say he found this ziggurat deep in the forest so we are looking for some place that is out of the way, tough to get to. It will likely be in the ancient forest, so we could encounter some interesting things along the way. Things that maybe have been out here a long, long time, and have no desire to be encountered."

Riana nodded. "So let's watch each other's backs and keep an eye out for trouble."

-28-

As they moved into the older areas of the ancient forest the trees grew massive in size. Each giant arboreal behemoth claimed a sizable chunk of real-estate for itself, yet the canopy of leaves and branches over their heads seemed to block out even more light than the younger forest, with its more tightly packed trees and foliage. The area between the trees was mostly dirt, with a few small plants strewn about here and there. Most of the space was hidden by the knee-high mist that was ever-present in the forest. No smaller or younger trees would dare to take root here for fear of being strangled to death by the giants that had been here for millennia.

The group picked their way through the maze of trunks, unable to see around even the smallest of them without taking half a dozen paces in one direction or another. They had no idea where they were going, but had resolved to keep going in one direction for as long as they could. All they really knew was that the structure they sought was somewhere in the ancient forest and that it was overgrown by the titanic trees. The mage's notes made no other mention of location or landmark.

"This is hopeless." Katrina said from Riana's right side, causing Riana to twist her head around and glare at her sister.

"That isn't helping Kat."

"I know, but this is like looking for a needle in a hay stack."

"This is one needle that *must* be found though. The lives of every person in Avian depend on it."

"Duck." Jumah said in his normal jovial tone from directly in front of Riana.

She ducked her head down and felt a branch pass over her. She had found that there was very little that her specialized vision could detect in the forest, which was odd because she had always been told that the Forest of Brume was one of the most ancient and magical places in all of Kalijor. Ancient sure, there was no disputing that from the descriptions of the trees the others had given her. But she could see no trace at all of any kind of magic here, except what they had brought with them. All of the time she had been able to navigate on her own, in Onoba, Rathalon, and then the tower, left her lost, blinded all over again. As a result, she had fallen back on Jumah to help her with navigation so as not to slow the group any more than was necessary.

"Thank you." She said, squeezing his shoulder with her hand as she straightened out again.

"My pleasure." He ran his fingers across hers softly.

"Still. It would have been nice if that mage had left *some* clue as to where he had gone…" Katrina never gave up on an argument if she could help it.

As she was about to offer some other bit of kindling to the fire Riana suddenly stopped short, dropping her hand from Jumah's shoulder and cocking her head to one side with her ears perked up attentively.

"What is it Riana?" Jumah's voice was full of concern again.

"It's that music again…" She mused as the haunting lullaby wrapped itself around her once more. It made her feel at once at ease and on edge. She recognized the song, it was one her mother had often sung to them at bed time when they were young. It made her long for those days again, with not a care in the world but where they could get into trouble the next day. Now however, it also made her uneasy. Where was it coming from? Why was it that only she could hear it? Was it some other strange new power that she was developing as a result of the loss of her vision?

"I still don't hear it." Jumah confirmed.

"Me either." Kat added from closer by.

"Nor do I." Exodus reported from somewhere near Katrina.

Riana put up her hand to silence them and slowly turned her head this way and that, trying to get a fix on the tune's point of origin. After a few minutes she slowly raised her hand and pointed in a direction. "What's out this way?"

"That direction leads further into the old forest. Not on our original path but not far from it either." Jumah replied, eyeing her.

"Let's go that way then." Riana said with no measure of confidence at all.

"We are not seriously thinking of following the music in Ree's head are we?" Katrina said with a note of concern for all their mental health.

"Do you have a better idea? It *is* a needle in a haystack after all." Riana offered her sister a wry smile.

"Point taken." Katrina gave up without a fight. It truly was better than nothing to go on at all.

"Very well then." Jumah gently picked up Riana's hand and set it on his shoulder again. "Please let me know if I should stop or change directions."

It wasn't more than half a day later that they burst upon the shore of the Great Inland Sea. Its dark, deep waters came right up to the ancient trees. Just beyond the roots, not more than a few feet out, the surface of the water was covered nearly as far as the eye could see with the same thick mist that lay constantly on the floor of the forest. Even in the full light of day the expanse of water looked forbidding as it stretched out of sight on the horizon.

More interesting to them, however, was the crumbling stone bridge that lay a few paces along what passed for a beach. The bridge seemed to defy gravity as it arched over the misty water, connecting to a large island. The island itself rose from the mists, seeming to waver under the towering trees and vegetation that covered it. The bridge looked like it hadn't been used in centuries. The surface was pockmarked and riddled with holes that showed the misty surface of the dark water below. If one had fear of heights, looking down showed a dizzying drop of a hundred or more feet to the surface of the water.

"Well that is something you don't see every day." Jumah quipped as the group tried to come to terms with what lay before them.

"That much is certain." Exodus said quietly from behind Riana.

"What are we dealing with here?" Riana asked with concern, her ears laid back doubtfully.

"It's probably best that you don't know." Katrina replied as the group slowly moved toward the bridge. As they approached, a large chunk of stone crumbled away from the structure and seemed to hang in mid-air for a moment before splashing into the water below. The mist swirled around in a vortex before hiding the disturbance completely.

"Definitely better that way." Jumah agreed as they all watched the debris disappear.

"That's not very reassuring."

"No. It isn't." Jumah replied, "And what are the odds that we don't have to go this way?"

"Not in our favor, I'd wager." Katrina chuckled.

"We need to head that way." Riana said as she pointed directly across the bridge, her ears swept forward to try and catch the music. "The music's coming from over there."

"Color me surprised." Katrina snorted as she gingerly pressed the toe of her boot onto the stone surface, causing a small bit to fall off somewhere up ahead of them.

"You think you can transport us to the other side Exodus?" Jumah shifted as he looked to the mage.

"No. I can only teleport to places I have actually visited. I can't even see the other side of the bridge. I'm sorry."

"Guys, what is going on here?" Riana asked, feeling a bit outside of the joke.

"I thought as much, but I had to ask. Riana, there is a stone bridge leading to a forested island. The bridge is… in bad shape."

"Of course it is." She replied with a sigh.

"Right, well we aren't getting across it by standing here looking at it." Katrina chirped as she moved out onto the stone structure with a false air of confidence.

The whole structure seemed to move under her slight weight. Masonry crumbled away as she moved slowly along its surface. Riana watched as her sister inched away from them, taking slow and careful steps. Then Exodus followed her a few paces behind, picking and choosing his way with great care.

"Ok Riana. Step only where I step. There are holes all over this thing and one bad step will put you in the water." Jumah said seriously as he turned away from her and placed one of her hands on each of his shoulders.

She squeezed him tightly and fell into his foot prints as they began to move forward ever so slowly.

It seemed as though hours had passed in silence before a deep rumbling sound overpowered the lullaby that had been leading them toward this ancient bridge. She was about to speak when the vibrations hit her, low, strong, and foreboding.

"Shit." Jumah hissed as he spun around and grabbed her by the waist forcefully. Suddenly, there was a rush of cold air around her, billowing past her ears as though she was suddenly in a gale-force wind. A hard impact jarred her body as the wind continued to foul her hearing and chap her skin. A second impact rang though her body, this one more forcefully, and the air was forced from her lungs. The tips of her ears began to feel as though they were freezing in the chill wind and just as it was about to become a debilitating pain, the wind stopped and she found herself sprawled roughly on the ground surrounded by the sounds of her friends coughing and wheezing and the unmistakable sound of an avalanche of stone cascading into the water.

"The hell was tha…" Katrina began to scream at them all before she was cut off suddenly, apparently by the sight of what was going on. As she turned around to take stock of the situation she watched the last of the bridge crumble away into the sea below them.

"Sorry for the rough treatment." Jumah said, his voice quiet and reserved as though he were ashamed of something.

"You did that?!" Katrina turned back toward him with her hands on her hips.

"Aye. I'm… Yes. I did that." He was obviously uncomfortable suddenly.

Riana got her feet under her and threw her arms around him, embracing him in a tight hug that threatened to force the air from his lungs. "Thank you Jumah."

His hands tentatively came to rest on her shoulders as he looked up at the other two with a searching stare.

Katrina seemed to be stunned into silence; A state that was only exacerbated by Exodus' next words. "Feline? Or canine?"

Jumah's muscles tightened and Riana closed her eyes tightly, hoping that the worst was not about to happen. Most people hated lycanthropes, hunted them in order to 'protect' themselves from the threat of infection with the disease. There were precious few of them left in the world, and Jumah's people were apparently all but extinct.

"Feline." Jumah said flatly. "My people once hailed from the steppes."

"Then you're… cheetah?" Exodus asked with a tone of amazement in his voice.

Jumah relaxed noticeably as he nodded in confirmation.

"That explains what just happened on the bridge. Thank you." Exodus thanked him heartily as he offered his hand to Jumah in gratitude.

Jumah took the offered hand and shook it solidly. "You're welcome. I'm sorry I didn't…"

"Think nothing of it. Public opinion is a difficult thing to overcome. Were I in your place I would have done the same thing."

"What is going on here?" Katrina finally managed to regain her powers of speech.

"Jumah is a werecheetah." Riana said simply as she tightened her embrace on his chest.

"Oh." Katrina replied, her tone somewhere between amazement and a complete lack of caring. "Well then… Thanks for the save. Should we get moving again?"

-29-

The island was something out of a story book. It was lush, green, and lacking the constant, ankle-deep mist of the Forest of Brume. It stood alone in the Great Inland Sea where the light of day could touch it on all sides, making the small open area the group had 'landed' on bright and welcoming. That was if you ignored the steep drop-off on the outside edge of the island, falling away into the waters below. The cliffside looked unclimbable due to the surface being composed of crumbling earth rather than any kind of stone. How the island had lasted this long against the surging tides of the sea was a mystery.

Jumah described the scene to Riana in as much detail as possible. Other than the small area where the bridge had once connected, there appeared to be no path or other indications as to why there had been a bridge leading here. The trees were thick and tall, without any branches close to the ground. Their canopy appeared to block out most of the light on the interior of the island, but not to the same extent as the mainland's forest.

"How's your music doing?" Jumah asked after finishing his description of their surroundings.

Riana, who had been listening intently to his description, was caught off guard. The music still tickled at the edge of her senses, and now that she re-focused her attention on it, it reasserted its place in her thoughts. She cocked her head to one side and perked her ears up to listen for a moment, turning slowly in place as she tried to determine the direction the music was coming from. She was hit by a wave of nostalgia as she confirmed that the tune was indeed the lullaby their mother used to sing to them when they were kids. Confusion waged war on her constantly as she realized that the melody was a song they had made up together and no one else would have known it. "It's coming from this direction." She finally replied, raising her arm and pointing toward the center of the island.

"That looks about right." Jumah said as he moved himself under her outstretched hand, placing it on his shoulder again. She gripped his shoulder with a gentle squeeze of thanks.

The group gathered themselves up, settled their things and forged ahead. The outer edge of the island was over-grown with thick vegetation around the bases of the trees, making their progress slow and uncomfortable. As they pressed on into the island's interior however, the thick carpet of plant life began to thin out, easing their passage more and more as they continued on. They had no trouble winding their way through the interior of the island as the tree trunks were widely spaced and had no low branches presenting obstacles to their progress. As they pushed further in, a new sound became apparent to Riana. Although she couldn't determine where it was coming from, it sounded like a low rumble that changed tone from time to time. It wasn't a constant noise either, only audible for a few moments here and there, and always coming from a different direction.

"Jumah…" She began.

"I hear it Riana." He whispered back, cutting her off.

"What is it though?" Katrina added in, her own ears twitching in agitation at the unknown source of the noise.

"What is what?" Exodus looked around himself with a tiny amount of concern showing on his face. His human ears were apparently not equipped to detect the sound at its present level.

"Some kind of rumbling or…" Katrina stopped suddenly as a realization hit her. The mage that had found this place had been chased off by some kind of creatures. "Growling."

"Yes. It seems the guardians of this ziggurat we seek have found us." Exodus replied.

"At least we've come in the right direction." Jumah's voice held a hint of false bravado."

Riana squeezed Jumah's shoulder at his comment. "We must press on."

He nodded, looking at each in turn, before moving into the forest with the rest of the group in tow.

For another hour they wove through the forest of the island. The entire time they were winding their way through the darker interior, they were pursued by the sounds of the growling creatures and Riana said that the music kept growing louder. They knew they were getting closer when more light began to filter down through the canopy and the smaller plants and ground cover began to thicken again.

When they finally came across the structure it surprised them all. They pushed through a wall of underbrush and there it was, a great pyramid of stone rising up out of the ground. The stone looked freshly quarried and set, but it was covered with trees and other vegetation that were at least a thousand years old. The stone structure was largely obscured from view because of the growth, but its presence was unmistakable. The structure rose several stories above the ground, its sides stepped and tiered with each higher platform being smaller than the one below it.

With some effort, they worked their way around the base of the structure. They came upon a long section stretching away from the central core of the ziggurat several hundred feet. At the end of the protrusion, they discovered a stone door in an archway that was surrounded by carvings of ancient runes and glyphs that looked very similar to the various tattoos covering Riana's exposed skin. In the center of the stone lintel above the door was the glyph they had all come to dread, the same one that floated in the center of the key they had recovered from the dragon.

No sooner had they discovered the doorway when the growling noise from the forest surrounding them intensified, followed by a rustling of leaves and branches and a shouted warning from Jumah.

"Get down!" Roughly, he dragged Riana down to the ground as

several loud howls pierced the air followed by three loud thumping noises as heavy bodies impacted with solid surfaces.

Turning toward the noises, Riana saw three purple-tinged creatures that looked like short, squat alligators, standing a couple feet high on at least a dozen boneless, tentacle-like legs. She could even make out mouthfuls of sharp, pointy teeth. Their growling and panting left no doubt that they were ready and willing to tear the group apart.

As she looked, one of the creatures coiled its tentacle-legs under its body and sprung toward her with its toothy maw open wide for the killing stroke. Her reflexes took over and she dove into a forward roll, kicking out her legs as she moved, forcing Jumah to tumble in the opposite direction.

He came up into a crouching position, swords in hand, ready for action. Riana followed suit, rolling to a crouching position and whirling around with Elkorine held firmly in her right hand and a crackling ball of lightning in her left. The creature was poised on the ground between them and growling loudly as its head twitched back and forth from one to the other.

"Katrina! Look out!" Exodus called from behind Riana as another of the creatures lunged at the other elf. Katrina raised her hand and recited a quick incantation that stopped the creature in mid-leap, leaving its many short, thick tentacles squirming and writhing, seeking purchase in the air. Riana twisted around and threw the ball of lightning in her left hand at the suspended creature. The energy slammed into it like a massive physical blow and caused arcs to race back and forth across its thick hide. The animal screamed out, whether in discomfort or anger she wasn't quite sure.

Both Katrina and Exodus began chanting incantations, their attention on the floating animal. Riana returned her attention to the creature still standing between her and Jumah. She felt a wave of heat wash over her from her friend's spells, just as Jumah dropped out of the air, sword points down, onto the creature that had jumped at them. The thing let out a yelp of pain as his blades drove home but it didn't look as though it was giving up the fight just yet. It twisted its head around to snap at its attacker, but met only empty air as Jumah deftly moved away from its ugly maw just before the strike.

"Mind your business!" Jumah hollered at Riana as he nodded toward the ziggurat. She turned around in time to side step a third creature as it leapt past her. It snagged her shoulder with one of its tentacles and spun her around roughly. In an instant, she had Elkorine up and thrust through flesh as the creature tried to pull her in. She staggered to her knees, looking up to see the creature turn around, growling and gnashing its jaws as it barreled toward her.

Her eyes flashed brightly and a rune on her arm glowed. A tangle of roots and vines shot up from the forest floor and wrapped themselves tightly around the animal's tentacles, pulling it to a rough halt in mid-charge. Not letting up for a second, Riana's eyes flashed again and a different glyph glowed as a bolt of lightning arced out of the clear blue sky and struck the creature in the head. Electricity arced across its skin and it howled, a long keening call directed at the other of its kind. It ended abruptly when Riana buried Elkorine to the hilt in its skull. The creature slumped to the ground, letting loose one last pitiful whine before dying.

Riana cast her gaze around the area as she slid her sword out of the creature's body. Jumah was just pulling his own swords from the first creature, while Katrina and Exodus were using sticks to poke and prod the charred remains of the one they had fought. They were engaged in a rather heated debate about what manner of animal it was and rather than interrupt them, or more specifically, get dragged into the debate, she moved over to Jumah and asked if he was alright.

"I'm fine." He replied jovially as he resheathed his swords and turned to look at the others for a moment. "As are they apparently."

"So it would seem." Riana said, casting a disparaging glance at them over her shoulder. "Now if only we could get them to put that much energy into figuring out how to open this door."

"And quickly." Jumah said in a hushed tone, cocking his head to one side and focusing on some far-distant item of interest.

"What is it?" Riana turned her head in the same direction before realizing what it was that had caught his attention. There were more of them. She could hear the growling as they approached. Lots of them. From every direction. "Crap." She hissed through tight lips as she tried to make out individual sounds in the approaching mass. "Thirty of them?"

Jumah grinned at her with a look of approval on his face. "Close. I make out thirty-four."

"Either way, it's too much for the four of us to handle. Hey you two!" She raised her voice as she looked toward Katrina and Exodus. "More company, we need to figure this door out post haste."

Katrina and Exodus both paused in their argument dropped their sticks as one, and bolted toward the door. Their hands went straight to the frieze surrounding the door and they began speaking to one another in hushed, hurried tones about the meaning of each of the symbols.

"We really need Ree's input here, she's a self made expert on these things." Katrina said.

Riana swept her gaze back and forth across the dark expanse opposite the door, her ears focused on the growling sounds that were rapidly approaching from all directions. The only things she could make out were her companions. "You're going to have to hurry up!" She said suddenly as a thick tongue of flames issued forth from her outstretched hand and enveloped one of the creatures as it leapt from the forest toward them.

The animal dropped to the ground and began wailing in pain as its scaly skin burned, but was quickly finished off by a slash from Jumah's swords.

All at once the growling in the forest came to a stop and the group stood in complete silence. Even the sounds of the forest seemed to stop, surrounding them in an unnatural quiet that made their skin crawl.

"The door!" Riana hissed through clenched teeth, causing Katrina and Exodus to resume their efforts suddenly.

"I don't like this sudden silence." Jumah remarked as he scanned the tree-line for activity.

"Nor do I. Something's up." Riana agreed.

"No! That one's key, this one's possess!" Katrina hollered suddenly from behind them. "Only those possessed by the key may enter!"

"Well the two runes are almost identical, and that makes no sense, how could the key possess someone?" Exodus replied calmly, turning to look at Riana.

"Will you two keep it down back there?" Riana hissed again. She was so focused on the forest that she had not heard a word they said, only the noise of their conversation. "We're trying to…"

She was cut off as loud snarls and yips erupted from around them. Her ears twitched around, trying to get a fix on where the noise was coming from but it seemed to be all around, and rapidly closing in on them.

In a panic she threw up her hands and a storm of lightning bolts began arcing away from her in every direction, catching the mob in mid-air. There were no less than fifty of the animals, all attacking simultaneously from the tree-line. The ball of lightning shot out writhing tendrils in all directions, catching the creatures in mid-leap and setting their bodies to convulsing. The electricity arced from creature to creature, blanketing the entire area with purple-blue discharges.

"Back!" Jumah shouted suddenly. "Riana get back toward the door, there're more of them!"

Her concentration shaken, the electrical discharge stopped abruptly and she could hear the affected creatures getting to their feet almost immediately, preparing for another assault. Looking over her shoulder toward her sister and Exodus, she began back-pedaling toward the door, keeping her ears open for creatures along the way.

"Can you put up a shield or a fire wall or something?" Jumah asked hurriedly as he moved up beside her.

"No. That's Kat's area and we need her to work on the door because I can't see the damn symbols!"

"Alright then we need to buy them some time. Do what you can."

"Right." Riana sighed under her breath, "what I can…"

The battle became a blur as she lashed out with her sword and spells at anything that she could see. She was growing weak from exertion and numerous fresh cuts and gashes, combined with some reopened wounds from the fight with the tower guardian and Malice. Her head was beginning to pound and there was no discernible slow down in the flow of animals. She had no idea how many of the things they had killed, but she could hear Jumah's labored breathing, indicating that he too was being taxed unmercifully. All the while Katrina and Exodus continued debating the meaning of symbols on the door frame, and had finally resorted to trying to pry the slab of a door open with Katrina's staff, Chavan.

The air was suddenly forced from Riana's lungs as one of the creatures got through her defenses, slamming into her body head first and driving her to the ground. With all of her remaining strength, she pulled her legs up between herself and the animal and pushed it off with her feet. It flew back towards the trees and caused her head to collide with the stone slab that was the door of the ziggurat. She yelped in pain as she made contact with the hard surface, but to her astonishment it wasn't the blow to her head that caused the outburst, but rather a sharp, tingling jolt that seemed to be originating in her belt pouch.

"The key!" She stammered as she stumbled back to her feet, leaning heavily against the door for support. She pried open the leather pouch and jammed her hand into it as Jumah backed into her, his muscles flexing and rolling as he worked double time to keep the creatures at bay. His back smashed into her and he forced the three of them into the door, trying to reduce the amount of area he had to defend now that Riana was no longer in the fight.

"If you have a plan…" he panted, "now would definitely be the time."

Riana's hand closed around the hard, crystalline form in her pouch and she pulled the object out to let the others see it. As soon as she glanced down at her outlined, purple hand, she saw the form of the key glowing brightly within it.

No longer in control, she slammed the crystal key against the surface of the door, pinning it between the stone and her hand and pushing with all of her might. She felt Exodus and Katrina pushing as well and they were rewarded with a low, rumbling vibration from within the structure somewhere.

Without warning the stone slab fell back away from them and the four fell into the opening, ending up in a heap on the cold stone floor. Before any of them could begin to get their feet under themselves, they could hear the sound of the slab closing again and then silence fell, leaving only the sound of their fatigued panting and groaning.

-30-

"Good thinking Ree." Katrina moaned as she picked herself up off of the floor and conjured a sphere of light at the end of her staff by rapping it against the floor a few times.

"I wish I could take credit for it. The thing damn near burned the skin off of me trying to get my attention. And then I couldn't stop myself from using it!" Riana replied as she too extricated herself from the pile of people on the floor.

"Either way, I am most pleased to be away from those creatures." Exodus intoned as he brushed himself off.

"Yeah. What he said." Came Jumah's cheerful reply. "So... What now?"

Riana looked around at their surroundings. Unlike the outside of the structure, which she couldn't see at all, the interior was glowing brightly in her vision. The hallway they were standing in seemed to be hexagonal in cross-section and about twice her height. She could see the hallway extending out away from where they stood and then abruptly turning right and disappearing out of sight.

"Weird." She commented.

"What's that?" Jumah asked as he moved up beside her.

"Well, I can see the walls in here even though I couldn't see the pyramid at all from the outside."

"Interesting…" Exodus mused from near one of the angled walls.

"What's that?" Katrina moved in closer to him.

"Well by all accounts this place has not been visited by a living being in millennia right?"

"That's what all of the documentation I was able to dig up would suggest."

"Then why is it so clean? There isn't a mote of dirt or dust, or a single cobweb to be found in here."

The group milled about for a moment as each of them seemed to be verifying his statement. Riana even ran her fingers along the lower face of the wall to see if she could feel anything there before Katrina finally said, "Yeah. That is kind of weird. So either this place just doesn't get dirty over time or…"

"There's someone here with us." Jumah said flatly.

"Exactly." Katrina agreed as she ran her own hand along the wall. "Which is insanity really, not even elves live that long. A dragon maybe. Or some elemental or demi-god perhaps, but I can't imagine any of those creatures having much interest in cleaning the place. Especially not to this extent."

"No." Jumah said, his voice still flat and matter-of-fact. "I mean, there is someone here with us. I can smell them."

Everyone turned to look at him simultaneously. Riana placed her hand on his shoulder and gave it a squeeze. "Can you tell anything about them?" She asked.

"Yes. Only one thing in all of Kalijor smells like this. A fire dragon."

"Wow." Katrina offered. "Is that all? No sweat right?"

Jumah looked at her for a moment, his expression unreadable. Finally, he turned away quietly and began leading Riana down the hallway toward the corner.

"What did I say?" Katrina looked to Exodus for help.

"I'm not entirely sure really. Although I must say that any dragon that has been alive for as long as this place seems to have been around, would have to be very powerful indeed. If we have to fight the creature…" He moved off after the others without finishing his thought, leaving

Katrina there to think about things for a second before she hurried after them.

They moved in relative silence after that, following the hallway around several ninety degree turns and eventually down a few steep ramps that put them well below where the water of the Inland Sea would reach. The hallways remained smooth and featureless, and strikingly clean. Finally, they stepped into a large chamber that was lit by a series of torches set into brackets carved in the shape of dragon heads on the walls. Opposite the hallway, a stone alter or table was just discernible behind the great bulk of a ruby-red dragon laying on the ground. The dragon was curled around itself in a comfortable position, much like a sleeping cat or dog. The creature was easily over one-hundred feet in length, although it was difficult to tell for certain with its neck and tail wrapped around its impressive body. Its great, leathery wings were folded against its back lazily, but looked as though they would block out the light of day if unfurled completely. Its head was as large as any one of them, with a pointy snout and long sweeping horns jutting out from behind its eyes which appeared to be closed. Its jaws were shut but several sword-length teeth were still easily seen peeking from behind a curled lip. The lance-like claws that tipped the digits of each of the creature's four powerful limbs were not readily visible, but nervous imaginings filled in the blanks nicely. Its entire body was covered in dark, ruby-red scales that reflected the torch light while the four companions stood in awe of the creature.

Riana sucked in her breath as she looked at the dragon. She had never seen anything so beautiful. Every detail of the creature, every single scale stood out in stark relief. While the Death Dragon had appeared to her as a sort of mono-chromatic, purple painting, with its details smoothed together, creating a sort of dragon-shaped silhouette in her vision, This dragon looked more like a very detailed line drawing. It looked a lot like wire-frame models she had seen in computer displays while learning the trade of being a Corporate Courier for Solidarity Online. This beast was no creature of magic or powerful wielder of the arcane. No, this creature *was* magic. The physical embodiment of the flow of mana in the world. It was every spell, cantrip, enchantment and potion, physically manifested for her to see. The creature was beautiful in its raw power and deadly potential.

"Long have I slept here. Waiting for the chosen." The voice rolled though the room, jarring their bodies. It was a low sound, just on the edge of hearing, although they definitely did hear it. It was more felt than anything else as it rolled across them.

"We mean no disrespect." Katrina moved forward a step and addressed the creature as it lifted its head slightly, extending it toward them on its long, sinuous neck before setting it down again much closer to them. Its eyes were open now and appeared to be two pools of molten gold with narrow black slits for pupils. It seemed to inspect her for a long moment before speaking once more.

"You are not the one. Only the chosen may enter the vault and retrieve what you seek."

Now they all looked toward Riana, who was sure she was blushing scarlet from head to toe. "What makes you think it's me?" She asked sarcastically.

"Who else would it be Ree?" Katrina poked her in the shoulder as she spoke. "You've got the key."

Riana sighed heavily, wanting nothing more than a normal life, a quiet evening in front of a fire with Jumah, or a joy ride around the moon in the Kestrel. What would she give to be…normal? But then what was normal? This life and these things were all she had ever known. Didn't that make them by their very nature…normal? She snapped her attention back to the room, as Katrina cleared her throat harshly. Looking around at the purple-outlined faces of her friends each in turn, she finally took a few tentative steps forward and addressed the dragon that was looking at her intently. "I am Riana Thorindal. Daughter of Ezrina Reyals and Kilishandra Thorindal."

The dragon exhaled two columns of steam from its nostrils, causing Riana's skin to prickle from the surprise and heat of the action. "What is it you seek Riana Thorindal?"

"We seek the Obscuri relic that is secreted away here." She didn't see any point in trying to deceive this creature. If she angered it, she knew it was more than capable of destroying them all without even standing up. Although, something about it didn't sit well with her. Something about it was not exactly right but she couldn't quite place it.

"To what end?"

"To keep it out of the hands of evil."

"It *is* out of the hands of evil. There is no safer place." Its voice rolled through them like an earthquake.

"The people of Avian are made to suffer for it. An evil person is holding the city hostage unless we bring him the key."

"And yet you have no intention of bringing the key, or the artifact." It was not a question.

"No. The Obscuri assured us that it would be disastrous if either the key or the artifact fell into the hands of someone like that."

"What do *you* think?"

She stopped short, thinking about what the dragon was asking her. What did she think about what? About the key? The artifact? The Obscuri? "I'm sorry, I don't..."

"The question is simple enough. What do you think? The Obscuri assure you of one thing. Your enemy assures you of another. You have friends and companions that are obviously loyal to you and your quest, so they apparently have some measure of faith in you and your abilities. But what do you think?"

She was still stumped. Yes she had friends that were traveling with her. Why? Because they were her friends. Where there other reasons? Deeper reasons? And what was all this about the Obscuri and her enemies? What did this creature want from her? "I... I don't..."

"You don't think? Or you don't know what I am asking you?"

Her face heated in embarrassment and frustration at the accusation. Was it really an accusation though? Or just an observation? Was she so transparent? "I don't understand the question. What do I think about what?"

The dragon's voice rumbled through her, "You put your life in jeopardy, your friend's lives as well. You accept the responsibility for the lives of every being in Avian. You have embarked upon a quest that has earned you the attention of some of the most evil people in Kalijor and you don't even know why. So I ask you again, what do you think?"

Riana stared straight ahead as the dragon chided her. It was right though, she had no idea what she had submerged herself in, and worse still, she still had no idea why, or even what the stakes really were. All she knew is that she had been swept up in the tide of events and one thing had been leading to another for so long that she had stopped thinking about 'why' a long time ago. Finally it hit her, she was tired of being pushed around. Tired of being a rudderless ship adrift in the currents and eddies of other peoples' conflicts. "I think I am tired of being everyone else's pawn. I think it's time the decision was mine." She looked back to her friends, all standing together proudly, willing to face death with her without a second thought. "And I think it's time my friends and I learned exactly what we are risking our lives for."

"I think you are correct." The dragon rumbled. "The relics locked away by the five crystal keys were introduced into the world of Kalijor by the developers shortly after the game's inception."

Riana looked at the dragon for a moment, its image shimmering in her vision, every bit as detailed as if she could see it normally. Finally, it occurred to her that the dragon had called them developers, and referred to Kalijor as a game. As if reading her thoughts, the dragon responded.

"Indeed. I am fully aware of the nature of this world, and furthermore, I do not have coding in place that prevents me from talking about it as such. Unlike others, such as your Master Gornin, who are aware on some subliminal level, but are unable to fully articulate their subconscious understanding."

"So Master Gornin has been programmed to refer to Kalijor the way he does. But you say he really knows the truth?" It was all a bit difficult to fathom, aware of the world but still… a program.

"That is correct."

Shaking her head, she decided to focus on the task at hand. "Alright. So about these items. What is so special about them? Why is everyone in the real world after them?"

"It is a complicated matter Riana. The relationship between your world and this one is more substantial than most people realize. The medium through which this game functions gives it power over your world."

"The medium? What are you…"

"Oh!" Katrina suddenly blurted out. "Sub-space! He's talking about sub-space!"

"Your friend is correct. Your scientists still do not fully understand the sub-space medium as yet. They are only now becoming vaguely aware of the connection between the game world and the real world."

"Alright. But what *is* the connection?" Riana asked with a note of impatience.

"Even though our worlds look and behave completely differently, each and every point in Kalijor is connected directly to a point in the real world. This connection is a direct result of the sub-space medium that the game uses for instantaneous communication across inter-stellar distances."

"Each point… Are you trying to tell me that by affecting things in Kalijor I can effect changes in the real world?" Riana's eyes opened up wide.

"In theory, yes. Although no one has yet managed to cause such an effect. The connections are usually much more subtle than that."

"Subtle… I'm afraid I am not following you."

"It is not surprising. Imagine if you will that a book in this world is the counterpart to a data file in a computer in your world. By altering the book in this world in the proper way…"

"…You could affect a change in the program in the real world!" Katrina blurted out again.

"Such would truly be an awesome power if used correctly." Exodus spoke quietly.

"And no one would find more use for such a link than the Conglomerate, or those that fight against it." Jumah breathed.

Riana looked back at her friends for a moment, soaking in the information as best she could. She was still so new to that other world, she didn't know everything she needed to about how things worked there yet. "So what do the artifacts have to do with all of this? What makes them so special that people are willing to kill each other for them?"

"Ah." The dragon replied sagely, "Most of the people who realize the intrinsic link between our worlds encounter the problem that the worlds take on such wildly different forms. A computer program in your world could be anything from a book to a bird bath in our world. And, once the corresponding object is discovered, one must then learn how to properly alter it in order to affect the desired changes. The five artifacts of the Obscuri are tools that make the identification, alteration, and understanding of this process much easier."

"So the artifacts are like hacker tools." Katrina spoke under her breath.

"Indeed. Only these tools allow people to hack the real world." The dragon replied.

"Suddenly, things are much clearer." Riana finally spoke again.

"So as you can see, the reason for these artifacts having been locked up is indeed sound. If the artifacts fell into the wrong hands, the person or people holding them would have incredible power, in both of our worlds. Each of the relics provides a different ability to the person holding it. Some make it easier to find the links between worlds, others make it easier to understand the nature of the links, and still others allow the manipulation to be performed much more easily. It is even said that one of the artifacts will allow its wielder to kill a person in the real world by destroying their avatar here."

Katrina gasped at hearing this. "Ree do you think that's true? Xavier's been looking for the keys. Why would he want something like that?"

Riana turned and looked at the ghostly outline of her sister, twisting her face up into a look of awe. "Kat, I know he has been a father figure for you since your parents died, but I think it's time you woke up to certain realities about him. If anything, this explains why he would be willing to sacrifice you for one of the keys."

"Ree I don't think he could do something like that..."

"Kat!" Riana shouted at her, startling the group. "He left you in here. Stuck where no one could find you. For *six months*! He did not lift so much as a finger to try and find you. What exactly is it that someone like that would *not* be capable of doing? It was 'business as usual' less than a week after you were kidnapped Kat. He didn't organize search parties, or even pull any GM's off regular duty to help me look for you."

Katrina looked at her sister for a long moment before spinning around in a whirl of robes, burying her face in Exodus' shoulder and breaking down into sobs.

Riana watched her sister's breakdown with mixed emotions. She knew Katrina needed to realize what Xavier was, what he was capable of. But she didn't like to see her suffering. Finally she moved over to the pair and wrapped her arm around Katrina's slender waist. Leaning her head in close to her sister's ear she spoke quietly.

"Kat... I'm sorry. I don't know Xavier. Not like you do. All I know is what I have seen of him. Maybe he has his reasons for doing what he did, but I still find it unacceptable. Even with the best of intentions, what he did to you was reprehensible."

Katrina continued to sob into Exodus' shoulder as Riana let go of her and turned to face Jumah and the dragon.

"Any advice you have here would be appreciated. I don't want these items to get out. But I can't stand by and let the people of Avian suffer and die. I gave my word I would return and help them."

Jumah smiled warmly and shrugged his shoulders slightly. "If you haven't got your honor, you haven't got anything as far as I am concerned. So not going back is not an option. As to the question of the artifacts..."

He turned and looked at Katrina and Exodus, "They have not even been released into the world yet and look at the damage they have already caused. Your boss, the guy who runs this whole world, and is apparently her father, threw her to the wolves, then, for whatever reason, refused to mount any sort of rescue. And you two are now at one-another's throats over the whole affair."

Riana ignored his pointed look. She could hear her sister's quiet sobs and knew full well what she would see if she turned. Instead, she forced herself to look at the guardian of the artifact. The great dragon looked at her impassively, showing no signs of concern for the events unfolding before it. "And what do you think?" She asked the creature bluntly.

The dragon raised a scaly eyebrow at her and then let its low rumbling voice spill out across the room. "It is not my place to advise you on your course of action. I am simply protector of the seals guarding the artifacts."

"Surely you must have an opinion." Riana retorted acidly. Her patience was fast wearing thin.

"I do and it will remain mine. No one can make this decision for you. It is yours and yours alone."

Riana huffed loudly, trying to express her feelings of abandonment in this situation. Turning to face her friends she started talking things through quietly. "So Avian is under siege by a powerful mage or hacker. They want the key or they will let the city die. If we give them the key then they can get the artifact, or *we* can get the artifact and try to use it to stop them. But doing so will put the artifact back in the open again. We could try and defeat this person without it but we have no idea who or where they are, or even how to deal with them if we *do* find them. If the key is any indication then this artifact could be the one that allows us to find the links between worlds, which could make it a lot easier to find this person."

Again she looked at Jumah, imploring him for help with her whole body. He looked back at her and smiled slightly. "Riana I will support you in whatever you decide. Personally I think we should leave this thing where it is. Even if it means Avian dies. Any players will already have left there and an NPC is just that... *not* a player. So what harm is there in a computer program dying?"

"I'm afraid you do not fully grasp the situation." The dragon interjected. "The links between our worlds are absolute. Every person here bears a direct link to a person there. Whether the link is active, as in the case of a player, or passive as in the case of an NPC. The link is still there, and still very real."

Riana looked at the dragon with a visage of horror on her face. Katrina stopped her sobbing and turned around suddenly to stare in awe at the dragon. Jumah and Exodus both looked in the same direction, their faces difficult to read, but definitely serious.

"So... If even an NPC dies here..." Riana began.

"Then the person linked to that NPC dies as well. In your world. There has only ever been one single case where an individual in one world did not bear a direct link to one in the other." The dragon looked directly at Riana as it spoke this last statement, almost as an accusation.

Riana's skin heated at the inference. She knew she was unique but she hadn't realized just to what extent. It seemed every single time she

236

turned around there was someone there telling her how different she really was from everyone else.

Jumah raised a curious eyebrow at the silent communication that had just taken place between Riana and the dragon. Memories of the rumors about a rogue program having been extracted from Kalijor ran through his head. Could such a thing actually be true?

"So if Avian dies then…" She breathed quietly.

"Then thousands of people in your world will die unexpectedly. Men, women, children, animals."

"Oh lord…" Katrina gasped.

Riana stared at the dragon fixedly. "Alright. How do we get at this thing? We have to find this lunatic."

The dragon seemed to take a deep breath, holding it for a second as it closed its eyes and concentrated. Finally it opened its eyes again and spoke dramatically. "Those who seek it know that those who have it would never admit it. Those who claim to have it may be surprised to learn they may never know its touch. If you spent a lifetime seeking it and never found it, it would be a lifetime well spent."

"What the hell is it?!" Riana seethed as she paced about the room. For good measure she kicked the stone table at the end of the room and immediately regretted it as her toes started throbbing. "Dammit!" She cursed. She knew better than to kick with her toes anyway, she deserved the pain. "What is this riddle all about anyway? I thought these things were protected by traps and monsters and other ugly stuff like that."

"The tests are designed to make sure the person that releases the artifacts is more than just physically capable." The dragon replied calmly.

She cast an icy glare at the shimmering purple form of the beast. She knew the creature was imperturbable but the simple act of it was meant to help her feel better. Unfortunately all it did was exacerbate her mood.

"Calm down Ree." Katrina said from where she sat on the floor facing Exodus. The pair had pulled out an impossible number of volumes from their robes and packs and were rummaging through them to find any information that might prove useful with the riddle.

Riana tossed her sister a disparaging glare as well just for good measure, even realizing that the look would be as wasted on her as it was on the dragon.

"She is right Riana. You need a level head to think this through properly." Jumah moved up behind her and gently wrapped his arms around her waist, pulling her in close to him.

She sighed as she felt the warmth of his body against hers and let herself fall into the feeling a bit. Looking from Katrina and Exodus, to the dragon and then down to Jumah's hands, Riana realized they were all trying to accomplish what had never been done before. This whole situation was crazy. In fact, her whole life was crazy. In the last two years, she had found out that she was born in a virtual world. She only discovered the truth after being transplanted into the 'real' world and being placed in a cybernetic body. She had learned that people in the real world were just as apt to kill one another over meaningless trinkets as they were in the world she had grown up in, proving that the 'human' condition was alive and well no matter what world a person lived in. Then she had been betrayed by a man that she had thought she could trust, again over a stupid trinket. Now here she was, back in the realm where it had all begun. She was faced with the knowledge that anything they changed here would have a real effect on the 'real' world. It was amazing to her how humans, real humans, not the virtual ones here in Kalijor, were so ingenious at innovating and creating, but never seemed to stop and reflect upon what they had done from time to time. Here they had an entire world they had created for their own amusement and yet they didn't have the wherewithal to understand the

240

ramifications of meddling with their own creation. How was it that an entire race of people could be devoid of even a basic amount of wisdom in these matters, the foresight to simply stop and look around every once in a while…

Then it hit her all at once, "Wait that's it!"

"What's it?" Katrina half shouted from the floor as she looked up suddenly at Riana's exclamation. Exodus' head snapped up as well and Jumah released her waist and stepped around beside her so he could see her face.

Riana beamed with delight at her revelation. "It's wisdom! Think about it! Anyone who is wise enough to know what wisdom really is would never admit to being wise. They would always be looking for something deeper wouldn't they? I mean it was your own Socrates who said that he was the only wise person he knew, because he was the only one who realized that he really knew nothing in the grand scheme of things. And anyone I have ever met who *claimed* to be wise, was in reality a blithering idiot!" She clapped her hands together loudly, spinning around to face the dragon, a grin spreading across her face from ear to ear as she looked at the creature.

"Well done Riana Thorindal. The prize is yours to take, if it is still your desire to do so." As it spoke, the dragon turned to look at the stone table in the room. The group followed its gaze, and saw a small gold circlet appear in the center of the slab. To Riana's eyes it was a brightly glowing circle of light, much like she would have imagined a halo to look, floating slightly above the surface of the table.

Cautiously, she made her way over to the artifact and looked at it much more closely. The object was by far the brightest object she had yet seen with her altered sight. It radiated bright purple light in a corona that seemed to ignite the rest of the room, washing everything in a bright purple glow. After a moment she looked, back toward her friends and the dragon, all of whom were looking at her expectantly.

"I'm still open to alternatives." Riana said flatly. She was fairly certain that there would be none, but she was still unconvinced that this was the correct course of action. She was more than willing to change the plan to something, anything, with less far reaching consequences. A long moment of silence followed her comment and finally she sighed once more and reached out to take the artifact.

The instant she touched it there was a blinding flash of light. It would have been enormously painful to everyone in the room had it not been so brief, but as it was it was over before anyone realized it had happened. As they all blinked away the discomfort it took them a moment to realize that the dragon was gone.

Riana stood up straight, holding the circlet in her outstretched hands and looked to her friends for advice on what to do with it. Reading her questioning look Katrina responded, "Well it looks about the right size to be worn on the head."

"You think that's a good idea?" Riana sounded very uncertain.

"No." Katrina said. Then she smirked as she continued, "But do you have a better idea?"

"Touché." Riana acquiesced, then took a deep breath and held it as she lifted the circlet up to her head and settled it just above her ears. For a moment, nothing seemed to happen. Then nothing else happened. After a few minutes she was fairly well convinced that she had done something wrong and reached up to take the thing off her head when things changed, eliciting a small gasp.

"What is it?" Jumah asked quietly. He had moved towards her, concerned by the noise.

"I can see... Lines of some kind. They are very faint, but I can definitely make out some kind of lines emanating from each of you.

"Lines?" Exodus remarked. "What kind of lines?"

"Yeah. What kind?" Katrina echoed.

"Well." Riana paused to try and think of some way to describe them. "They are kind of a wispy yellow, or gold color. They sort of emanate from your mid-sections and then trail off into nowhere. Although now that I look at you both a little more intently I can see smaller, fainter lines connecting each of you to your spell books."

"That is odd." Exodus finally replied, falling silent again as he pondered the meaning of the lines.

"No. No I don't think it is." Katrina replied suddenly. "Here Ree let's try something real quick. Tell me what you see when I cast this spell." Then without waiting for a reply she chanted a few simple words and a sphere of light appeared next to her, floating in mid-air lazily.

Riana looked on as the magical sphere appeared. She sucked in a deep breath, straining slightly, as she focused on her sister more intently. She could see a faint wisp of gold connecting the sphere to her sister's outline. She described what she was seeing to the group and Katrina snuffed out the sphere of light with a satisfied giggle.

Everyone stared at her for a long moment before she began to explain her amusement. "It's describing a link between a person and their energy."

"What?" Jumah asked as politely as he could.

"Look. When you cast a spell, you use some of your energy to channel into the environment and magnify with intense focus. We then force it into whatever useful service we can come up with. Well, there has to be a connection of some kind between ourselves and the energy we expel, don't you think? Just like when you exhale, the column of air remains connected to you, at least until you finish exhaling and break it off. This thing just allows the wearer to see that faint connection between the user and the magic."

"I guess that makes a certain amount of sense." Exodus replied.

"Ok." Riana added with a note of panic in her voice as she tugged on the circlet. "Now can we work on why it won't come off?"

-32-

After nearly an hour of trying to remove the artifact, they had finally decided that since it seemed to be doing her no harm they were better off leaving it alone. Jumah had reminded them that the lives of everyone in Avian hung in the balance and Riana admitted that she would rather see them in an improved situation and worry about herself later.

As they began discussing how they would go about getting to Avian, Exodus reminded them that his area of magical specialization was the creation of gateways and portals and quickly conjured up a column of floating rings for them all to use.

In another moment they had all stepped through the portal and were immediately beset upon by the winged guards in the Avian portal chamber.

"Halt! Who dares enter Avian in this dark time?" An angry voice shouted at them as Riana felt the frigid air of Avian surround her. The effect was very much like diving into a cold lake, minus the water.

She gasped, trying to catch her breath in the suddenly chilly air. Finally, gathering her wits she looked around and saw a few small purple outlines in the room. A dagger or sword here and there. A magical pendant of some kind, a ring, and a bracelet seemed to float about the room, but none of the people wearing or carrying the items could be discerned from the background of blackness in her vision. When she looked harder, she could see a dozen or so wispy golden trails emanating from what had to be their bodies. Each wisp wound off lazily in different directions, some connected to the magical items and others stopped abruptly or disappeared into what she assumed to be a wall or some other unseen solid object.

Spinning around, she quickly accounted for her three companions. All of them standing back to back with her in a tight formation, ready for the worst. Jumah had his swords drawn and his muscles were tensed and ready to be uncoiled in an instant.

Riana took a deep breath and stepped forward with her hands raised, trying to look as unthreatening as possible. "I am Riana Thorindal and these are my companions. I made a promise to return here and help your city once my sister was found and now I am here to fulfill that promise."

There was a brief moment of silence. Then she heard the sound of weapons being sheathed and feathered wings being ruffled. Finally a commanding voice addressed her. "Riana Thorindal. I am Captain Tal'il. His highness said you would arrive in the city soon. He also said to escort you to him once you had. If you and your companions will follow me please?"

Riana let her breath go in a long stream, she hadn't even realized she had been holding it. "Of course. Thank you." She replied as she reached behind her for Jumah. Quickly he snatched up her hand and placed it on his shoulder as he stepped in front of her. Together the four of them followed the Captain out of the room.

As they left the portal building, a wave of frigid air washed over them. Riana staggered, nearly falling to her knees as the cold washed over her exposed skin. In a flash, Jumah had her cloak out of her pack and wrapped around her tightly. He pulled her close, trying to share his body heat. It helped, but not much. They walked through the deserted streets of the city, slowly making their way to the top tier where the palace was built in the highest branches of the mighty, petrified tree.

As they moved along the cobbled streets, Riana felt that something here was very, very wrong. Aside from the obvious issue, there was something about the city that just felt… wrong. Careful to keep her hand on Jumah and trusting him to detour her around solid objects, she tried to focus her concentration on the guards that were escorting them through the streets. Looking around slowly she directed her attention to each of them in turn. There was something different about one of them. A much thinner, less discernible wisp extending from the body of the guard to her right. She looked at the space around the wisp, determined to see why there was a difference. As they trudged through the frigid streets, she forced herself to see deeper into the person that she knew was there. Suddenly, she was rewarded with a flash of gold-white light in the shape of a winged person. The image slammed into her like a physical blow and then was gone again an instant later.

The explosion of light caused a wave of nausea to wash over her and she dropped to her knees, gasping for breath and trying to keep her stomach down. Jumah snapped up her hand again and Katrina shouted out in concern. The others gathered around to see what was going on. As she looked up, she pushed her mind back to where it had been just as the flash of light had hit her. With a little effort it happened again, only this time she was able to maintain it for more than a split second. It was gone again before she could do much else.

As she allowed herself to be helped up and offered some token assurances that she was OK, she tried again. This time, the image stayed. The guard in question now showed up to her as a brightly glowing golden shape. Very obviously human, with a pair of wings folded up loosely across its back. She gasped as she saw the figure, without even realizing the extent of what had happened at first. After a moment she realized that more was going on here than she knew. She finally tore her eyes away and scanned the group again. This time she was amazed by what she saw. Every other person, her friends included, was now visible as a more or less solid red form, golden wisps reaching out from their cores. Only the one with the weaker wisp trail differed. She could think of only one thing that all of her companions had in common, but it made no sense to her why, or even how, the rest of the guards would have that in common as well.

"Are you alright Ree?" Katrina asked as she moved up alongside her. She put her arm around the shoulder Jumah wasn't already supporting. Her voice was heavy with concern for her sister.

"I'm fine." Riana panted. It seemed to be taking considerable effort to maintain this new perspective. Finally she let her concentration slip and breathed heavily as she refocused on her friends. "Listen." She said, almost under her breath. She spoke so quietly that she could barely hear herself, forcing Jumah and Katrina to move their heads in even closer in order to hear her. Although she knew they both had much keener hearing than those surrounding them and so her words would most likely remain unheard by anyone else.

"Something fishy is going on here. I just managed to access some new power from this thing and it showed me something very strange. Although I'm not sure how such a thing is even possible..."

"What is it Ree?" Katrina whispered back as she looked around the group suspiciously.

"I don't know how to explain it other than to say I think that only one of these guards is an actual NPC." She responded, knowing it sounded as unlikely as it felt. No one would ever want, or choose to play as a city guard, and so the game world was designed to set up all guards as NPC's, in order to allow players to play, rather than have jobs they needed to report to in the game.

"How can that be?" Jumah hissed. "I thought the system was supposed to set up all players as adventurers or crafters of some kind, not guards and support people."

"I thought so too." Riana answered under her breath. "But that is the only explanation I can come up with, as unlikely as it seems."

"All players *are* supposed to be adventurers or crafters." Katrina added. "I probably know the rules better than anyone here and there is no way the system would allow a player to be a city guard, even if it *was* a desirable position to someone. Something strange is going on here."

"I know." Riana agreed. "It doesn't feel right here. Even for a place that is under the influence of a powerful curse. But I can't put my finger on what it is exactly."

"Can you use your new powers to find out more?" Jumah asked.

"I can try." Riana answered, "but it really seems to take it out of me. I'll need you two to support me as we go, I don't want to draw any more suspicion from these folks."

"Understood." Jumah responded, tightening his grip on Riana's slender body. "Kat you go tell Exodus what is going on. I'll keep Riana moving."

"Alright." Katrina said, sounding concerned, "you be careful Ree."

"I will." Riana smiled at her sister as Katrina disengaged herself from them and slid back in the group to huddle up next to Exodus and bring him up to speed.

Riana wrapped her arm around Jumah and pulled herself up against him tightly. She was pleased to feel him tighten his grip on her as well. Reassured, she began shifting her focus again, trying to force her vision into a range where she could see something, anything, new. It took a few more minutes of trying before she found another 'frequency' to tune in to. Now she could see the red silhouettes but they were much less bright. When she concentrated on a person, she was washed through a series of images of places she had never been, as though she was on a fast-forward journey to somewhere. Some of the places she had seen in images before while studying Earth history, space stations, colonies, vehicles. After a moment the wash of images would come to a halt and she would come face to face with a blurred image of a person in a gaming pod, tied into the system in a sleep-like state. But when she reached out to touch the image it would shimmer like a reflection on the surface of a pool that someone had dropped a stone into. Suddenly the image would fade and she would be staring at their silhouette again.

When she looked at the golden silhouette of the guard she suspected was actually an NPC, the same series of images flooded past her, but when the rush of imagery stopped she was looking at a small child playing in a park with his friends.

"They are PC's Jumah." She whispered under her breath. "I can see them in their gaming pods!" She almost let her amazement get the better of her. Jumah's soft admonishment to keep it down, reminded her that she wasn't entirely certain if she could trust the people she saw.

"What about the NPC? What do you see there?" He whispered back at her.

"A young boy playing in a park somewhere."

"Interesting. Have you been able to find anything that might help us with the curse on Avian?"

"You mean aside from the fact that there are PC's pretending to be NPC's?" She asked.

"Of course dear." He grinned as he spoke under his breath.

Riana blushed scarlet beneath her cloak at the term. She had no idea what, if anything, he meant by the comment, but it made her feel strange to think what it *could* mean. Shaking her head slightly to clear her thoughts, she turned her thoughts back to the task at hand. She stared, not at the people, but at the space between them. Following the theory that the wisps were energy, she felt certain that she could see the energies of the spell that was causing Avian such distress. To her surprise, a moment later she saw a bright blue aura surrounding a silhouette of the city. As she focused on the glowing halo surrounding the city she saw that it had a thick blue wisp streaming into its center. A wisp that, from the look of it, originated from a red silhouette of a person within the palace at the top of the city.

She gasped sharply as she realized what she was looking at. "Jumah. It's amazing! I can see the curse! I can actually see it surrounding the city. And more importantly I can see the person it is connected to. The one that seems to be controlling it."

"Where is this person?" He responded, his voice reminding her of their surroundings. He slowly began reaching for one of his swords with his free hand.

Riana felt the movement and quickly snatched his hand with hers, holding it down to his side and leaning even further into his muscled body. "Just wait. It looks like we are being led straight to whoever it is."

"Then we should escape these impostors now and not be led into their trap." He hissed roughly.

"We could do that. But the person seems to be in the palace. There are only a few reasons I can think of that they would be there." She ticked them off on her fingers as they continued forward. "Either they are a member of the royal family, or on staff there. Or they have somehow taken the city hostage and are holding the royal family hostage. Either way, we need to handle the situation with a touch of delicacy."

A low growl emanated from Jumah's chest as he mulled over the idea of walking into the unknown and certainly dangerous situation ahead of them. "Yes. But do you remember the part where it's likely a trap?" He finally mumbled in weak protest.

"Yes. And one of your own early philosophers once said that the first step in avoiding a trap is knowing of its existence. Now that we know, we can plan accordingly and move forward."

"I don't like it."

"Noted. Now play along or I'll take away your ball of yarn." She smiled slightly as she teased him.

"Why Riana. If I didn't know any better I might think you were flirting with me…" He seemed happy at the change in the conversation.

"Maybe I am…" She let it stand at that.

-33-

As they were led into the palace, Riana concentrated on the people around her. With the circlet's power allowing her to see their true nature, most of them were a bright yellow/gold color, but quite a few were red which she was now certain meant they were players. She squeezed Jumah's arm tightly as they were ushered into a large room and informed that someone would be with them soon. Quickly, the group huddled together in the center of the space, trying to keep their voices low and out of earshot of the people watching them from the edges of the room.

"What are we up against here?" Jumah asked almost casually.

Riana scanned around the room once more before answering. "All six of the guards in here are players. If I had to guess, I would say that nearly half of the people we've seen in the palace so far are as well."

"What are they doing here?" Katrina wondered aloud, craning her neck to look at one of the guards. "And more to the point how did they get wings like that? That has never been an option for player characters."

"Now *that* is a good point." Exodus added, smiling at Katrina. "How does one go about building an avatar that the system does not allow?"

"I think it's safe to say that we are dealing with a hacker here, not just some powerful mage." Katrina finished.

"Alright. Well a skilled hacker would be much more difficult to deal with than a mage. So what is our line of attack here? How do we deal with this?" Riana asked the group.

"Well I don't know how to deal with hackers." Jumah offered, "but I do know how to kick some ass in Kalijor. And one other thing I know is that even with a hacker on their side, all of these players will still have to fight for themselves, and even the best gear in the game is not going to keep my blades from their flesh."

"Fair to say." Exodus chimed in again, "but that still leaves the hacker himself for us to deal with. Riana? Can you still see the person that the curse is emanating from?"

Riana looked around slowly until she found the image she was looking for. A brightly lit red silhouette surrounded by a swirling blue maelstrom that twisted up and away from them, growing larger and curving around until it became a great cloud of blue light enveloping the entirety of the city. "Yes." She replied. "They seem to be speaking with another player about something. About a hundred yards that way." She pointed casually toward the figures as she faked a languid stretching motion for the benefit of their keepers. She still had yet to figure out why she could see some people through walls and not others.

"So the question becomes, how do we deal with *that* person." Exodus added. "In the end, these others are merely pawns standing between us and the king."

"Maybe..." Katrina began to speak but suddenly fell silent again.

"Maybe what Kat?" Riana prompted, looking at her sister pointedly.

"Well I'm not sure..." Katrina seemed reluctant to speak.

"Kat if you have something we can use, now would be the time for it." Riana pressed on.

"Alright, I'm not really sure about the specifics, but an engineer on the station once tried to explain to me how the system monitors for hacker activity. I didn't really understand most of it, which is why I am reluctant to talk about it. But one of the things he said is that the game's magic and hacking aren't really all that different. Mostly they are doing the same things but magic is very subtle, and it is used to produce results that are expected by the system."

They all stared at her for a moment, playing with the words in their minds, pulling them apart to see what parts were of use. Finally Riana spoke up. "So if this person is going to hack the system, they need to be very low key about it. They can't do things like blow us up instantly or conjure up an army of dragons or anything."

"I think so." Katrina replied uncertainly. "Again, I'm not sure I fully understood what he was saying. I really just got him talking about it to stop him hitting on me."

Riana gaped at her sister for a moment as a twinge of something stirred inside her stomach, what was it? Jealousy? Why would she be jealous? How could they be in the middle of a dilemma like this and her mind was reeling about a comment from her sister concerning her social life? After a moment she realized that the conversation was moving on without her and she shook her thoughts aside to focus on the task at hand.

"…manipulating the weather patterns. If they did it very slowly over time the system might not have taken notice of it." Katrina was saying.

"Well that makes sense I suppose, but wouldn't they have to stay in relative proximity to the target of the hack for the entire time?" Exodus responded. It gave Riana a headache whenever she listened to these two theorize together, but she knew this was important and so, focused her energies.

"Yes, more than likely." Katrina agreed.

"So we are looking for someone who has been in Avian for a while. Since just before the climate started to change. Someone whom no one would suspect, or even take notice of."

"Ok, so it's someone no one here would have suspected." Riana chimed in testily, "why do we need to puzzle this bit out? I can *see* the person in question. They are heading this way by the way. What we really need to know is who are they in the real world, and how do we fight them here?"

"Well can't you see them in the real world now? You said you could see these other people in their gaming pods." Katrina said.

"Apparently I need to be a bit closer for that to work, and I wasn't able to make out their faces or anything, just a general image of them. Maybe I need more practice or something."

"Maybe so. Or maybe that is all the artifact allows. Did you say they were heading this way?" Exodus asked calmly.

"Yes. Yes, I did." Riana replied equally calmly. "They are at the door now from the look of it."

And then the door opened and Riana's companions collectively gasped.

-34-

"So. You have returned as promised." A familiar voice spoke as the figure entered the room and stood before them. It took a moment for Riana to realize where she recognized the voice from, but finally it clicked. The voice belonged to the person who had helped them escape Avian before. She felt Jumah reach for his swords. The collective sliding of metal on metal as all of the guards surrounding them drew their weapons and brought them to bear on the group caused Jumah to relax again.

"How are you doing this?" Riana asked flatly.

"Oh I admit it has been difficult to orchestrate, but it has also been quite amusing to know you all are running around at my behest. Did you know that no one has seen that death dragon and lived to tell about it in over a millennium? And here you four managed to not only see it, but neutralize it and steal its treasure! Spectacular really."

"You planned all of this? From the beginning?" Katrina sounded disgusted, but a hint of amazement was edging into her voice as well. It seemed as though he didn't know the extent of what they had accomplished.

"And you let us go…" Riana began.

"Because I knew that you could get me what I wanted." He finished for her.

"And we fell into place exactly the way you wanted." Katrina said acidly.

"Exactly. Now. The key, if you please?"

Riana chuckled openly then. Her lilting voice bordering on outright laughter. "Well," she giggled, barely able to speak, "not exactly according to plan."

The man twisted around and threw Riana a look that she could feel burning into her. She had no need of her sight to know what was going on. "What happened?! What did you do?!" He shouted at her, hatred dripping from his voice as the realization began to dawn on him.

"Well, we didn't see the point of running out after the key and then not opening the door." Riana quipped through her giggles.

"You didn't!" He screamed at the room.

Riana turned to look at his silhouette and pointed to the circlet on her forehead casually.

"You bitch!" He screamed at her as he drew his sword, its blade radiating a bright purple in her vision. The sound of several other weapons being drawn around the room followed his action and Riana knew that this was the moment of truth for them. The next few minutes would be the ones that determined the fate of Avian and its people.

"Cursing at me won't help you any. What's done is done, and now it is out of your reach. I am curious to know how you have done what you have done here, but in all seriousness I just want to fix your damage and get the hell out of here." Riana gripped the handle of Elkorine and slid it out of its sheath.

As if on cue, Jumah's swords slipped from the sheaths on his back and he locked the pommels together, creating the longer sword-staff weapon she had first seen him with back in The Bramble what seemed like a life time ago. Katrina slipped her long, slender dagger from beneath her robes and began chanting a spell of protection while Exodus removed a medium length wooden stick from his belt. He too began chanting some arcane phrases. Riana's eyes flashed and she felt the kiss of her own magic swirl around them. In a moment each of them was covered in a thin, flexible layer of ice armor.

"I don't know what your hold is over this city and its people. But I am only giving you one chance to give it up and walk away."

The man looked at the four of them for only a moment before stepping back a half step. For the briefest of instants the group thought they might have pulled it off, but it was not to be.

"Kill them all." He said as the various guards in the room moved in to seal the opening he had left in their circle. "Bring me her head."

Riana sighed heavily. All at once, the room became a cacophony of metal on metal and explosions. She would have thought things would be moving along quite quickly but it seemed that fighting other players was actually a lot more difficult than fighting 'computer controlled' creatures. Unlike NPC's, the guards didn't follow a strict path or method of attack. The guards did seem to move in unison, but more like an organized combat unit galvanized together by years of relying upon one another for survival. Then, who was to say that wasn't the case? When she followed their wisp trails back into the real world all she had seen were game pods with people in them. No indication of where they were or what they looked like really. They could easily be all together in the same room. In fact that would seem to make sense since they all seemed to be working together.

She dodged out of the way of an incoming sword and jammed Elkorine forward catching a bit of flesh as the guard backed away in a hurry. Focusing her attention on the task at hand, Riana conjured up a ball of fire in her left hand and hurled it at the guard confronting her. Without waiting to see what happened, she dove in behind the fire ball with Elkorine in the lead. Guessing the man would try to dodge to his right based on his closed stance, she adjusted her trajectory and was pleased as he attempted to move out of the fireball's way only to be met by the tip of her sword. The weapon drove to the hilt in his chest drawing a surprised gasp from his lungs before they deflated permanently and he slumped over onto her shoulder.

"Dammit get off!" Katrina hollered from Riana's right side. Sparing a glance in her sister's direction Riana saw two of the silhouettes bearing down on her, weapons glowing purple and slashing back and forth through the air. On instinct Riana spun around to her left and, putting as much inertia into the body on her sword as she could muster, sending the dead guard flying. They barely had time to react to the body impacting them as they were bowled over.

Wasting no time, Katrina chanted a few power words and a great stone fist rose up out of the floor to smash the guards and their dead friend repeatedly. The sound of the assault reverberating off of the walls actually slowed the fight down as others took hesitant glances at what was going on. By the time the stone fist sank back into the floor again, there was nothing but crumpled armor and bloody soup left where the people had been and suddenly Riana was glad for the loss of her sight for the first time.

The sound of a lightning bolt tearing through the room drew their attention to where Exodus was fending off another of the guards.

"Go get your man." Riana said to her sister as she turned around to watch Jumah spin around in a dance that looked as though it had been expertly choreographed weeks in advance. "And I'll go get mine…" she said under her breath.

As she moved closer to Jumah she watched as his glowing purple sword-staff spun in graceful arcs at impossible speeds. She had no idea how he could possibly control the weapon and quietly vowed to ask Master Jonin about it when she got back into the real world. Surely this was a skill he could pass on to her.

Jumah seemed, at worst, to be having a good time, and at best she thought she could actually make out a smile on the purple outline of his face. He seemed to be toying with their opponents as he easily held three of them at bay. Any time one of them began to gain ground, Jumah's weapon would be there an instant later to force them back again. His actions seemed to be frustrating the guards, as their advances appeared to be becoming more erratic, less coordinated, driven by emotion rather than skill or team efforts.

"You OK Jumah?" She asked almost casually.

"Fine thank you. Be done here in a moment." His voice was full of good humor and he didn't miss a beat.

Satisfied that everything else was under control she turned to look at the man that seemed to be the source of all of their troubles.

"You can't hurt me!" He spat at her. "My powers come from outside the system. You can't possibly defend yourself against me."

"Let's just see shall we?" She stared at him coldly as she slowly advanced on his position. Holding Elkorine at the ready in her right hand, she conjured up a crackling sphere of black energy in her left and took another step toward the impostor.

He moved faster than she could see. One instant he was standing there in front of her gloating, the next he was standing off to her side jabbing at her mid-section with his sword.

Her instincts took over and without thought she moved Elkorine up to parry the attack. She managed to deflect the blade partially and move slightly, but the tip of his sword still managed to chip away at the icy armor covering her body. Wincing in surprise she stepped back away from him as she hurled the sphere of annihilation at him.

This time her enhanced vision caught a flash of blue around the man as he vanished from her sight and the spell ball passed harmlessly through the spot he had been occupying an instant ago. Instead of disintegrating her intended target, the deadly projectile evaporated a large portion of an outside wall and let in a frigid, gale-force wind.

Riana lurched forward as her senses began setting off alarms in her head. Her dance partner seemed to be behind her again, so she tucked into a roll coming up facing the opposite direction, but it was already too late, he was gone again.

"Dammit! Hold still!" She cursed at the room.

"Not likely." She heard from behind her even as she felt his foot strike her in the ribs.

She opened herself up to lessen the impact of the fall then quickly rolled back into a crouching position. Suddenly an idea struck her and she instantly activated the spell. The area around her increased in temperature several hundred degrees in the span of a second. A tapestry nearby burst into flames and the rug she was on instantly turned to ash. Most of the surrounding furniture followed suit and a symphony of candelabras and decanters could be heard raining to the stone floor as the solid surfaces they had previously been perched upon disintegrated under the onslaught of the heat wave.

"Augh!" She heard him howl briefly but when she turned to look, he was gone again.

"So. You aren't invincible after all uh?" She scanned the room as she taunted him.

"Close enough to deal with you, bitch!"

"Shit." She rolled away from the blade as quickly as she could but it wasn't enough, the blade shattered the flexible icy armor and bit deeply into the flesh of her upper leg. Clenching her jaw against the pain, she clutched the wound with her left hand, trying to stave off the bleeding as she looked for him. Focusing through the pain, she saw the answer she had been looking for. The blue energy seemed to be an indication of how he was moving around the system so quickly. It flowed from one spot to another and as it stopped, he appeared for just an instant, then the faint cloud would roll across the room to another location where he would appear again for the briefest of heartbeats.

'So you DO have a weakness.' She thought to herself as she watched the cloud move. As it began to slow down, she raised her hand and willed an arc of lightning to cross the span between them. The timing was such that the instant he appeared, the electricity struck him dead center. There was a loud popping sound followed by the crash of his body bouncing off the wall.

She smiled to herself as she saw his body hit the wall like a rag doll. Her moment of satisfaction faded quickly when, instead of slumping to the ground, he landed on his feet and straightened up again, leveling his sword at her once more. "You'll pay for that."

"Sure I will." She quipped. Looking around the room for anything she could use against him, she sighed as nothing presented itself to her immediately.

Too late, she realized he had disappeared again. She didn't have time to look for him and had no idea where he would appear, so in an attempt to present as small a target as possible, she dove forward into a roll. An instant later, she felt the bite of his sword in the flesh of her right leg and yelped in pain. She finished her roll awkwardly and pulled herself up into a crouching position. Waiting only a heart-beat, she conjured a dome-shaped shield around herself in time to stop his next swing. Listening to him curse, she smiled to herself and forced the shield to explode outward from her. Again, she heard his body slam forcefully into a wall. Turning to face the noise, she scowled when he regained his feet almost immediately. Her mind raced to find a solution.

"Need a hand?" Jumah's voice was music to her ears as it came up behind her.

"Do I ever." She replied through clenched teeth. Squeezing her free hand over the fresh wound on her calf, she indicated the smiling impostor with a nod of her head. "He seems to be using whatever hacker abilities he has to warp around the room. I can see him move, but only barely."

"Let's just see how fast he really is." Jumah's voice carried its usual humor again as he pressed a soft leather pouch into Riana's hand.

"What… Oh!" She squeezed the pouch tentatively and after a moment realized what was in it. It was the same pouch Master Gornin had given her in Cohai a while back, the one full of Brume Tree seeds. She looked up at their adversary with a smirk on her face.

"Laugh all you like, even the both of you can't defeat me!" He postured as he hefted his sword again and vanished once more.

As she watched the faint blue wisp move about the room she slipped one of the spiral shaped Brume Tree seeds out of the pouch and held it gently between her thumb and fore finger. The instant the wisp stopped moving she threw the seed at it.

In an instant it was over. The man appeared, sword poised to strike out at her flank. As his body materialized, the flying seed found its mark, striking him in the center of his chest. He sounded almost stunned by it, sharply inhaling his breath as it struck him. It was as though he was expecting something more to happen. When nothing did, he disappeared again, reappearing in time to have another seed smack squarely into his chest, he seemed to decide that it was a ruse and regained his confidence. In one swift movement he swept his weapon up over his head and grinned down at her crouching form. In a flash, the air was forced out of his lungs as Jumah's twin blades buried themselves in his chest up to their hilts. He stood there for nearly a minute, with his sword poised over his head, as he seemed to contemplate what had just happened. How had his adversary moved so quickly? Finally, his body slumped to the floor in a heap and the sword clattered to the ground in one final bid for attention.

Riana wished she could have seen the look on his face as it happened, but she was happy with the result none-the-less. The rush of freezing air through the damaged wall was replaced with a slower moving warm breeze and the entire room seemed to become calmer, somehow less hostile. Then, she was surrounded by Exodus, Katrina, and Jumah, all exchanging hugs and quiet congratulations. She knew things were looking up.

-35-

The next few days passed in a blur. The weather in Avian reverted to its normal state within the first eight hours after the battle. Within twenty four hours, the city's crops began to turn green and show signs of life again. The actual royal family of Avian was discovered to be secreted away in the lower levels of the prisons on the second tier of the city and, once released, bestowed titles of knighthood upon the four of them in a grand celebration that ended in a city-wide feast.

Riana found Xanthe in the royal stables where he had apparently been living happily with several of the city's griffons. He seemed overjoyed to see her again. He had been cared for by the entire stable staff since they had been less then busy with their normal chores of daily griffon maintenance when the city had more or less shut itself down. The two greeted each other emotionally and quickly shared one another's experiences through their empathic link. The stable staff said he was more than welcome to stay there whenever they visited and seemed sad that he might be leaving them soon.

The people of the city, outside adventurers and craftsmen returned in droves when word got out that it was returning to normal. As soon as the citizens learned what had happened, they too showered the group with accolades, offering them basically anything they desired in exchange for the great deeds they had done. Save for the services of a healer and some general equipment repair however, they all refrained from taking anything from the people of the recovering city.

It seemed impossible to find a moment of peace as everyone constantly sought out the heroes of the city, but Riana and Jumah finally managed to secret themselves away for a few moments. She smiled at him demurely as he closed the door behind him, sliding the lock home with an exhausted sigh of relief.

"I'm not sure I can take any more of this Riana. It really isn't my style to be worshipped." He turned around to face her with his typical smile in his voice as he spoke.

She grinned at him now. "But you take it so stoically! One would never know you for the introvert you really are!"

He crossed the room in short order and wrapped his arms around her, pulling her tightly against his body. She flushed as new thoughts began to fill her mind, thoughts of them being... much more intimate together. Her body tensed as she tried to focus.

"What's the matter?" There was a note of concern in his voice.

"Nothing..." She lied, and badly at that.

"Riiight…" he called her bluff.

"It's just… We have to go. We've been in Kalijor for over a month now and there are things we have to take care of in the real world. But I…" She stared out the window into what she knew was the clear blue sky surrounding Avian.

Jumah set his chin on the top of her head and squeezed her reassuringly. "It's OK Ree. I'll message you and we can talk offline. But we can always meet in Kalijor if we want to…" His voice trailed off, letting her fill in the blanks with her own pictures of what they might do together. The thought stirred something deep inside her. A shiver ran through her as she considered the possibilities, eliciting a wide grin from Jumah.

"Where are you? I mean… you know… in the real world." She felt strange asking for information about his life outside Kalijor. Part of her wanted to remain in Kalijor, in his arms, forever.

He was quiet for a moment before he answered her. "Earth Station. I run a small shipping company, mostly local Earth space stuff, not many long hauls. You?"

"I live with Kat. On the Tyconderoga." She leaned her head back into the crook of his neck and chin and closed her eyes, sighing again as she realized she could still see through her closed eye lids.

"Wow. You live in the belly of the beast uh? Kalijor central operations." He sounded impressed.

"I guess so…"

"Well look, I know you two need to log out so I won't hold you up. I've already sent my contact info to your message center, so contact me OK? We're close enough we can have dinner or something right?"

Suddenly, she twisted around in his arms. Wrapping her arms around the back of his head, she forcefully pulled his head down and pressed her lips against his. It started out as a rough, uncivilized kiss, but as it continued they both began to relax and it evolved into a passionate, loving expression. Finally, after what seemed like an eternity, they broke apart and she looked up into his eyes, wishing with all her might that she could see them again, see them as a normal person would. For a long moment neither moved.

Then a knock at the door snapped them back to reality. "Ree are you in there?" It was Katrina.

Riana sighed again before answering, trying not to sound annoyed by the interruption. "Yeah. I'm coming Kat."

"Ok, I'm logging out. I'll see you in a minute or two OK?" Her voice filtered through the ornately carved door.

"Alright." She pressed her lips together as she looked at Jumah longingly. Then to him, "I guess I have to go. Thank you Jumah… for everything you have done for us… for me…"

He smiled down at her again and hugged her close before letting her go. "Hey. It isn't the end of the world. We'll see each other again, maybe sooner than you think. Go on, go catch up with your sister, I am sure you have a lot to do, all things considered."

She smiled at him and nodded her agreement. "OK. Soon then. Thanks Jumah." And she triggered the disconnect command.

In a flash her world went completely dark, then slowly she began to be able to make out some shapes, outlines of people, the game pod she was in, the computers in the Kalijor game level of the Tyconderoga station and... all in a sort of purple wire-frame on a deep, black background. "Oh no!" She hissed to herself... "I still can't see!"

-36-

"What do you *mean* you still can't see?!" Willhelmina accused as the door to her quarters slid noiselessly closed behind her.

Riana scanned the room with her altered vision. It was strange really, she could still make out everything in the room, including Willhelmina, but none of it was right. Everything was still in shades of purple, and mostly just outlines. There were no fine details to be seen, only the purple lines, highlights, and the black spaces in between.

She plopped down on Willhelmina's couch nonchalantly, the furniture groaning in protest under the unexpected weight of her slight frame, a side effect of having a man-made, metal and composite body. "I would have thought the statement was fairly descriptive on its own. Do you really want me to elaborate?"

Willhelmina glared at her for a moment. She moved into the room like a tornado and made her way toward the kitchenette where she tore through the cooling unit and cupboards in search of food. "Just because you are frustrated doesn't give you the right to treat me like that Ree." She managed to sound fairly intelligible around the mouthful of breakfast cereal she had managed to cram into her mouth in the few seconds she had been in the room.

Riana sighed dramatically. "I know. I'm sorry Kat. So, what did the medical staff say? Clean bill of health?"

Willhelmina almost choked on her cereal, finally managing to get enough down to speak again. "Those idiots wouldn't know healthy from a broken oxygen hose!"

Riana grinned across at her friend in the kitchen. "Not an agreeable prognosis then?"

"They said I was horribly malnourished and my muscles were beginning to atrophy from lack of use. Despite the IV drip and electro-muscular stimulation they had me on while I was in the pod."

"Kat you were plugged in for over a month. An IV can only do so much to keep you healthy. We should go to the gym and get some exercise tonight."

"Yeah OK…" Kat said dismissively, "When did you have that done?"

"What?" Riana looked down at herself, trying to find what had drawn her friend's interest.

"That! On your wrist!" Willhelmina was pointing at her now, as if she could make Riana follow the line of her finger from all the way across the room.

Looking down at her wrists, Riana saw the mysterious purple glyph representing the elven word for 'secret' on her left wrist. On her right wrist however, was a new glyph. Vivid green, even in her altered vision, was clearly the elven glyph for 'knowledge'.

"I've no idea." She finally managed. "I didn't 'have it done.' This is the first time I've seen it." She rolled her arm back and forth in her lap, inspecting the new image from every angle.

"Does it seem in the least bit odd that every time you come into contact with one of those keys you suddenly grow a new tattoo in the real world?" Now she was speaking around a mouthful of some kind of cookie or cracker.

"Not as much as it bothers me to have my vision go all crazy spontaneously." She dropped her hands into her lap and rolled her head backwards onto the back of the couch. Turning her head toward the kitchen, she saw Willhelmina eating something and her own stomach began to churn. "Do you have any chocolate or anything? I could use some glucose."

"Um…" Willhelmina rummaged though her small pantry and finally removed a couple of the chocolate bars that she had begun keeping on hand for Riana. Her body didn't need much in the way of nutrition, mostly complex sugars for her highly tuned nervous system.

"Here you go." She said as she tossed the candy to her friend.

Riana snatched the bars out of the air with little effort and tore into one with no ceremony at all. "Thanks, I had no idea how hungry I was until you started eating."

"Well your condition certainly hasn't hurt your reflexes any."

"So…" Riana prompted not so subtly for a change to more serious conversation.

"So?"

"So… What are you going to do?" She knew the subject would be exceedingly sore, but it had to be dealt with, Xavier still hadn't made any effort to see Willhelmina, even after they had logged out and spent half the day in the infirmary being poked and prodded.

"About what?" Willhelmina dropped her food container roughly on the counter and stuck her head back into the cooling unit under the pretense of looking for something else that might pass as appetizing.

"Kat!"

"What Ree?! What do you want me to do about it?" Willhelmina slammed the door of the cooler roughly, causing a symphony of tinkling and crashing noises to issue forth from its hidden interior, then stood up straight, folding her arms across her chest and glaring at Riana.

"I don't know Kat! But *something* needs to be done! He left you in there! You would probably still be tied up in there if Jumah and I hadn't come looking for you."

"So what? Do you want a medal or something?"

"No Kat! It isn't like that and you know it! And just because you are frustrated doesn't mean you can take out your aggressions on the refrigerator!"

A moment of silence fell over the room before they both suddenly burst out laughing. It took several minutes for them to collect themselves again and get back to their conversation.

"Seriously though. I have no idea what I would even say to him. Ree, he has given me everything. A home, a family, an education, a job, *you*! What *can* I say to him?"

"Well for starters you can ask him why he didn't come after you. He didn't even order a search. That's what really concerns me about it. I am sure he can make the whole situation make sense from some perverse business standpoint, but to just leave you in there? Trapped?"

Willhelmina looked at the wall behind Riana suddenly, her green eyes clouding slightly as she seemed to be watching some far off scene or memory flit by.

"What's going on Kat?"

"Huh? Oh. Nothing. Sorry. Just thinking about all of it. You're right of course. I do need to talk to him."

Riana could tell something was bugging her. She had spent more than thirty years with this person. Whether in this world or a virtual one, that kind of time gave a person certain insights. However, she also knew enough to let her keep her thoughts private, she would come around when she was ready.

"Alright, so how about that workout?" She offered instead, opting for another change in subject.

Immediately Willhelmina's face brightened again. "Ok, but no taking it easy on me, I have to get back into shape again if I am ever going to keep up with you."

"Fair enough." Riana agreed as she stood up and moved toward the door with Willhelmina sliding in behind her.

-37-

Willhelmina circled slowly around Riana, looking for some weakness in her defenses. It had been nearly an hour now and she had yet to land a blow of any kind on her. She was beginning to think Riana was more advanced than anyone had really thought when suddenly she moved one of her hands slightly, lowering her guard on her left side.

She acted without thought, lunging in with a blindingly fast back fist that would have surely knocked the consciousness out of anyone unlucky enough to get in its way. She smirked to herself as her knuckles approached Riana's temple, but suddenly the gym became a streak of grey and white as her stomach lurched. She felt a pressure in her elbow and shoulder and suddenly her whole body jarred as she impacted fully with the unforgiving floor of the ring.

Riana looked down at her with a grin on her face that stretched from ear to ear as she held out her hand to help Willhelmina up. "Had enough sis?"

"Not on your life." Willhelmina said as she accepted the hand and hoisted her lithe frame back to a standing position. She turned to face Riana and they measured off again, taking fighting stances. "The piezoelectric stimulators seem to have kept my muscle strength in pretty good condition."

"Yeah, your over-all conditioning has slipped though. That means more work-out time for you lady!" Riana grinned as she set her hands slightly out of place, begging Willhelmina's attention, but she would not fall for it twice. Instead she stepped in with a round kick aimed at her friend's waist, only to have it slapped away and followed up with a series of light blows from Riana's right leg to her own left flank. Stepping back again after the assault, she made sure her hands were in a solid position and forced herself to breathe regularly. *"She's playing with me. She could take me any time she wanted to..."*

Riana grinned widely. She could indeed take Willhelmina at any time, but she wanted to provide her enough challenge that she would learn from the experience, but not so much that she would be discouraged. She wanted to get better, so Riana would do her best to help. She set her feet slightly too close together and lowered one of her hands to create a few openings for her friend to take advantage of and waited for the inevitable to happen.

As soon as she moved her foot, Willhelmina lunged in with a flurry of punches and back fists, trying to get even one through Riana's defenses. Once or twice, she thought she got close but, in the end they were all swatted away harmlessly. "Damn it!" She swore. "Ree stop toying with me!"

Riana frowned. "I thought you wanted to learn. How will you learn if you are constantly getting your butt kicked?"

"I'll figure something out. Just you stop going easy on me!"

"Alright." Riana sighed. Setting her stance properly she narrowed her eyes, taking in the high-contrast, purple relief image of her friend in the ring, focusing on nothing, and yet, seeing every single detail. Willhelmina dove in with a front kick and in an instant Riana had snatched it up and yanked her friend forward, pulling her off balance, then spinning her around and sliding a foot under the flailing mass which caused her to completely lose her balance and topple face first into the floor.

Not waiting even a second for her to regain her composure, Riana lunged at her downed friend, leaping into the air and tucking her right foot up under her butt as she came down, driving her knee toward her friend's back. She knew how to control the impact so she wouldn't cause any serious injuries but she hoped she wouldn't have to. At the last second, Willhelmina rolled away and Riana's knee drove full force into the floor of the ring, causing it to buckle with a loud cracking noise.

In a flash, they were both back in fighting stances, eyeing one another and waiting for the next waltz to begin. When Willhelmina dropped her guard for an instant, Riana pounced again, driving at her with a series of punches that forced Willhelmina back against the ropes. Finishing up the combination with a powerful reverse punch, Riana forced it past Willhelmina's defenses and was just about to pull the punch when she heard the distinct sound of someone trying to get her attention by clearing his throat.

She looked up an instant before the punch landed. Thankfully her fist followed her eyes, missing Willhelmina's head by less than an inch. Instead, she drove the limb though the turnbuckle, snapping it like a dried up twig, and sending the top rope flying toward the adjacent corners with a loud popping noise.

The person she saw made her stomach twist into a knot and bile rise in her throat. He stood in his usual manner, stock still, straight as a ram rod, his perfectly manicured hands resting one atop the other on the pommel of his gnarly wooden cane. He was dressed in his usual designer suit, perfectly situated with not so much as a single dark hair out of place on either his head or the immaculately trimmed goatee. To her altered vision he looked like some sort of three dimensional computer model of a man that had yet to be animated and made to seem alive. It hadn't even been given color or texture yet, still existing as nothing more than a wire-frame model of a man.

"Xavier." She said simply as she stood up and faced him, her hands dangling at her sides.

"Ms. Thorindal." He replied without an ounce of anything but business in his voice. "Good to see you off the game deck again."

"I'm sure." She narrowed her eyes at him.

"Playing a bit rough aren't we?" He said off-handedly as he turned his head slightly and raised an eyebrow at the smashed turnbuckle.

"Not especially. She can take it." She said, suddenly remembering her friend and offering her a hand to help her off the mat.

"Thanks Ree." Willhelmina said as she hoisted herself to her feet. Straightening herself up a bit, she looked at Xavier. To him, she nodded her head and said, "Xavier, thank you for letting Ree help me out."

"She did not give me much in the way of choices." He responded without the slightest hint of remorse. "I am however, glad that things turned out well. It is good to have you back."

"It's good to be back." She admitted, turning to face Riana who was staring back at her with a look of startled bewilderment on her face. Willhelmina blushed scarlet, she knew Riana wanted her to confront Xavier, but somehow she just couldn't seem to muster the courage. She turned away from her friend, knowing that they would be having words later.

"So, to what do we owe the honor of your visit?" Riana finally hissed out the side of her mouth as she continued to glare at Willhelmina, finally turning her head very slowly to face Xavier as she finished speaking.

"I have come to inform you both that the prototype processor stolen by Mr. Shantal has been located. I am sending the two of you to see if you can retrieve it this time." There was a certain venom to his words. His voice did not sound as if he was upset, but more like he simply could not believe that he had been made to ask for this thing more than once.

"And what was in the case I brought back from Mars station?" Riana asked sarcastically.

"Nothing." Xavier said simply.

"Nothing?" She repeated with a tone of disbelief.

"Nothing," he repeated, then added, "at all."

"This seems like the sort of thing you may have mentioned at some point." She began to raise her voice at him as the feelings welled up inside her.

"You were busy trying to find Willhelmina. Every time I tried to speak with you, you threatened me or refused to deal with me. So, now that Willhelmina is free and we have more definite information on its whereabouts, I bring you the information. I hope that you will now be more receptive."

Riana looked at Willhelmina who was standing there next to her, looking for all the world like a lost child in a crowded market. She knew what working for Xavier was about now. She knew he would sell them out at the drop of a cloak if it served his purposes. And yet, she felt compelled to take the assignment, if for no other reason than to take another shot at the mercenary that had destroyed her hands. Gregory Shantal, with his overalls and his wispy grey-white corona of hair. She looked down at her completely regenerated hands and sighed heavily. Then, without looking at Willhelmina again, said, "Alright, you win. Give us the details."

-38-

"The processor is equipped with a radioactive isotope tracking mechanism. Unfortunately the case it was being transported in was blocking our attempts at locating it until late last week."Xavier's voice was calm and commanding. "Now however, it appears to have been removed from the case, most likely for the purpose of reverse engineering it. We can not allow this to happen and we have precious little time to stop it. They may already have learned more about it than is acceptable." He stood at the front of the briefing room in his normal 'at attention' stance, with his gnarly cane set solidly in front of him. Pressing a button on the podium next to him, the room lights dimmed as the holographic display winked to life, displaying an image of the planet Earth and its system of interlocking orbital rings.

"The processor has been taken to Earth Station, Xaman-Otoch." As he spoke the three dimensional image zoomed in to the point above the North Pole where two of the three inter-locking rings came together to form a gigantic city complex. "It took a couple of days for our agents to narrow down the search but we eventually tracked the processor to the doors of our competitor, Aegis Online."

The image further zoomed into the structure until it showed a series of chambers and hallways that were highlighted against the rest of the mega-city. The highlighted area was easily as large as the entire Mars Station Riana had visited over a month ago.

"How did they get it?" Riana asked.

"Presumably our Mr. Shantal sold it to them. Alternatively, he could have been working for them the entire time. At this point that is irrelevant. What we need to know is that they haven't copied the technology. So we need you two to get in, retrieve the original unit and destroy any copies or attempts at copies they may have there, as well as any computer records of their research."

Willhelmina dutifully copied the information they were being given into her wrist computer, retrieving the schematics for Xaman-Otoch and the rest of Earth Station and setting to planning out a route to the Aegis Online facility. Riana looked at her briefly, then turned her attention back to Xavier and narrowed her eyes at his image.

"We signed on as couriers Xavier, not spies or some kind of combat unit. This place is built like a fortress." She tapped at the holographic display on her own wrist computer, calling up the specifications for the AO facility's entry and egress points into the rest of the city. "These doors look tougher than starship hulls."

She was still learning things about this new world she lived in, but she learned quickly, especially with her ability to connect directly to computers when she wanted to and access information at the speed of thought. One thing she had figured out pretty quickly was that anyone installing doors like these would not stop at tough doors to keep their secrets inside. There would certainly be even more defenses within the facility.

"You're asking us to fight a war for you. A war that we can't win."

Willhelmina looked up at Xavier to see what his response would be. She had reservations about going as well, especially in light of the things she had learned about him recently, but she was still having a hard time believing he was capable of what she had been told he was doing.

"Nonsense." He said flatly. "We have secured all of the necessary credentials and uniforms to get you both in and out safely. Because there is the possibility of some unforeseen trouble, we would prefer to have people capable of handling themselves in there. Just to deal with any possible problems that may arise."

"Fine." Riana acquiesced then changed the subject abruptly. "So what do you know about these people that were attacking Avian? They were hacking the system somehow and the servers did nothing to protect Kalijor."

"I assure you Ms. Thorindal, that I have people working on it as we speak. Once we arrive at a solution, rest assured that we will let you know." He offered her a wan smile before adding, "If it turns out that you need to know for some reason."

Riana glowered at him irritably, jumping slightly when Willhelmina's hand touched her wrist. Twisting around to look at her friend, Willhelmina smiled at her comfortingly. Turning back toward

Xavier she eyed him suspiciously. "Alright. In the mean time, we'll go get your trinket."

"I would expect nothing less of you." He smiled at her. "The Kestrel will be prepped and ready before the hour is out."

Riana stood up and headed for the door, looking back to her friend who slowly stood up and looked toward her. "You go ahead Ree. I'll catch up with you in a minute."

Riana nodded and strode out into the hallway, heading toward her quarters to get ready. As she moved down the corridor, she began to hear the same haunting music that had led them to the ziggurat in Kalijor. Cocking her ears up and focusing on the sound, she closed her eyes, realizing for the first time that she could no longer see through her eyelids. Focusing on the melody she followed it down the hallway, dragging her finger tips down the wall as she moved, listening intently as the sound grew louder.

Her finger tips finally came across an open doorway and her ears told her that the music was coming from within. Standing there and listening to the melody with her eyes closed she focused in on the powerful voice of the singer. She sung on about the stars in the night sky watching and protecting her loved ones always. There was a moving symphony of instruments underneath the voice, but the separate parts all blended together into a stream that seemed to bore straight into Riana's mind and open up her memories. Memories of her mother sitting on the edge of her bed and singing the same song to her on nights when she had been particularly concerned about the monsters under the bed wafted through her mind's eye, carried by the melody. She had no idea how long she had been standing there listening before she finally felt the presence of someone standing inside the doorway. At some point, she had turned

292

around and leaned against the wall in the hallway and set her head against the wall with her long, tapered ears perked up, listening to the music.

She turned her head slowly and opened her eyes to reveal the outline of a small man leaning against the jamb of the open door, looking at her calmly. There wasn't really enough in the image for her to determine who it was, but the feeling of his presence told her everything that the sight of him did not. In a flash she stood up straight and faced him, placing her hands together in front of her, below the belt and bowing deeply with her eyes averted. "Master Jonin. I'm sorry, I didn't mean to intrude."

"It is alright Riana, I would not have left my door open if I had not wanted company. I have been expecting you."

She stood up straight again and raised an eyebrow at him doubtfully. "Why?"

"Because it is time. All things happen in their time Riana, that is your next lesson." His voice was smiling as he spoke. "I have something for you."

She looked at him quizzically. "For me? Master Jonin I…"

"It is alright Riana, it is a small thing really, and I would not trust anyone else with it. Only you have the skill and reflexes necessary to master it." At that he held out a small cylinder to her.

Tentatively she reached out and touched it, it was cool and smooth to the touch. "What is it?"

"A monowire sword. This switch activates it. It is a formidable weapon Riana, please be cautious with it."

She picked it up gently and wrapped her hand around it, feeling its slight weight. "Master Jonin... I can't take this. I have read about these and they are terribly expensive." She had read about them, they were composed of a power supply and a magnetic field generator that would uncoil and suspend a monomolecular wire that was capable of slicing almost any substance known to science. It was particularly destructive because it actually disrupted the bonds that hold molecules together, cutting on a near-atomic level.

"I insist. It is no longer of any use to me and as I said, any of my other disciples would only maim themselves with it. I have missed you in the dojo." His change of subject seemed to finalize the matter, so Riana slipped the device into a pocket and sighed.

"I'm sorry sir. I've been...busy..." She looked away as she finished speaking, not wanting to tell him about the loss of her sight. True she was learning to work around it, to live with it, but she was certain it would be a disqualifying handicap and she didn't want to be forced to quit studying with him. After a moment of uncomfortable silence, she finally decided that the truth would be better in the long run and turned back toward him, ears drooping.

"Master Jonin I..." She stopped again, unable to continue for some reason.

"It's alright Riana. As I said, all things in their time. Would you do me the honor of sharing a cup of tea?"

Her ears perked up slightly at the opportunity to talk about something else; if he wasn't going to pressure her then she certainly wasn't going to push the issue herself. "Of course sir, I only have a few minutes though, Kat and I are supposed to leave for Earth soon."

"Of course. Please come in." He bowed and stepped aside for her to get through the door.

She returned his bow and stepped through the door into his spacious quarters, following him to the table. Sitting on her knees on the floor next to the low surface, she asked the question in the back of her mind. "Master Jonin, may I ask where you got the music? Who is the singer?"

He sat down across from her, set about selecting his tea leaves and depositing them in the pot, pouring hot water from another container gently atop the leaves, and covering the pot again. Without looking up at her he replied, "What music? I have been preparing my tea."

She looked at him as he performed the tea ceremony with flawless precision. "That music I was listening to outside. It's what brought me to your door sir."

"I always prepare my tea in silence Riana. I'm sorry but there was no music." He carried on with the ceremony as if nothing strange was going on.

"Something troubles you." He stated as he set the water container down on the table and oriented it perfectly.

Riana looked down at her hands, folded over one another in her lap and sighed. "You mean aside from the fact that I am hearing things? Yes. A few things."

"I find that a hot cup of tea is usually all I need to help sort things out when I am troubled."

"Master Jonin, I appreciate your hospitality, but I'm not really sure a cup of tea is going to help me out here. I mean, Xavier wants us to go raid some rival facility, and he didn't lift a finger to help Kat when she was stuck in Kalijor. Not to mention the fact that I keep hearing this music everywhere and…" She stopped herself again, unable to vocalize it to anyone but Kat.

"Yes, all of this is true, but you are both alive and well now, if anyone is capable of doing what he asks, it is the two of you. As to the music and your other problem, well… All things in their time."

He picked up the tea pot and slowly filled her cup. She sat there mulling his words over in her head for a moment until she realized that he was over-filling the cup. She couldn't see the liquid in her altered vision, but she could hear it pouring over the edges of the cup and the saucer then finally onto the table.

Reflexively she reached out and placed her hand on his, tilting the pot back so that it stopped pouring.

Without sounding surprised at all he looked at her and asked, "Why did you stop me?"

She looked at him incredulously for a moment then finally answered, sounding as though she thought he was insane. "Because my cup was full, it couldn't hold any more."

Quietly he stood up and bowed low to her. "Exactly. Please, have a safe and prosperous journey."

-39-

The conversation was still haunting her as she sat in the pilot's seat of the Kestrel, rolling the metal cylinder over in her hands and waiting for Willhelmina to join her for their voyage. "What the hell was that all about?" She said quietly to the device.

"What was what all about?" Willhelmina's voice lilted in from the equipment bay just behind the cockpit door.

"Oh. I had a strange conversation with Master Jonin on the way here. Not really sure what to make of it to be honest." She looked over her shoulder at Willhelmina as she entered the cockpit of the small shuttle. She smiled as her sister slid gracefully into her seat and spun it around to face the controls.

"So…" Riana prompted, having flashbacks to their discussion.

Willhelmina sighed heavily, dropping her hands from the controls half way through her pre-flight check. "I don't know what to tell you Ree. He's the closest thing to a father I have and despite what has happened I can't just sever all ties with the man."

"I wouldn't expect you to. I was just wondering if you had actually talked to each other about what *had* happened." Riana purposefully averted her eyes and resumed the pre-flight check so that her friend would feel less pressured.

"Yes. We talked about it. He said that he knew you could handle it and had wanted you to be the one to find me since you were so familiar with Kalijor, and definitely more determined than a normal paid employee."

"Sounds like a dodge to me. But it's a damn good one, I'll give him that."

"He *also* mentioned that you were terribly rude to him. I've never seen him so upset at someone before Ree, I don't know how you managed that."

Riana tried not to let the venom creep into her voice again, "Did he tell you what his reasoning was for putting you into that position in the first place?"

"You mean the fake key I was given?"

"The same." Riana rolled her finger down a bank of soft-switches that lit up in a colorful cascade as her finger tip touched them each in turn, causing the ship's compact power plant to hum to full power in preparation for departure.

"He said he gave me the only key he had. He swears he had no idea it was a fake and he is looking into it." Then she tapped her headset and changed her tone, "Tyconderoga this is Kestrel requesting departure clearance and escape vector from shuttle bay three. Flight plan ES-1701 bound for Earth Station."

Almost immediately they both heard the soft female voice of the flight deck computer system respond, "Kestrel this is Tyconderoga flight control, you are cleared to depart shuttle bay three, escape vector three degrees azimuth, twelve degrees declination. Please maintain harbor speed until you have cleared the final marker and have a safe flight."

"Thank you Tyconderoga flight control, Kestrel out." Willhelmina snapped off the comm and nodded to her friend.

Riana quickly snapped up the controls and after only a few feet of elevation, gunned the throttle. The tiny silver bird of prey roared through the small shuttle bay, knocking over several stacks of cargo crates before slipping through the electro-magnetic force wall that held the station's atmosphere inside despite the open door that allowed ships to pass easily from space into the hangar.

In the absence of atmosphere, the timbre of the ship's engines changed dramatically, As they sped through the station's local space, dipping and weaving through the constant streams of small loading craft and the much larger intra-system cargo haulers, the Kestrel moved like its namesake. The small ship spiraled around in a graceful arc as it crested the top of one of the large cargo haulers, before Riana nosed it down into a steep dive, dodging in and out of the streams of cargo boxes and automated labor pods. Twisting and turning, she pushed the engines harder and harder as she pulled up along the hull of the Tyconderoga, its sleek white skin sprinting past the cockpit's view port.

Suddenly the hull of the station was gone. For a brief moment there was a transparent geodesic dome with a tall man clad in an elegant silk business suit sitting at an equally transparent desk watching calmly as the ship hurtled past his office.

"You know… If you keep doing that they will suspend your license." Willhelmina admonished her friend.

"They can suspend it all they want. It won't stop me from flying. I love it too much." Riana answered with no hint of concern in her voice. Riana tapped a few buttons on her navi-pad and set the ship's auto-pilot to follow their flight plan toward Earth.

"Why doesn't anyone talk about the Earth Kat?" Riana said wistfully as she stared at the orb growing steadily larger in their view port.

"It's a long story Ree. Haven't you looked it up in your data terminal yet?" Willhelmina leaned back in her acceleration seat and placed her hands behind her head as she too set her gaze on the Earth.

"Just the basics. Something about a world war?"

"Yes." Willhelmina confirmed. "Late in the twenty-first century there were a lot of disparate political entities on the planet. They were always at one another's throats over one thing or another. Seems like money and religion were the real gating factors. Some things never seem to change." She added off-handedly.

"Anyway, at one point, in the late 2200's I think, several of the world's largest corporations banded together and bought up all of the bad debt for all of the major nations of the world. They gave them a few months to repay their debts, which of course none of them could, and then they foreclosed and sort of took over the whole place."

She tapped a blinking light on her panel that seemed to be vying for her attention. "Ninety minutes to Earth Station. I guess a few smaller political entities tried to rebel against corporate rule and launched a first strike on their seats of power. This would have been around 2500 somewhere. All of the missile defense systems were still in place and the automated retaliation kicked in. Next thing you know the Earth is a radioactive wasteland. Not fit enough for animals, let alone us."

Riana sighed heavily, thinking of the depths of depravity to which people so easily stooped when they felt wronged. "So you haven't been able to live on your own planet for over 500 years?"

"There-abouts yes. We only survived as a species because of our off-world colonies; Earth was a total loss, everyone died. Billions of people gone in an instant. We quickly learned to live anywhere we could, we'd had a good start at it by then, although there were some tough times when it looked pretty bad."

Riana sighed, looking at the elusive beauty of the blue-green orb fast approaching them. "It doesn't look dangerous."

"I know." Willhelmina sighed as well. "But they say that the radiation levels are still too high for us to return. The plants have been growing steadily over the last few hundred years but scientists say it will take thousands of years more for the environment to clean itself up to the point that we can reinhabit the planet."

"No one's been there for hundreds of years..." Riana's voice trailed off for a moment, finally her ears perked up and she turned to look at Willhelmina hopefully, "Do you think I could survive down there? The doctors said I could withstand thousands of times the radiation levels of a normal person."

"Whether you could or not is irrelevant really. You see that fine grey mist that seems to be just visible throughout the atmosphere?"

Riana focused her eyes on the planet, to her it was all just a tangle of purple lines but if she focused her eyes just right she could see what looked like a thin shell around the planet, a shell that seemed to be composed of tiny purple dots. "Not really." She responded, "But I see a series of... some... things... covering the planet in the upper atmosphere."

"That's the stuff. That is a mine field. It was placed there to keep people from getting on or off the planet. The radiation-borne diseases and mutations that could result from people visiting the surface can't be allowed. So the Conglomerate put that mine field there to keep people off the planet. Even if you could survive the surface, you'd never get there in one piece."

Silence fell between them as the Kestrel hurtled through the void between the Tyconderoga and Earth Station. Riana looked on as the great artificial rings surrounding the planet came into sharper and sharper focus. She had seen images on her terminal, studied their function and purpose, but never until now had she had a chance to see them up close.

There were three rings, each one double the diameter of the Tyconderoga. They intersected one another on three axis, set at ninety degree angles to one another. The effect was the appearance that the Earth had been sliced into eighths by the immense grey tubes. At each intersection there was a giant mass of metal, a mega-city, each one playing host to hundreds of millions of people. Extending down beneath each of the cities was a thick tube that disappeared into the planet's atmosphere far below. These were the old orbital elevators, tubes used to lift cargo on and off of the planet's surface at a greatly reduced cost to the alternative, which at the time would have been some form of solid or liquid fuel rocket. Of course the elevators were long out of use, having been shut down immediately after the radiation levels on Earth became lethal.

There were thousands of ships swarming around the rings as they approached the system in their tiny shuttle. Even though the Earth itself was no longer habitable, it had still managed to remain the center of the human race. People swarmed to and around it for all of their major commerce and the resident population on the station was still far greater than on any other single installation in the solar system.

"Earth Station control this is the Kestrel, registration number SO-1138 on approach from Tyconderoga, requesting clearance and approach vector for landing." Willhelmina's voice chirped into the comm, startling Riana out of her reverie.

"Kestrel this is Earth Station flight control. We have you on approach and you are cleared for docking in bay N-112, repeat N-One-One-Two. Stay on current vector and reduce to port speed please." A pleasant male voice responded.

"Roger flight control, staying on course and reducing speed."

Riana almost didn't throttle back the shuttle's powerful engines, but decided the better of it considering their mission. Sighing to herself, she took over manual control of the vessel and steered it toward the designated berth.

-40-

Riana stepped through the door of the hangar and into one of the three massive rings that encircled the planet. Instantly, she felt more at home than she had since the day she was first ripped from Kalijor. There were people everywhere, buying and selling everything she could imagine. They filled a massive hallway that would have taken five minutes to walk across and extended out of sight into the curve of the ring in either direction. The ceiling was the only giveaway, aside from their clothing, that she wasn't at home in Rathalon, wandering the enclosed bazaar.

The people here were also much more like those she had grown up around. While the majority looked like normal humans, there were a great many that had pointed ears—much like her own—and even more with strange hair colors, or eyes with strangely shaped pupils and garish colors. Some of them had tails, horns, fins, even what looked like gills and scales could be seen. As she stood staring at a man walking past her with bright orange hair and foot-long horns growing out of his forehead,

Willhelmina came up behind her, sealing the door to their docking bay, and poking Riana in the ribs.

"Hey!" Riana nearly jumped out of her skin as the jab shocked her out of her reverie.

"It's not nice to stare. And I would think that you, of *all* people, would be pretty comfortable with a scene like this." She grinned as she chided her friend.

"Well, I guess you're right but… It's just so…"

"Strange? Different?"

"Yeah. That." Riana nodded. "I guess I am just so used to people in this world being so… human… that I have grown to expect it. Why are there so many people here like this as opposed to everywhere else we have been?"

"Not sure really," Willhelmina began as they stepped into the flow of people and began moving down the massive corridor. "Some people say it is the lack of direct sunlight, since windows in a space station are more of a potential for disaster than anything else. Some say it's the lack of good old terra firma beneath the feet." She shrugged noncommittally. "Either way, you see more of these types of folks on space stations and ships than you do on planet-based habitats."

Riana marveled at the diversity of appearance in the people present, all going about their business as if everything was normal, which she supposed it was really. "But Mars Station wasn't like this at all."

Willhelmina made a face somewhere between sadness and disgust. "That's sort of a special situation. The Mars Station is even older than most of Earth Station. It's been there a *long* time and through the decades it has sort of become the "Plain of Sorrow" of the solar system."

Riana shuddered at the reference. They had spent a great deal of time in the Plain of Sorrow not too long ago and it wasn't an experience that she particularly relished. Of course, neither was her trip to the Mars Station. There, she had lost her hands to Gregory Shantal and her sister to Malice all within a five minute span of time. It had not been enjoyable.

"Well that sort of says it all doesn't it?"

"To be sure. Here's a transport station up ahead." Willhelmina diverted their path to the side of the corridor where a set of transparent doors were set into the wall. Beyond them Riana, could see a transport train similar to the one they had ridden on Mars loading people up for a quick trip to somewhere else in the station.

As they made their way into the depot, Riana checked herself over one last time. She was unused to being on assignment with so little gear. She was wearing simple 'street' clothes, nothing fancy or special about them, although they were a nice change from the normal attire of the Tyconderoga personnel. Her outfit was splashed with color, although not excessively so, and much more generously cut for her frame than the jumpsuits she had grown used to. The other glaring difference was the equipment. She wasn't strapped with combat webbing, carrying weapons or any other specialized gadgets for that matter. Really, it was just the small bag with the AO uniforms and badges in it and the monowire sword Master Jonin had given to her, tucked away in a pocket.

While Willhelmina hummed a quiet tune to herself as they waited for the next transport to arrive, Riana tied her thick purple hair up into a loose bun on the back of her head. Doing so revealed her long, tapered ears and fine elvish facial features to those around her, causing several people to glance at her out of the corner of their eyes. Others simply stared outright at her and she blushed a bit as her body flushed with embarrassment.

Leaning in close to her friend she whispered, "Kat, is it normal for people to stare like that?"

Willhelmina stopped humming and looked at her friend. Grinning widely as she brushed a few stray locks of her own raven hair behind an ear. "I suppose it is pretty normal for someone like you."

"Someone like… me?"

"Yeah Ree. You aren't exactly unattractive you know? People like to look at attractive people. I suppose you get used to it after a while." She shrugged as the next transport pulled in to the terminal. "Hey. Didn't you say Jumah lives here somewhere?"

Riana's eyes brightened and her ears pointed straight up at the mention of his name. Her cheeks flushed deeper red as that familiar feeling of giddy warmth washed over her. "Um, yeah. He said he ran some kind of cargo business or something out of Xaman-Otoch."

"Maybe we should drop by and see him while we're here…"

"I'm not sure that's a good idea…"

"Why? You don't think he'd want to see you in person?"

310

"No. It's not that…" Riana's voice trailed off as if she was lost in some weighty thoughts. "It's just that we're on assignment and we shouldn't be taking any detours or anything."

"Yeah… On assignment… Right…" Willhelmina leveled her gaze on Riana, who ignored her scrutiny by staring determinedly at a spot on the floor as though it was about to do something worthy of the attention.

"Stop staring at me." Riana's ears cocked back in annoyance as she spoke to the spot on the floor.

"What's the problem Ree?"

"What makes you think there's a problem?"

"Ree I've known you for like, thirty years. You can't honestly think I wouldn't recognize your 'something's wrong' face can you?"

Riana sighed heavily, her ears drooping down low as she turned her violet eyes toward her friend. "I'm still scared I might hurt someone…"

"Ree everyone gets hurt in relationships sooner or later, and rarely does it happen intentionally."

"I know that Kat, but that's not what I mean. I still don't know the limits of my strength. I don't want to actually *hurt* someone. Physically."

"What? Are you planning on getting in the ring with him?"

"Not exactly…" Riana replied quietly as she continued her study of the spot on the floor.

"Oh." Willhelmina nodded sagely. Then the implication hit her full force, like a physical blow to the brain, "*Oh!*" She flushed a little bit as well and an uncomfortable silence fell between them for the rest of the transport's short journey.

When it came to a smooth stop, they moved out of the tube into the station with the other disembarking commuters. They had moved half way across the platform, toward the door, before Willhelmina stopped and placed her hand on Riana's shoulder.

"You are so controlled when we spar. Don't you think you can control your strength when… Well you know."

Riana looked at her friend forlornly then away again quickly, finding some other spot on the floor worthy of her intense scrutiny. "I don't know. I've never done anything like that before. And what if he doesn't… Like me… Here. I mean, he doesn't really know who… what… I am."

"I guess I can understand that. But I still don't think you should let it stop you from seeing him. I mean you really seemed to hit it off together. It would be a shame to let it go without at least trying." She steered them toward the near-by facility and slipped through the door. "Here. Let's duck into this restroom to change."

Moments later, they reappeared wearing the purloined uniforms and ID badges that had been provided to them. Quickly checking one another for anything that might identify them as anything other than Aegis Online employees, they headed out of the area and into a large, enclosed lobby that played host to a small park with a grassy area, several trees and a small fountain in its center. A great many people, in every conceivable style of dress and appearance, went about their days here. Children played in the park while parents sat in the grass and read or talked to one another. Others moved around the park, heading from one hallway to another on the outskirts of the large room or to the lift doors that lined the wall on the edge of the open space.

Quickly scanning the chamber, Riana located the lift they needed and she headed in that direction confidently, knowing Willhelmina would step in behind her. One integral part of this operation was for them to always give the impression that they belonged there. Standing around looking for where they were supposed to be would be a big indication that they didn't belong.

Stepping into the lift Riana selected the appropriate destination on the control panel and then looked at her friend. "I mean it isn't as if I don't *want* to, you know. I just don't want to hurt him, or anyone else in the process."

"Well that's very noble and all, but how long do you think it will be before you go insane from the lack of it?"

"Insane?! That can happen?" Riana's ears splayed out in concern as her eyes widened and she looked at Willhelmina.

Willhelmina turned slowly to look at her friend, the look on her face was a cross between amazement and mischievous. She rolled her eyes as she spoke. "Oh yea. Happens all the time. People getting so hot and bothered that their brains start to melt. Terrible business that, wouldn't wish it on my worst enemy."

Riana punched her playfully on the arm. "You rat! You had me worried for a second there. I thought you were serious."

Willhelmina grinned from ear to ear. "Well not totally serious. I guess some people go their entire lives without it. Sometimes I wonder if I could make it a month."

"You just made it a month. You were stuck in a game pod for nearly two, remember?"

Willhelmina screwed up her face and looked at the ceiling in an overly dramatic way. "And look, my brain is already melting. Hey! Maybe we should hit a club or something before we leave…"

Riana flushed again. She thought of Jumah and was certain that even if he didn't like her, she didn't want to pick up some guy at a club.. "I'm not sure that's such a good idea. I want to be with someone I care about."

Riana hugged her arms around herself tightly and shifted on her feet a bit as the thoughts swept her up.

"Don't we all." Willhelmina said flatly as the lift stopped smoothly and the doors slid silently open to reveal the main lobby of the Aegis Online facility.

-41-

The pair slipped through the labyrinthine hallways and rooms that made up the AO complex with relative ease. Riana had memorized the map they had been given and her recall seemed to be one-hundred percent accurate. The complex itself was gargantuan in proportions, easily as large as the entire Tyconderoga. Their ID badges had opened all of the necessary doors. The various people they had passed in the hallways had not given them a second look as they moved toward their objective.

They chatted as they moved, trying to make it sound as though they were just going about their usual business. Keeping the conversation light and their senses sharp, looking for anything that might require immediate action.

They arrived at the lab in question just as a group of people exited it on their lunch break. Slipping through the thick double doors, Riana turned around and entered a new encrypted door lock code as they closed behind them.

As the sharp metal-on-metal snap sounded, signaling the bolts sliding into place and sealing them in the room. Riana and Willhelmina sprung into action. Willhelmina moved straight to the processor prototype locked into a scanning apparatus in the center of the room. Deftly she popped it out of the mechanism and slid it into the custom, shielded case that she had brought in with her. Quickly, she slipped it into a pocket in the clothes she wore under the uniform for safe keeping and turned her attention to the rest of the lab, looking for any copies of the processor they may have been working on.

Riana, on the other hand, moved straight to the main computer console in the room and began tapping away at the controls looking for any schematics or other information about the processor. She snorted a couple of times as she ran into some rudimentary security protocols and deftly found her way around them, but when she finally found what she was looking for she narrowed her eyes and cocked her ears back in frustration.

"Kat there seems to be some new kind of encryption locking up these files we need. It isn't like anything I've seen before."

Willhelmina moved quickly to the terminal and scanned the display. "That's odd." She finally said as she tapped a couple of controls and watched the display change slightly.

"What?"

"This looks like game AI code."

"Artificial Intelligence?" Riana started reviewing the display in more earnest.

"Yeah. I'm not sure what it's doing in a research computer, but that is definitely what it looks like."

"Oh hell."

"What?" Willhelmina shifted her focus to Riana's display and narrowed her eyes at it as she took in the information. "Is that what I think it is?"

"Certainly looks that way. Assuming you are thinking it looks like a dragon."

"They have a dragon guarding the files." Willhelmina said in amazement. "How the…"

Willhelmina's musing was cut off by Riana suddenly ducking her head under the console and prying a metal panel off the base of the unit.

"Ree what are you doing?"

"Looking for an ODN port. I don't think I can get around this with this interface." She continued rummaging around in the myriad of fiber optic and electrical cables behind the damaged panel until she finally found what she was looking for and yanked it free of the console. The controls winked out, becoming a featureless, shiny black surface. Sitting upright in a chair, she held the glowing fiber in her hand and eyed Willhelmina seriously. "Hopefully it's a young dragon." With that, she held the connector near her wrist until the tiny flap of skin receded, revealing the ODN port in her arm, then jammed the cable home in the jack before Willhelmina could offer protest.

In a flash of bright light, Riana's consciousness lifted out of her body and she found herself standing in a shiny, gleaming silver room. Crouching in front of a door in the far wall was a large blue dragon, staring at her intently with deep cobalt eyes. Looking down, she saw that she was in her normal adventuring leathers from Kalijor, complete with sword belt and Elkorine on her hip. Her tattoos were present and glowing in sharp relief to her lightly tanned skin. It took her a moment to realize that she was actually seeing normally.

She didn't have time to spend wondering why, so she shrugged and took a few tentative steps toward the creature, causing it to raise its hackles and hunch its head and neck down between its shoulders, still staring at her relentlessly.

"I do not know you. What is your purpose here?" The creature's rough basso voice rumbled through the stark chamber, echoing off the walls.

"I have come to retrieve the information concerning SO's processor." Riana replied confidently.

"What you seek does not belong to you. Leave here or face the consequences." The beast exhaled a small cloud of green gas as if to punctuate its statement.

"I don't want to hurt you, but the data you protect is stolen." Riana's eyes flashed as a thick, flexible layer of ice incased her body.

The dragon snorted a cloud of acrid pea-soup gas as it rose up on its four legs and reared its neck up, now towering over her. "You are not allowed here!"

Snaking its long neck out, it snapped dagger sized teeth toward Riana. Instinctively, she stepped to the side and drew Elkorine from its scabbard, swinging it in a wide upward arc that brought its tip through the scales on the dragon's neck, leaving a deep furrow and a trickle of blood.

The dragon recoiled in surprise and narrowed its eyes at her before exhaling a thick, viscous cloud of the toxic green gas. As it quickly began to fill the room, Riana sucked in a lung full of air. Her eyes flashed again and a wave of intense heat rippled outward from her, igniting the gas and sending an explosion through the room that slammed them both against opposite walls.

Riana staggered to her feet as the ice melted from her body. She stooped down to snatch Elkorine up from the floor, her eyes flashing as she looked up at the dragon picking itself up from the ground. Another explosion resounded through the chamber as a bolt of lightning arced out of the ceiling and coursed through the dragon's body, sending the thing into convulsions. Moving across the space toward the flailing dragon, Riana prepared to bring her sword to bear on the creature. She was caught off guard when its hind leg kicked out violently and smashed into her ribs, launching her across the room and into the wall again. She hissed as the air was forced from her lungs and glared at the dragon while heaving and wheezing as her body tried to get enough air to breathe.

The thumping sound of the dragon's footfalls alerted her to its charge and she rolled forward just in time to get bowled over again, but it was better than being trampled. She rolled up into a crouching position and spun around, eyes glowing as large sphere of crackling black energy appeared in her left hand. The dragon rounded on her and reared up on its hind legs, flapping its wings menacingly and roaring.

As the beast came down, trying to slice her with its wicked sharp fore-claws, she dove to the side and flung the sphere of annihilation at it with all her might. The sphere of energy slammed into the dragon's chest, eliciting a panicked, pained wail from the creature as it lost its footing and crumpled to the floor in a great heap, legs and tail twitching reflexively.

Rolling to her feet she turned around, ready for the next attack. When it didn't come, she moved toward the dragon. Her eyes went wide as she saw the hole burned clean through its chest.

"Not much of a dragon." She wheezed through her still-recovering lungs as she staggered toward the door on the far side of the chamber. When she touched it, the door opened to reveal several shelves stacked high with rolls of parchment. Quickly she snatched up the papers and jammed them haphazardly into her large belt pouch. When the vault was empty she mentally triggered the log-out sequence and in a flash she was sitting in the chair in the computer room again.

"Ree that was awesome!" Willhelmina cheered as Riana reached over and pulled the optical cable from the port on her wrist.

"Which part?" Riana asked as she rubbed her ribs soothingly. She didn't even register the fact that they actually felt sore from the kick, even though she was no longer in virtual space.

"The whole thing! I mean, I've never seen someone use a game AI to guard files before but it makes perfect sense really, as long as you have a computer capable of handling the code, but actually logging in and beating it face to face was a stroke of genius! How did you know to ignite the poison gas?"

Riana looked at the purple outline of her friend and pressed her lips together. "Because the poison gas of blue dragons is flammable, we were taught that at the Magic Academy years ago Kat."

"Oh. I guess that's true." She moved to a smaller terminal and began tapping on the controls, rooting out any remaining research files pertaining to the processor and deleting them. "Wait a sec Ree. You mean you *saw* the dragon?"

"Of course I saw it Kat. I've been seeing things for quite a while now." She stood up from the chair and moved up behind Willhelmina. "And hearing things, and feeling things..." she added under her breath.

"Ree you don't get it. You *saw* the dragon. You saw its true color, not whatever you have been seeing of things recently. You really *saw* it!"

The realization hit her harder now that she had time to think about it.. She *had* seen it, and everything else. Just like she used to before the loss of her vision. But now, back in the real world, she was once again seeing only wireframes in her vision. No texture, no substance. "What the hell? Why can I see normally in this thing..." She kicked the large console suddenly, leaving a large, boot shaped dent in the metal panel, "and nowhere else?"

"I don't know Ree. Let's get out of here and then we can discuss it. I think I've got the rest of the information scoured out of their system."

"Good plan." Riana acquiesced as she moved to the door and tapped out the code sequence she had set earlier. The bolts could be heard retracting into the doors which then slowly and silently slid back into the walls to reveal a lone figure standing in the opening looking at them. A corona of wispy silver hair framed a too-happy smiling face and his overall clad body looked impossibly frail despite what Riana knew to be his actual strength.

Riana's gasp caused Willhelmina to swivel around in her chair to see what was going on. "Oh shit." She managed to say.

"Now now my children, let us not forget our manners. It simply isn't polite for a lady to swear."

-42-

"Gregory Shantal." Riana said, venom lacing her voice. She glared at him icily, opening and closing her hands reflexively in anticipation of battle.

"Riana Thorindal." He replied happily, grinning widely. "And I see that you have found your little friend. Xavier's puppet.

"Stuff it dragon breath. What's your business here?"

"My business here is accomplished. I was to get you here. Now I have only to keep you here long enough for you to be taken apart and reverse engineered."

"You'll have the devil of a time getting me to stay." Riana stepped back into a fighting stance, ready for the fight she now knew was coming. Willhelmina moved up beside her and moved into a similar stance.

"Oh how precious!" The mercenary cooed at them, clasping his hands together in front of him in a childish gesture of glee. He stopped just short of bouncing up and down. "You know this need not resort to violence, all you have to do is lie down and shut your eyes. They have promised to put you back together again once they are through with you."

"So this was nothing but a ruse to get me here? The processor, Kat's imprisonment?" Riana's violet eyes seemed to glow in the artificial light of the lab.

"Of course it was! Look at yourself child! Nowhere else is there such a machine as you! The pinnacle of engineering and programming, come together in one single vessel. And to think it is wasted on one such as yourself. A pity really." He made a tsk-ing noise as he shook his head almost imperceptibly.

Riana made to step forward but Willhelmina placed a hand on her shoulder, stopping her before she got away. "You're trying to provoke us. It won't work." She said as she looked to her friend's raging eyes.

"You don't think so?" He mewed, "that's too bad, I worked *so* hard on the routine!" He put a hand to his chin then and stroked it as one might expect to see a wizened old gentleman stroke his beard. "Let me try once more before you slink off the station..."

"There's nothing you can say that will make us attack you," Willhelmina said as she stepped closer and put her other hand on Riana's, squeezing it reassuringly.

"Just the same allow me to try once more... Ahem..." He stood up straighter and held his hand to his throat as he made the noise, putting

324

on a show for his audience. Before speaking again, he locked his steely eyes with Riana's, "I killed your mother."

Riana's whole body tensed and her enhanced muscles coiled instantly, ready for action. Her eyes flashed and Willhelmina thought for a second that she saw the tattoos on her wrists glow for a second. "Ree, don't. He's only trying to provoke you."

"Oh I did too. Of course that was after I raped her in the Burning Expanse. You know I think it was the first time she ever had a man before? Difficult to imagine, looking the way she does, her never having had a man before. Anyway, I took her virginity, then I took her life, and left her body to be eaten up by the sands of the Burning Expanse."

There was nothing Willhelmina could do to stop it. Riana leapt across the distance in the span of a heartbeat. She lashed out at him with a flying kick that would have torn a hole in a starship bulkhead, but Gregory dodged it with little effort, stepping lightly to the side and grinning at Willhelmina like the cat that ate the canary.

Not to be deterred, Riana landed lightly and swung her right leg around in a reverse round kick that caught the man in the ribs and put him into the wall ten feet away with a crash that reverberated up and down the hallways of the complex. The wall folded in around him under the force of the impact. She smiled wickedly as she slowly put her leg on the floor and set herself into a stance, ready for a fight.

"I see you have been practicing." He said lightly as he extricated himself from the mangled section of wall plating and dusted his ugly overalls off dramatically.

"Quit your babbling and let's get this over with." She spat.

"Riana, we should go. That noise is going to bring more people and we don't have the stuff to deal with armed guards." Willhelmina was edging toward the door now that the opening was no longer blocked.

"You go ahead Kat. I'll catch up to you." She never took her raging eyes off of the man, standing there calmly, waiting for the conversation to come back around to him.

"Ree, I'm not leaving you here." Willhelmina put a hand on Riana's shoulder and squeezed it, pulling her friend toward the hallway but Riana shrugged it off.

"Go Kat. Take the processor and the data back to SO. I'll charter a ship or something when I am done here, but I need to do this."

"You're being stupid Ree. You can't believe anything he says, he's a liar. A paid warrior who takes hostages and breaks deals. You don't owe him anything, let alone an honorable fight. What would Master Jonin say?"

Riana glared at the man, standing there with his hands in his coveralls, rocking back and forth from heel to toe playfully. "He would say that *everyone* deserves an honorable fight."

The sound of booted feet began filtering through the winding hallways as they spoke, just by listening they could tell that the local armed guards were closing in on their location.

"Go Kat. I mean it." Riana looked at Willhelmina finally, certainty, in her eyes. "Finish the job and buy something nice for dinner. I'll be right behind you. You'll need me to cover your escape anyway."

Willhelmina stole a glance down the hallway one direction, then the other, before turning her gaze to Riana. Riana mouthed the word 'go' to her and finally she sighed. "All right. But if you aren't home right behind me…"

"I'll be home." Riana reassured her. "Now go finish what we started."

Willhelmina looked at her one last time, turned on her heel and ducked down the quieter hallway, away from the sounds of approaching boot-steps.

Turning back toward Gregory, Riana set her stance and narrowed her eyes at him once more. "Alright, let's finish this."

The mercenary was looking at his fingernails intently when she spoke. He continued doing so for a moment, before finally turning toward her and opening his eyes up wide. "Oh. Oh I'm sorry child, we're you talking to me? It's difficult to tell sometimes, you should work on that. Very rude."

"You've no idea." She said as she launched herself at him again, diving in with a flurry of kicks and punches that he batted away with minimal effort.

"Still playing the children's version of the game I see." He commented in a bored tone as he calmly fended off her attacks then launched into a flurry of his own. He was faster than she remembered. His arms and legs moving at blinding speed, she was barely able to block them. The fact that she was still very angry didn't seem to help her any.

She tried to force herself to calm down but flashes of her mother laying dead in the Burning Expanse kept fueling the fire inside her. She needed to clear her head, knew she didn't stand a chance if she kept this up. Stepping into his stance, she quickly feigned a front punch and instead grabbed him by the overalls, shifting herself around into a front stance, facing the other direction. The result was quite satisfying. Gregory lost his balance and was flung bodily across the lab where he smashed into a computer console, tearing it from the floor and showering the room in sparks and flashes of light as he skidded to a halt against the far wall.

Taking advantage of the momentary lapse in combat, Riana dropped to her knees and closed her eyes, inhaling deeply and forcing her mind to clear itself of any thoughts but those of the here and now. As she focused her energies she heard the approaching storm of boots clattering to a halt in the open doorway, followed by the hum of energy weapons being powered up.

"There they are! Freeze! Don't move!" A burly man shouted at her from the doorway.

Calmly, she opened her eyes and raised her hands over her head to show that she was unarmed, but she kept her eyes on the spot where her true adversary was now extricating himself from the destroyed computer console.

"She shouldn't be a problem. Private Reynolds, cuff her!" The man shouted at one of his troops.

A skinny looking man with a young countenance responded instantly, stowing his rifle on his back and taking several confident steps forward with a pair of hand cuffs that had appeared in his hand from one of the myriad of pouches on his impressive looking armor. "Yes sir!"

"WAIT!"

The young man skidded to a halt half way to Riana as Gregory Shantal's voice sliced through the room. A moment later the damaged computer console lurched up into the air and crashed down onto the floor some ten feet away, its smooth interface panel shattering into a thousand pieces across the floor as it landed. The mercenary stood up slowly, disentangling himself from a mass of cables and wires that looked to be trying to swallow him whole as he stared at Riana.

She met his gaze evenly, the hatred gone from her for the moment. Master Jonin had seen a measure of success in teaching her how to clear her mind it seemed.

"She's mine. Get back." He finished as he dropped the last of the offending cables to the floor at his feet. He moved forward intently, his feet thumping heavily on the deck plates of the lab as he moved. When he was within feet of her, she stood up lightly, letting her hands fall to her sides as she watched him.

The soldiers immediately stepped back into the hallway and stood more at ease, but kept their weapons in hand and pointed generally in Riana's direction. It was apparent they had seen this show before and knew the rules.

Shantal stepped into an offensive stance and motioned for her to attack him with his forward hand.

She smiled at him sweetly and shook her head, she wouldn't let herself be baited again.

"Fine. We will play it your way child." He sneered as he lunged at her.

He approached her at blinding speeds, extending his fist only at the last instant. She stepped to the side and grabbed his fist with her right hand. As he traveled past her, she yanked on his arm, wrapping his arm back behind him as he passed her, then forcing his head toward the floor. He flipped over as he fell, landing face up on the metal floor with a deafening metal-on-metal bang before sliding to a stop a few feet from her.

In a snap, he was back on his feet again. He leapt at her, this time extending his foot toward her face. Calmly, she ducked under the approaching limb only to realize too late that it had been a ruse. As she ducked, he shifted his stance mid-air, bringing his lower leg up and kicking her hard in the chin as she moved toward the floor, amplifying the force of the impact.

Her world spun as his kick lifted her fully off the ground and sent her a few feet back where she crashed onto a table, scattering lab equipment as she rolled over backward onto her feet on the far side of the table.

"Not bad old man." She complimented him as she ran her hand under her chin and pulled it away, inspecting the blood on her fingers with interest. It wasn't bad, but she could tell that her jaw had been dislocated by the impact. Placing her hand on her jaw again she wrenched it until it popped back into place with a loud cracking noise. "Looks like we are in for a fight here."

"Indeed we are child." He sneered at her. He was clearly less impressed with the competition than she was, but the muffled comments from the armored guards meant this was unexpected fare.

Riana calmly walked around the lab table toward her adversary in the center of the room. She took a fighting stance, nodding her head at him ever so slightly to indicate her readiness to proceed.

The dance that followed was one that would have shamed some of the choreographed battles she had seen in films from the twenty-first century. The two fought on for the better part of an hour, neither ever getting tired, and exchanging blows equally. They seemed to be evenly matched now that Riana had a level head and at one point the soldiers began exchanging credits, betting on who would land the next blow or who would be the ultimate victor.

As the fight continued, even more spectators showed up. They lined up in the doorway but none were so brave as to actually enter the room. The combatants had long ago smashed the furniture to bits and trampled those bits into the deck. Anything that was more resilient had been bent, broken, or simply relocated to one of the far edges of the room, including a pile of smaller pieces of test equipment, forming a nice knee-high wall between the crowd of on-lookers and the combatants.

They had both taken something of a beating over the course of the fight, but Riana seemed to be faring better as her bio-mechanical body was less susceptible to permanent damage and physical impairments than his hydraulic and micro-servo enhanced body. As a result, he was growing more and more upset with each passing moment. Riana exploited every tiny little mistake he made to its fullest, much as he had when they'd fought in the depths of Mars Station.

At last, he reached his breaking point. She threw him, head first, into a pile of destroyed equipment and when he stood back up again, he was brandishing a large beam of metal that he had dislodged from the pile.

331

He swung it menacingly as he stepped from the pile, eyeing her with murderous intent. His childish demeanor had long since faded, leaving nothing behind but the cold, hard killer that he truly was.

"Time to put this to an end. You will never beat me, not in this world, or any other." He stepped toward her, swinging the metal beam with immense strength. Almost on instinct, Riana pulled the monowire sword from her pocket and flicked the actuator. She heard a soft hum as the magnetic field extended the atom-thin wire. As she brought her own weapon to bear, the sound of the metal beam being cut in two reminded her of how the craftsmen of Kalijor would use a thin wire of steel or some other hard metal to shave flakes and leafs of softer metals from blocks.

The tip of the beam came to rest against the wall behind her, after bouncing off two walls and the floor multiple times with a clatter. The silence that followed was almost deafening. Even the spectators were eerily silent as she looked up into her opponent's furious eyes. He held the remains of his metal beam in his left hand, eyeing the smoothly cut end with a curious expression. Finally he seemed to come to a decision and raised it up over his head. With a scream of rage he brought it down again, aiming straight for her head.

She heard Master Gornin's voice in her head from more than a year ago, when he was teaching her how to use her sword... *"The best way to handle an enemy's weapon is to never be in its path."*

She shifted to the side and twisted her body toward Shantal's, dropping her weapon down on top of him as he moved through the space she had just been occupying.

"Fight with honor, but leave your opponent no weapons with which to attack you. When your life is on the line, it is yours or theirs, make no mistake…" The troll's voice rumbled through her mind as she finished her sword stroke, flicking the actuator again and standing up straight. She was at the door before his severed hand even touched the floor.

The gathered crowd of people stood in awe, too stunned to stop her from squeezing through and moving off down the hallway toward the nearest exit.

Quietly she slipped the sword into her pocket and stepped out of the AO facility and into Xaman-Otoch proper, intent on finding a ride back to the Tyconderoga.

-43-

She slid around the corner recklessly as another hail of gunfire erupted behind her. One or two stray bullets impacted on her shoulder as she slipped around the cover but they were fired from far enough away that the damage was minimal, especially on her armored skin. She took in her surroundings quickly and seeing several people near her she screamed at them, "Run! Get out of here!"

She barreled through the small crowd of onlookers and around another corner just as the small group of pursuers rounded the corner and fired a short burst into the crowd.

"These guys are serious. They don't care who they hurt trying to get me." She muttered to herself as she scooped up a briefcase that some fleeing pedestrian had dropped on the ground. Turning around mid-stride, she flung the case as hard as she could toward the corner she had come around. As planned, one of the soldiers rounded the corner just as the briefcase arrived and it connected with his face. If he hadn't been wearing the helmet he would have been killed outright by the force of the blow. As it was, he was knocked back into his companions, bowling them all over as they bunched up behind him trying to round the corner.

As they went down en mass, a couple fired their weapons and one of them got lucky. She knew they had scored a direct hit on her left shoulder just above the breast. Thanks to the sharp pain streaking through her body, she knew that it had penetrated her armored skin. After an instant, the nanites in her blood stopped the pain transmission cold, allowing her to think rationally instead of being driven by pain and fear.

Spinning back around, she dashed toward a nearby lift and dove through the closing door, taking three more shots to her right shoulder and back before the doors closed fully.

She slumped against the wall, closing her eyes momentarily before speaking to the lift's computer, "Level twenty-three please." She moaned into the wall, trying not to think of the cool liquid running down her back in shallow rivers. The lift began to move and she rolled herself around, leaning against the wall and probing the hole in her left shoulder with her index finger. It sank into the hole up to her second knuckle before she felt the back of the bullet that had caused the wound.

"Damn armor piercing bullets! Who are these AO people?!" Her knees weakened a bit, causing her to slide down the wall. She was losing energy fast and needed a place to rest and hide while her nanites worked their magic on her wounded body.

Without warning, the lift lurched to a stop, causing her to slip and fall the rest of the way to the floor. Looking up groggily at the display panel she could see the lift had been stopped not even half way to her designated floor. "Bastards are quick." She mused as she forced the fog from her mind. She didn't have time to think about passing out just yet.

She looked around the tiny little coffin for any sign of hope. Finally, she got her feet under herself and stood up. Looking at the ceiling of the lift, she found the thin lines denoting the maintenance access and jumped up, smacking the release stud that was recessed inside a light fixture. The panel swung down into the lift and she grabbed it, hauling herself up onto the roof of the lift before reaching in behind herself and pulling the hatch closed again.

The lift shaft was an acrophobic's nightmare, extending out of sight in both directions with barely enough room between the car and the shaft wall for a person to squeeze through. There would be no chance of surviving if she had to be in the shaft while a lift was passing at speed, she decided, the tolerances were just too close. Quickly, she located the maintenance ladder and in sixty seconds, was three stories above the jammed lift car, opening a service access door and crawling from one nightmare to another.

"Twenty minutes of crawling around in these damn tubes and I've no idea where the hell I am…" She muttered as she found another service hatch and slowly opened it just enough to peek through the crack and try to get some idea of where she was. She wasn't sure, but she thought she might have blacked out a couple of times. There were some discrepancies between what she remembered and what her internal clock were telling her, but it had been mere moments. She had to find a safe place to recuperate or she was going to pass out right here and they would find her for sure. As it was, she was leaving a trail of blood through these maintenance tubes.

Scanning the other side of the hatchway, she saw a stair well, with a large number nineteen painted on the opposite wall in large, friendly numerals. "Finally a break," she breathed as she opened the hatch the rest of the way and threw herself onto the landing with a thud.

Slowly, she pushed herself to her feet and secured the maintenance panel, then made her way up a few flights of stairs before she heard the sound of boots tromping down from above.

"Hell. Here we go again…" She looked up the gap between the stairways and saw the black booted feet of the AO soldiers flooding down toward her in a great wave. Forcing herself back into high gear, she turned around and made for the nearest door, next to it was the number twenty-one. "Why does that sound familiar?" She wondered as she yanked the door open and slipped through into a nice, clean hallway lined with doors. Just above her head she saw a sign that read, 'Welcome to A block. You are on level 21.'

"Twenty-one A… Why is that so familiar?" She staggered down the hallway looking at the numbers on the doors as she made her way past them. Finally it hit her. "Twenty-one-eighty-seven!"

She nearly gasped when she saw the number and remembered its significance. Her hands fumbled with the panel next to the door, her eyes going blurry on her. The purple-outlined keys kept dancing from side to side when she tried to press them, but she finally managed to press the call button.

A moment later the panel began to slide open. The instant it had retracted far enough for her to fit through, she lurched over the threshold and landed face first on what felt like a nicely woven dwarven rug. She heard the door close behind her and called out to it deliriously, "Door,

338

lock. Do not disturb." She heard a tone that meant the mechanism had indeed locked and then gave some more serious consideration to a month-long nap when she heard a soft footstep near her head.

Opening her eyes slightly, she saw a bare foot not more than a few inches from her face. Forcing herself to roll up onto her side, she followed the foot past its ankle where it transitioned into a nicely muscled calf and shin, followed by a strong knee and well defined thigh that disappeared into a pair of silk boxers and then reappeared as a toned, but not overly-muscled stomach and chest with a pair of strong arms folded across it. Atop this tower was a perfectly situated head with long, flowing blond hair that was pulled back into a loose pony tail. A somewhat familiar face looked down on her with a strange mixture of amusement, concern, and sheer horror.

Before she blacked out, she managed to smile weakly and say, "Hi Jumah. You said I...should stop b... some time... s'okay if... I... need to... I'm sorry..."

And then her world went black.

-44-

Consciousness returned slowly, fighting her every step of the way. As she opened her eyes, the first thing she saw was the ceiling. It was smooth and roughly the same design as what she was used to waking up to, for an instant she thought she was back in her quarters on the Tyconderoga. But, the ambient sounds in the room weren't right. Suddenly, it all came back to her in a flash and she sat up in a flurry of bed sheets. Looking back and forth around the room to take in her surroundings all at once.

She was in a bedroom, an unfamiliar bedroom, sitting on a large bed that dominated the back wall of the room. On one wall of the room was a low dresser and on the opposite wall was a small entertainment/ computer area with some media scattered around in little piles. There were three doors in the room. One was partially open and looked as though it dead-ended in a small, unkempt closet. The second door was open and revealed a darkened bathroom. The third was tightly closed, but she was comfortable assuming that it led to the rest of whatever residence she was in at the moment.

Which was her next line of business… Figuring out where she was. She knew she had punched in an entry request on a door but she couldn't remember who's door, or why she had known the owner might be sympathetic to her plight. Then she had passed out because of blood loss.

"Oh crap." She hissed as her hand went to her shoulder, feeling for the hole the AP bullet had made. Looking down she saw a whole, undamaged T-shirt in place of the damaged, bloody one she knew she had been wearing. Stretching the neck open, she looked down and saw that her skin was smooth and undamaged where she knew the bullet had gone in. She'd been out long enough for it to heal, which meant hours at least, maybe a day or more.

Kat! She dove for the computer terminal and punched in the number for Willhelmina's quarters on the comm application. The dull tone sounded three or four times before Willhelmina finally blinked into view on the display.

"Hello?" She said tentatively, not recognizing the caller's information. When she saw Riana looking back at her she gasped, "Riana!! Where have you been?! Are you alright?"

"I'm fine." Riana reassured her friend quietly, trying not to draw the attention of her unknown benefactor. "I have no idea where I am, I just woke up and I wanted to make sure you got out OK."

"Yeah, I had a little trouble in customs because of the alarms going off at AO, but they eventually let me by. I waited for nearly an hour before I left Ree, but they started searching ships so I had to take off before they stopped me. That was three days ago."

"Three days?!" Riana sighed heavily, "It's OK Kat, so long as you are safe." Riana ran her fingers through her hair, dragging the thick purple mass to the back of her head where she tied it in a loose bun to keep it out of her face. "Is everything else there OK?"

"Yeah, aside from everyone wondering where you ended up, we are all OK here. The processor checked out and it looks like they hadn't made too much progress based on the data we recovered. How did you make out with that bastard Gregory?"

"I uh… I beat him." She tried to skirt around the subject. Suddenly it seemed as though she had done a great wrong in cutting off his hand. She knew he wouldn't have hesitated to do it to her, especially since he had already done it once, but still… "I have a sneaking suspicion that we will be seeing him again though."

"Well now that we know you can take him, we don't have to worry about that do we?" Willhelmina grinned widely. "Now, do you need me to come and get you?"

"No, I think I'm going to look around here a bit and then find a charter back to the Tyconderoga, what time is it?"

Willhelmina glanced away from the camera for a moment then looked back. "It's nine."

"Ok. I'll try to get a flight out of here around six or seven. Expect me back after dinner."

"Sounds good. I'll let Xavier know."

Riana grimaced at the mention of his name. She didn't like him keeping tabs on her all of the time, even if she *was* his employee. "Alright. Now, I need to find out who I owe the big favor to. I'll talk to you tonight Kat."

Without waiting for a reply, she terminated the transmission. Shifting herself out from under the heavy covers on the bed, she set her bare feet on the cool floor and stood up. Taking stock of her situation, she looked carefully at what she was wearing, a T-shirt and boxers. Nothing at all like what she had been wearing when she was last conscious. Whoever she owed the favor to was going to get a thorough trouncing for their efforts unless they had a pretty good explanation for her current state of dress.

Quietly, she padded over to the closed door and keyed the open button. The panel silently slid aside to reveal a medium sized living room area that was decorated modestly with a few pieces of furniture. A large view screen dominated one wall and numerous swords and other ancient melee weapons decorated the walls between pictures of fantasy characters doing fantasy things. Opposite the screen was a moderately-sized kitchen that was exuding the heavenly smells of cooking food.

Her stomach twisted itself around and made a noise, betraying her presence in the room. At that point she didn't care, she was suddenly ravenous and in desperate need for sustenance. As she eyed the kitchen hungrily, a man stepped into view from behind a cabinet door, his blonde hair was pulled back in a ponytail and his eyes glowed in the light of the room as he smiled at her.

"Well hello there! Welcome back to the land of the living." He quipped as he closed the door and set whatever he had retrieved down on the counter. "Can I interest you in something to eat?"

She couldn't help herself. She lunged toward a stool at the counter, sitting quickly and looking over at the stove abutting the bar. The furniture protested slightly under the weight of her body, but seemed to be holding up as she crossed her arms on the counter and leveled a roguish smile at the man. "Could you ever. I am famished. What are we having?"

He smiled back at her as he grabbed a spatula and flipped a couple of round objects in the skillet over then tended to some sizzling strips of meat in another pan.

"Pancakes and bacon. I'm afraid I don't have much else in the place right now. You caught me just back from a long trip." He spoke casually, almost as though he hadn't found her bleeding on his rug.

"Sounds great." She smiled up at him and gladly accepted the plate he offered her.

Three helpings later she began to feel the hunger pangs fade a bit and they began to talk as she finished off the last of the food he had prepared.

"Thank you." She said, sopping up the remaining syrup with the last bite of pancake.

"You're very welcome. So uh… You want to talk about it?"

She looked up at him, ready to ask what he meant until she realized how silly a question that would really be. She sighed and set her fork down on the plate. "Sure. What do you want to know?"

He looked at her for a moment, puzzling something over in his mind before answering. "Let's start simple." He reached forward with his right hand outstretched toward her. "Hi. My name is Vincent Torres, my friends call me Vin."

She accepted his hand in hers and gave it a healthy squeeze, then smiled again. "Riana. Riana Thorindal. My friends call me Ree."

The handshake broke off somewhat uneasily as he retreated back to his own stool and looked at her in contemplation for another long moment. Then he finally spoke again, "You know if this is going to work at all, you are going to have to be completely honest with me."

She looked awkwardly at him, unsure what he was talking about. "What do you mean? We just started talking about it."

"Yes we did. And already the communications are breaking down. Please, tell me your name."

It was one of the most confusing things anyone had ever said to her. Hadn't she just told him that? She cleared her throat and wiped her lips with her napkin, setting it aside then looking back at him. "My name is Riana Thorindal."

He sighed and leaned back into the wall behind his stool. "That's funny, because I know a nice girl named Riana in Kalijor, and as far as I know the system won't allow you to use your real name in the game. So either you are an impostor, or there is something very different happening right here."

She stared at him, open-mouthed. She had never even thought that people would be forced to use different names for their avatars in Kalijor. Now that she considered it though she supposed that even Willhelmina's name was different in the game, she just called her Kat because that was how she had always known her. She chuckled as she thought about it, which caused Vincent to raise an eyebrow at her. She supposed there was nothing for it but to tell him her story, at least in brief. She owed him that much at the very least.

Half an hour later, they had moved to the more comfortable furniture in the living room and Vincent was leaning forward with his elbows on his knees listening to her describe the trip from the AO complex to his door. When she finished, he leaned back against the soft cushion of his chair and ran his fingers through his hair. She couldn't get past how much he looked like Jumah.

"I have to say that sounds pretty wild. I wouldn't believe a word of it except that I watched those bullet holes close themselves up with my own eyes. That and in talking to you I can tell you are the same person I met in Kalijor. So you're really... from there? Like really born in Kalijor and moved out here?"

"Yes." She said simply. She didn't really know what else to say.

"And now you're in industrial espionage..."

"NO!" She almost stood up out of her chair as she shouted the word. "I am a courier! Kat and I are *not* fighting SO's wars for them!" She was ready to go on, but she finally noticed his wicked grin and caught herself up short. Sitting back down again she picked up a throw pillow and tossed it at him. At that, he burst into laughter.

"Anyway," she continued along a different course. "Thank you very much for taking care of me. I really didn't mean to drop in on you like this."

He continued grinning at her playfully. "Don't worry about it. I have no love of those Aegis folks. They never pay an invoice on time and that's just rotten business. If there's one thing I have learned in my life it is that rotten businesses are run by rotten people. Besides which, you have made an impression upon me that I doubt any other woman could match. Riana, I'm afraid you have already spoiled me."

She eyed him suspiciously then. "That reminds me buster… Just how exactly did I get into these clean clothes?"

His grin faltered for an instant before returning and then growing even wider. "We magicians never reveal our secrets m'lady. T'would be bad for our reputations." Then he stood up abruptly and began tidying the place as he continued, "So, do you have any plans for the day? Maybe get shot at some more? Pass out in some other stranger's living room?"

She 'tsked' at him, standing up and helping him with the few dishes they had dirtied. "No. I'm afraid that was a one-time show. Anyone not there to see it is just going to have to buy the book."

"More's the pity. You could make a fortune selling tickets to the follow-up act." He admonished her.

She eyed him curiously, "What follow-up act?"

"The one where the bullet holes magically close themselves up and you wake up fine."

She stopped and looked at him, still unable to tell when he was joking and when he was serious, just like Jumah. "You know. If anyone else ever finds out…"

He grinned at her, stepping in close. "Well, I guess you'll just have to do something to keep my mouth occupied."

"Why Mr. Torres, are you flirting with me?" She smirked.

He stared at her for a long moment, then seemed to make up his mind, taking a step back and smiling. "How about some music while we get cleaned up, and then I shall take you on a whirlwind tour of the Earth Station." He stepped to the entertainment center and punched a couple of buttons. The room was suddenly filled with the same elvish lullaby that had been haunting Riana for weeks now. "Although we may want to get out of Xaman-Otoch and see the rest of the station considering your popularity with the constabulary in these parts…" He trailed off as he turned to look at her, and saw that she was simply standing there, staring off into space.

The music filled her being so completely that she could not even begin to describe it. It wasn't just her mother's words, but her voice as well. And she was actually singing in elvish, exactly as she had always done when she sang to them as children. The sound was different now though, it was coming from all around her, instead of echoing around in her mind, just on the edge of actual hearing. Now it was there for real and she knew it. She looked toward Vincent to ask him something and realized he was speaking to her.

"Riana are you alright?"

"Huh? Oh. Yeah, yeah I'm fine. What music is this?" She nodded toward the entertainment center.

Vincent offered her a concerned look before he glanced back at the console briefly and replied, "It's a new singer. She calls herself Resonance. I just picked it up on my way back in from the moon the day you arrived."

"A new singer?" She absently rinsed the plate she had been holding under the water for five minutes now as she looked at Vincent.

"Yeah, you know, these folks come and go. Especially the ones that try to make a career singing in fantasy languages like this lady."

"Fantasy languages?" She glanced back and forth between him and the entertainment center.

"Yeah you know. Elvish… It's from the Kalijor…" he stopped suddenly as he realized what she was thinking. "Oh. Riana, I'm sorry I didn't mean anything by it…"

She smiled weakly at him, forcing herself to focus on her dish washing. "It's OK. You get used to it." She lied.

"No it isn't." He replied as he moved up beside her and took the dish from her hands, setting it in the washing machine and then looking her in the eyes. "Look, this is obviously a pretty new situation for me. And while that's no excuse, I'm going to play the card anyway. I'll tell you what. I saw an advert that said Resonance is going to play today so how bout we go get you something to wear, then I buy you dinner and we go to the concert."

Riana looked at him for a long moment before she finally nodded at him, still unsure what to say as the song flooded through her being and awakened feelings in her that she had never really known she possessed. Feelings of need and… desire. She watched him smile warmly as he pushed her gently away from the kitchen sink and took over the dish washing.

"There's clean towels in the bathroom. Go grab a shower and get cleaned up. Help yourself to anything in the closet until we get you something proper."

She smiled warmly at him as she moved off toward the bathroom, still listening intently to the sound of her mother's voice ebbing and flowing around the room, caressing her just as it had so many years ago when she was a youngling in Rathalon.

-45-

Before she knew it the bulk of the day was gone. Vincent had taken her to one of the other hubs of the Earth Station and they had spent hours going through shops for clothes that Riana could wear to dinner and the concert. She was, of course, no stranger to shopping and actually managed to pay what she thought were some very reasonable prices for her findings. She was again amazed at the varieties of cuts, styles, and colors that were available. She was simply in awe of the fact that some people would actually wear some of the things they encountered.

She had decided upon a simple skirt and top that fit her well and revealed a bit more skin than she was comfortable with of late, mostly owing to the lack of her tattoos. She felt somehow, incomplete without them. She wouldn't have purchased the outfit, except that Vincent seemed to really like it, and not in a lecherous sort of way. Now, as they were finishing up dinner at a very nice restaurant, she was having second thoughts about the choice as she noticed half the men, and some of the women in the place grabbing secret, or even blatant looks at her.

Her ears splayed out and flushed as she caught someone's eye and quickly snapped her head back around, locking eyes with Vincent. Clearing her throat sheepishly as she poked at her food with her fork. "I may never get used to this..." She said, half to him and half to herself.

"Get used to what?" He replied with his trademarked smile spreading across his face.

"All of these people looking at me. They were doing it the other day in a transport too."

"Well I'm afraid that is something you will definitely have to get used to. Because unfortunately, men are pigs. And you, Riana, are a very attractive woman."

Her whole body flushed at his compliment, and she swore she could feel her internal temperature rise several degrees, although her bio-readout confirmed it was still dead-on normal, just as it had been since she woke up in this body.

"Especially when you blush like that." He added for good measure.

"Well, you don't strike me as being a pig." She said, almost to herself.

"Oh no. Make no mistake. I am as big of a pig as the next guy. I just have the good sense to admit it, and to try and curb the habit." He pressed his thumb onto the surface of the data pad that was displaying their evening's meal selections and the associated costs. The pad beeped its acceptance of payment at him and he grinned at her as he wiped the screen with his napkin and set the pad on the table.

She blushed a shade deeper and then smiled at him, her ears perking back up a bit. "Well thank you. For everything you have done for me the last few days. But most especially for today…"

She wasn't sure how it happened, but the next thing she knew, she was leaning forward over the small table. She could feel his warm breath on her lips and cheeks. She had no idea what to do next and so she just closed her eyes, her ears cocking back in anticipation of what was to come next. As his lips brushed across hers, electric sparks arced across her skin from head to toe and again, she felt her body heating up.

It lasted mere moments, and yet it felt like an eternity. When they finally broke apart, she remained there with her eyes closed for a long moment, reveling in the feeling of the kiss. She had no idea it could feel so wonderful, and scary, and fulfilling. Yet, it created such a gap in her when it was gone. Finally, Vincent's shuffling on the other side of the table caused her to open her eyes and look at his outlined form. He was scooting his chair back and preparing to stand up, but his eyes were still locked on her.

"We uh… should probably get going if we wanted to make that Resonance concert. It's just right around the corner but these things can fill up pretty quickly."

"Ok." She acquiesced, not really wanting the moment to end. She rose to her feet and pulled her new jacket from the back of her chair, slipping it on as she watched him do the same with his. They stepped around the table and he snatched up her hand, giving her his roguish smile. Then he led her out of the restaurant and down the cavernous corridor toward a freestanding structure the size of Kalijor's great arena. It looked as though it could easily seat more than eighty-thousand people.

As they drew up to the stadium entrance, Vincent thumbed the reader at the gate and it opened to admit them. They quickly made their way through the numerous hallways and various ramps to find their seats. They were set up directly across from the stage, just off the floor of the arena in the first row of seats. She wasn't sure how it worked in this world yet, but she knew that in Kalijor, these would be very good, very expensive seats.

"I hope this didn't cost too much. I know I've been sort of a burden on you." She looked at him seriously.

His outline shrugged and that ever-present grin spread across his face. "Nonsense, I've no one else to spend it on since I am away most of the time on business. And besides, I can't think of a single person in this world, or Kalijor, that I would rather spend the day with."

She couldn't be sure, but she thought he might be blushing. Grabbing his hand she interlaced her fingers with his and snuggled against his shoulder to watch the rest of the seats fill up. As the lights in the arena began to dim, signaling that the concert was about to begin, a hush fell over the stadium. The lights winked out and the silence that fell over the enormous crowd was astonishing, especially in a space as huge as it was. After a long moment, a single mote of light appeared in the center of the stadium, floating in mid air some fifty feet above the floor of the stadium.

Slowly the light expanded in gently pulsing waves while an enchanting melody crept into Riana's hearing, barely noticeable even to her enhanced senses. The melody steadily increased in volume as the light expanded and grew until it finally coalesced into the form of a beautiful, radiant elven woman with long, elegantly tapered ears and fine features. As she came into sharp focus, the melody shifted into a more dramatic sweeping movement and she began singing a powerful ballad in elvish.

Riana didn't realize she was sitting there with her mouth open until Vincent gently pushed her chin up to close it. Embarrassed, she thanked him and resumed staring at the figure in the center of the stadium as she swayed hypnotically and drove the song with her powerful voice.

There was no mistaking it now, it was definitely her mother, Ezrina. But how could that be? She hadn't been seen by anyone in over three years Kalijor time and Riana had seen a vision of her laying dead in the Burning Expanse. How could she be here, in the real world, performing in front of eighty-thousand people?

The first song ended with a brilliant display of lights that issued forth from her mother's hands like some sort of spell effect and then she crouched down, almost into a ball as another powerful movement began. This time she began singing while crouched down, a song about love and loss, and the need to go on in the face of terrible pain. As she sang, her voice shifted from sad and lilting to powerful and driving. She stood up again, unfurling her arms and sending off more sprays of light that whisked around the stadium, surrounding people and enveloping them in cocoons of light that shimmered for a moment and then vanished.

Throughout the entire concert Riana was transfixed. Each song performed was like a personal message to her specifically. It was her mother, she was sure of it. And she was telling her to go on, to keep her friends close and her enemies closer, to learn all she could from anyone that would teach her, and to be compassionate when no one else possibly could. By the time the lights came back up she was close to breaking down completely. She knew that if she still had tears to cry, her face would be streaked with them and her eyes would be red and puffy. As it was, she had a lump in her throat that she swore should have been visible to anyone standing near by and she had trouble standing up from the dry sobs that were wracking her body.

At a complete loss for anything else to do, Vincent just sat there and held her, his arm wrapped around her shoulder, squeezing her to him as she let it all go. When she finally started to calm down, he spoke softly so as not to draw attention from the throngs that surrounded them as they waited to exit the stadium.

"Riana I'm sorry. I had no idea this would be so powerful for you. This was a mistake…"

She looked up at him with an unreadable expression, somewhere between glee and gloom. After a long moment, she smiled and leaned in to give him a hug. Careful not to crush him by accident. "No, this was exactly what I needed. Thank you. I've been looking for her for so long now, I was starting to give up hope."

"Looking for… You were looking for Resonance?"

"No. I have been looking for my mother. That was her. That was Ezrina! Although I don't understand how she could be here. I need to talk to her… Do you know how I could talk to her?" She looked up into his eyes hopefully.

"I'm not sure. I've heard that nobody sees her between concerts, not even her agent or manager. They handle all contact via comm unit or electronic messaging."

"But she has to be here somewhere right? I mean, she was just there…" She pointed to the empty space in the center of the stadium where her mother had been performing.

"No, that was a hologram, I think she was broadcasting from Tranquility but I don't remember for sure."

"She's on the moon?"

"I think so. It's difficult to tell these days where someone is performing from. Here, I think we can get out now." He stood up and offered her a hand as a gap formed in the exit line.

Standing up and taking his hand, Riana cast her gaze back around the massive chamber that was the stadium. Only once before in her life had she experienced such a moving, emotional episode, and that was when Master Gornin had introduced her to her other mother, Kilishandra, back at the Cohai Observatory in Kalijor more than a year ago. Now, as then, she was leaving the experience feeling changed, purposeful, and for the first time in a long time, full of hope.

Turning back toward the front of the line, she grabbed Vincent's arm and snuggled up against him again as they awaited their turn to leave the stadium and head out into Earth Station once more.

-46-

The trip back to the Tyconderoga was uneventful. Riana was able to make a call to the station and convince someone to hire Vincent to haul some piece of equipment to the station. Doing so made her feel better about his refusal of payment from her when he insisted she return on board his ship, the 'Neophyte's Serendipity'. Along the way, they talked about Kalijor, 'real' life, Willhelmina, and numerous other things. The one thing that seemed strangely conspicuous to her was the lack of conversation about her origins and present state, as yet.

When she had asked him about it, he had simply smiled his winning smile and replied, "It isn't nice to talk about such things. I figured you would talk about it if you were interested in talking about it, and while I must confess to more than a little bit of curiosity in the matter, I am really just more than pleased to be spending time with you."

So she had decided to spend a little time talking about herself, imploring him to ask a few questions. After much poking and prodding he managed to come up with a few.

"Alright," he finally acquiesced, "Is your body totally artificial? Because it looks pretty normal to me."

"It's mostly artificial, yes, but all of my skin, hair, eyes, all of the stuff you can see is real, organic, living tissue. As is my nervous system."

"Ok. So please don't take this the wrong way, because you look great, but… When I moved you from the living room to the bed room, you weighed more than anyone I've ever moved. And I've moved some pretty big passed out folks before, I used to work in a bar."

She sniggered a bit at him before putting on her best wounded look, "Why mister Torres! How dare you impugn a lady's honor by being so forward about her weight!"

To this, he groaned and rolled his eyes melodramatically. She let silence fall for a few moments to make him think she was actually upset. When she saw him casting her little nervous looks she finally let him off the hook. "I weigh about three-hundred pounds. My bones are all titanium alloy shells with carbon-fiber structural reinforcement and my muscle tissue is some sort of top secret semi-metallic composite that behaves like organic muscle tissue but has much higher tensile tolerances and compression ratios than the real thing. I understand that is where the bulk of the weight is since my internal organs are pretty simple and very light weight cybernetics."

"Wow that sounds pretty technical. Do you really understand all of that?"

"Most of it. I seem to have an increased capacity for learning. Something to do with how the computer interfaces with my nervous system. It seems to make pretty much everything work at a higher than normal level. I learn faster, move faster, process information faster, there are numbers associated with all of it, but I'm still learning what all of that means."

"I see. So uh… Are you…" He suddenly grew very uncomfortable and started fidgeting in his seat and poking randomly at the controls of the ship.

"Am I…" She prompted him.

"Er… What I mean to say is… if we… you know… start seeing each other for a while and eventually we decide to… you know…"

Riana flushed through, heat coursing from head to toe and visions flashing in front of her eyes. Her ears splayed out in embarrassment and she looked out the starboard view port at empty space, trying to find anything of interest to distract her from her sudden series of day dreams. "I uh… My data doesn't include that information. I… I'm not sure… I guess I'll have to ask…"

The remainder of the trip was completed in relative silence with each of them trying to reconcile the feelings brought on by that simple question. Riana had no idea if she was even physically capable of the act of sex, and she had honestly never really even thought about it before then.

Now that she thought about it though, it really helped explain a lot of the feelings she had been having of late, especially when she thought about Jumah, or Vincent now. It caused that strange heat to flush through her body. She would have to find out soon if she was 'equipped' to handle such situations, because it was suddenly obvious to her that eventually there would be a desire, if not an outright need to go there.

As the 'Neophyte's Serendipity' was unloaded in the Tyconderoga's landing bay, Riana and Vincent said a reluctant good bye. Promising to see one another again as soon as was possible, they hugged one another for a moment. As they separated, he kissed her lightly on the lips before slipping back inside his ship and closing the door behind him leaving no opportunity for her to even think about saying anything to him. The kiss still burned on her lips and in her mind as she dropped onto the protesting couch in Willhelmina's room five minutes later.

"Now I *have* seen everything." Willhelmina grinned at her as she entered the living room and saw her friend sitting on the couch staring dreamily at the far wall.

"Huh?" Riana looked around toward Willhelmina as she moved across the room and sat down next to her.

"So. Tell me all about it."

"All about what?" Riana tried to play it off as though nothing had happened.

"What could she possibly tell me about..." Willhelmina trailed off in mid-sentence and feigned deep thought for an instant before grinning at Riana and continuing, "about the kiss maybe?"

Riana couldn't help it. She flushed through again, her ears splaying out in embarrassment as she looked away demurely. "Is it that obvious?"

"Well let's just say that anyone with eyes in their head could see it across the shuttle bay. So, no, not really that obvious at all…"

Riana groaned and pushed playfully on Willhelmina's shoulder, careful not to push too hard. Willhelmina rocked backwards onto the couch and then back up into a sitting position again like an old wooden toy Riana had when she was a youngling in Rathalon. She sniggered at the thought, causing Willhelmina to eye her suspiciously. Finally, she calmed down and sighed heavily, not a sigh of frustration, but one of… she wasn't really sure what… contentment? "Kat, he was amazing! I don't know what else to say. He's just like Jumah really, which isn't that surprising I suppose. I mean he looks different, and he isn't a were-cheetah, that I know of, but he really is the same person!"

Willhelmina grinned at her. "Well what did you expect? Jekyl and Hyde?"

"Who?" Riana raised a curious eyebrow.

Willhelmina laughed loudly at that. "Nineteenth century literature. Look, the interface for Kalijor pulls features from the real life person and works them into the avatar.. It uses 'residual self image' and is really more about the sub-conscious than the computer, but that is where that comes from. And as far as how he acts… Well I guess you got lucky, not everyone is like that. But I would go so far as to say that people in Kalijor tend to take some portions of their real personality and amplify it for their character."

"What do you mean?"

"Well people who are generally nice may tend to be really goody two-shoes in Kalijor, while people with a couple of dark leanings may be really evil, or just live on the wrong side of the law in Kalijor. It gives people a chance to play out fantasies, to let loose that side of themselves that they just can't let people in the real world see."

"Huh. Well I am glad! He was really sweet. I literally stumbled in on him. Totally unannounced, riddled with bullet holes and he just cleaned me up and hid me away from the AO soldiers until I was on my feet again. Then he made me breakfast, took me out shopping and to dinner, then to a concert! And oh-my-god Kat!! Have you heard this singer Resonance? It's mom I swear!! I saw her, and heard her, and it was Mom! She's out here in the real world somehow!"

Willhelmina looked at her friend with a suspicious face of her own. "That's all very good Ree. But Ezrina? Out here? I don't see how that's possible." She sat back a bit and looked thoughtful for a moment. "Resonance you say? Did your new friend say where she was performing from?"

Riana looked at Willhelmina skeptically. "How did you know she wasn't there? I didn't say that."

Willhelmina sighed. Sometimes she forgot how new Riana was to this world. "Ree most performers do tele-presence performances now. With so many people and places out there, it would be next to impossible for someone to perform everywhere even if they spent a lifetime touring."

"Oh." Riana replied simply. "He said he thought she was performing on the moon somewhere."

"The moon… Ok, no sweat." Willhelmina sat down in front of her computer terminal and began tapping away at it. A few minutes later she leaned back in her chair and started tapping at her temples they way she did whenever she was frustrated with the machine.

"What's the matter?" Riana asked as she slipped off the couch, much to its relief, and made her way to the chair next to Willhelmina's.

"I can't find any sign of her having been checked in to any hotels on the moon. Nor do I see any other celebrities that fit the profile of a singer. Either she wasn't on the moon or I am just not looking for the correct info."

"Maybe she lives there?" Riana asked hopefully. "If she is a resident then she probably wouldn't be using hotels."

"True." Willhelmina responded as she bent forward once more and resumed tapping at the interface.

"How do you think she got out here? Who else could have done something like that?"

"Huh?" Willhelmina snapped her head around and focused on Riana after a moment. "Oh, sorry. Um… As far as I know no one else is even close to the kind of technology that produced your body. The genetic and cloning stuff is pretty well understood though, as you saw on Earth Station. The really big concerns would be how they got the wet-ware to accept the download, and how they managed the download at all."

"What do you mean?" Riana looked at her quizzically.

"Ok here's the deal, you know your specs right?"

"For the most part…" Riana trailed off, remembering her conversation with Vincent.

Willhelmina quirked an eyebrow at her, obviously picking up on the change in thought process. "What's up Ree?"

"Nothing." Riana lied. She didn't really want, let alone know how, to discuss the matter with anyone just then.

"Alright…" Willhelmina touched Riana's hand. "Well when you want to talk about it you know I am here for you right?"

Riana squeezed Willhelmina's hand reassuringly. "I know. Thank you Kat."

"What are sister's for?" She smiled, then changed gears suddenly, "Ok, so in your specs there is a computer that interfaces with your nervous system right?"

Riana quirked her head to the side a bit as she recalled the information she had studied about her body's construction. "Yes, something about hardware to wet-ware interface and sub-control?" She looked at her friend questioningly.

"Don't ask me. I don't know the specifics. All I know is that the techs told me it wasn't possible, at least not with today's technology at any rate, to make a computer program, no matter how advanced it was, make heads or tails of human brain tissue."

"What does that mean?" Riana sounded as lost as she looked.

"I think he meant that there is no way to download an artificial intelligence directly into a human brain, regardless of how advanced the program was. They are just too fundamentally different for it to work."

"Ok, so how did they... Oh, the computer in my skull..."

"Exactly." Willhelmina confirmed. "The processor in your skull is one of the most advanced processors in existence, with the exception of the one we just recovered from AO. What that processor does is allow your 'program' to access and use the biological nervous system in your body."

Riana stared at her friend for a long moment. She wasn't sure how to take the statement that she was a program. She supposed it was true really. And if things were reduced to the lowest common denominator, she supposed humans were really not much more than programs either, they were just specifically designed to run on the hardware of the human nervous system, whereas she was designed to run in a computer system of a much different design. Finally, she shrugged it off, she knew Willhelmina meant nothing by it. "Ok, so what's the big deal there?"

"Well, the big deal is that the processor in question is a)Specifically designed for use in *your* skull. From the ground up it was designed to do what it does and nothing else, and b)It is the only one of its kind in existence, anywhere. Not to mention that the person responsible for its creation is most assuredly *not* ever going to spill its secrets to the competition."

"Why? Who designed it?" Riana raised a curious eyebrow.

"Xavier did." Willhelmina said with a sheepish smile. "And I'm pretty sure he wouldn't let anyone in on the magic."

"Ok, so someone could clone the necessary biological parts, but the hardware necessary to allow software to interface with those parts is uncommon at best. But still it *is* possible that someone else came up with it right? I mean... here I am and all."

"Right." Willhelmina acquiesced. "Which brings me to my second point of concern. We were only able to pull you out of Kalijor by channeling the download through several internal network nodes in order to circumvent the Kalijor server's firewalls and ICE, and we actually had to take the servers down to do it. Anyone attempting to do such a thing from outside would not only meet with enormous resistance from the security systems, but it would also cause unprecedented problems with the world server *and* tip us off to their activities since we monitor the system twenty-four seven for exactly that sort of thing."

"So you are saying it's impossible." Riana sighed heavily. But it *is* her. I know it with all my heart!"

"Calm down Ree. I never said it was impossible. I just said I have no idea how it could actually be happening. We'll get to the bottom of this, don't worry."

Riana's eyes lit up with a thought then, eliciting a gasp of delight.

"What?" Willhelmina asked, raising an eyebrow at her sister.

"What if she was a player. A real person, like we are. Someone who logs in and plays Ezrina?!" Riana gushed.

Willhelmina leaned back and considered the thought for a moment. She seemed to be rolling the possibility around in her head, chewing on her lower lip for several long moments as she considered. "Well, Xavier can certainly keep a secret with the best of them…" She leaned forward and tapped at her computer for a few minutes, calling up the Kalijor NPC husbandry records and scanning through them before leaning back again and pointing at the file. "The problem is that the server registry says she is an NPC, born in Pandoria to two NPC's."

"Could that record be falsified?" Riana asked.

"I suppose it's possible." She admitted. "Although it really doesn't change the root issue here."

"Which is?" Riana prompted.

"Whether she is a real person who was playing Ezrina, disguised as an NPC in the system, or an actual NPC from Kalijor that has been somehow downloaded from the system into this world, we still don't have any idea where she is now." Willhelmina swept her hands across the floating displays, scattering them around the desk so that all of their search information could be seen, lain out in a line.

The pair of them stared at the displays long into the night, puzzling through the various, improbable possibilities.

-47-

Riana deftly slipped past Willhelmina's kick, stepping inside her stance and applying a light push to her friend's shoulder, forcing her to fall on her back with a thump. They had been at it for an hour now and Willhelmina still had yet to land a single blow, but it wasn't from lack of effort. She was glistening from head to toe with sweat and breathing heavily from the constant exertion, but she kept trying without complaint.

Offering her friend a hand, Riana was taken somewhat off guard as Willhelmina kipped up and then dropped down again into a leg sweep. Not to be caught completely off guard, Riana swept over backwards through a hand stand, landing on her feet lightly and grinning at Willhelmina.

"Now you're getting desperate."

"No I'm not. I'm improvising!" Willhelmina panted back as she stepped in with a series of kicks and punches.

Riana snatched one of Willhelmina's punches out of the air and twisted her body around. Locking her wrist behind her back, Riana kept her on the threshold of pain for a moment before pushing her forward and letting her stagger a bit allowing her to regain her balance. "I see. I'm sorry I thought it was something else. Like exhaustion setting in or something."

"We should get something to eat when we're finished here." Willhelmina changed the subject as she suddenly lunged forward with an impressive jump kick.

Riana stepped aside and caught her friend's ankle in mid-air, again guiding her to the ground with a rough tumble. "Ok, but you're buying."

Willhelmina kipped up to her feet again and spun around with a reverse hook kick that grazed Riana's shoulder as it sped past. Riana grinned as she watched the foot go by.

"This is getting annoying. Are you even trying?" Willhelmina panted as she stood back and eyed Riana.

"You asked me not to 'let' you hit me. So I haven't been letting you hit me. You said nothing about me hitting back."

Willhelmina glared at Riana menacingly for a moment before her face softened a bit and she stood up straight. "You know… Sometimes, I really hate you."

Riana responded with a taunt. "What are sisters for?"

"Aggravation apparently. C'mon let's go get that meal." She waved Riana toward the locker room as she moved herself off in that direction.

Riana stood there a moment before responding. "Can I meet you on the promenade? I have… an appointment I need to get to really quick."

Willhelmina stopped and looked back at Riana with a raised eyebrow. "An appointment?"

"Yeah, it's with Gayle, nothing serious. I just had… a couple of questions…"

Willhelmina walked back over to Riana and placed a friendly hand on her shoulder. "Are you OK Ree? Is anything going on?"

"No! I mean… It's nothing serious. Just a question or two." She hedged, trying to avoid the conversation.

Willhelmina eyed her for a moment, seeming to sense her trepidation, then squeezed her shoulder and turned around again, heading for the locker room to clean up. "Ok then. I'll see you on the promenade in twenty minutes."

"Ok, I'll be there." Riana replied, relief in her voice. She turned around and snatched her gear bag off the floor and sprinted for the nearest lift.

When she stepped off the lift and into the promenade twenty minutes later she could not contain her giddiness. She was grinning widely and her ears were perked up toward the transparent domed ceiling. She waved and said hello to everyone she passed as she picked her way though the scattered tables and chairs. Willhelmina watched her approach with a quirky grin on her face.

"I take it you got some good news?" She prompted the jubilant Riana as she slid into the metal chair across from her.

"I did!" Riana replied happily.

"I don't suppose you want to talk about it?" Willhelmina raised an eyebrow at her.

Riana flushed a bit and turned away from her friend, her ears splaying out a bit. "Um… It's kind of… That is I…"

Willhelmina couldn't stand it any longer, she suddenly burst out laughing, which only caused Riana to turn a deeper shade of red.

"What?!" She managed to ask indignantly.

"Nothing Ree. It's just that you're priceless. That's all." She wiped the tears of laughter from her cheeks and tried to straighten herself up as much as possible, still stifling the occasional chuckle. "So uh… I was talking to Xavier and he said we could go to the moon for a couple of days if we want. I thought maybe we could go try and find Resonance. See what is going on there."

Riana's eyes brightened even more at the news, her grin widening and her ears perking back up again. "Kat! Thank you!"

"My pleasure sis. I have a crew prepping the Kestrel now. We can leave after dinner if you want. I know a couple nice hotels in Tranquility and some other sights we can see while we are there. It should be fun."

Riana couldn't remember eating a meal that fast since she was a youngling trying to get out the door to play with her friends in the alleys of Rathalon.

-48-

Riana almost danced her way down the ramp from the spaceport to the monorail station outside. She couldn't put into words how pleased she was to be away from the station doing something that wasn't work related. Willhelmina was grinning at her and shaking her head as they stopped at the platform and Riana shifted from foot to foot and hummed a song to herself while they waited for the train to arrive.

"You'd think you were excited or something…" Willhelmina quipped at her friend as she poked her in the ribs.

"It's been a long time since we have just gone somewhere." Riana breathed as she moved to the music in her head.

"We go places all the time." Willhelmina grinned, knowing the response she would get before Riana spoke.

"Yeah, but that is for work, this is for *us*! Even with trying to track down Resonance and see if she really is mom, this trip is all about us!" Riana nearly sang.

The train pulled into the station silently and its doors slid smoothly out of the way to permit them inside. As they found seats and watched the other commuters bustling about, getting on and off the train, Riana still couldn't stop smiling.

The train moved out of the station, smoothly accelerating away from the spaceport and into Tranquility. The tall buildings whizzing by in a blur in the setting sun.

"We were going to head straight to the hotel, but I talked to a couple of friends here and got a line on where Resonance may be staying. I thought we'd stop by there first." Willhelmina almost whispered in Riana's ear, trying to keep the other passengers out of the conversation, especially while mentioning the name of the rising star.

"Kat this is so great of you. I really appreciate you helping me out like this."

Willhelmina shrugged nonchalantly. "Hey. What are sisters for?" She poked Riana in the ribs to punctuate the statement, eliciting a giggle from her friend.

As the monorail came to a fluid stop, Riana and Willhelmina stood up. Stepping onto the platform and into the early evening air of the city, Riana stretched, raising her arms above her head and looking up into the night sky. She experienced an instant of vertigo and when she snapped her head back down, she realized with a start that she was standing on a path

380

in the middle of a green grassy field that looked suspiciously like the Plane of Serenity.

Turning around in a whirl she saw the closed gates of Rathalon directly behind her. But something was different from how she remembered it. There were no guards at the gate. When she pulled at the huge doors they did not budge. She banged on the stone surface of the doors with her fist, but it produced no noise other than the sound of her flesh slamming into a solid stone surface.

Looking up she saw the hundred-foot-tall stone wall stretching away above her, bordered on one side by the starry, moonless night sky of Kalijor. "What the hell?" She murmured out loud. Looking down at herself she realized two things. The first was that she was again wearing her normal leathers, revealing her tattooed skin, Elkorine at her side. The second was that she could see normally again. Everything was as it had been before she lost her sight in the tower of the Death Dragon.

For a long moment, she simply inspected herself, reveling in her normal vision.

An explosion behind her startled her out of her fond remembering, causing her to whirl on her heel and see the fading remnants of some kind of flash off in the distance. Without a second thought she headed off toward the receding light, just as another flash appeared, followed a moment later by the sound of thunder.

She dashed madly across the distance, pushing herself to the limit. When she finally did catch sight of the scene, her heart wrenched and she suddenly found herself running even faster, heart pounding in her chest.

Just ahead was an area that had been blasted clean of the native long grass of the Plane of Serenity, presumably by the magic spell-balls that were being hurled back and forth by the two occupants of the clearing. With his long black sword in hand, and clad in inky black armor, one of the combatants was clearly Malice. He prowled around the scorched clearing with his sword held aloft, batting spell-balls back at the other person. Just barely visible to Riana's keen elven vision, she could see well enough to know who it was that stood against Malice.

"Mother!" She screamed as she charged toward the pair, throwing caution and any chance of a surprise attack to the wind. The woman in the circle was wearing an elegant wizard's robe. Her long platinum hair was pulled back in a tight knot on the back of her head, revealing long, tapered ears and finely sculpted elven features. However, the golden eyes that flashed in the light of each explosion were the clenching proof.

Ezrina was furiously chanting away, hurling glowing spheres of energy at Malice one after another. She showed signs of fatigue and Riana could tell by the diminishing effects of the spell-balls that she was rapidly tiring.

The pair circled around each other as Riana charged onward. Malice sneered at Ezrina as he batted away another sphere of lightning, watching as it exploded into the ground and sent a shower of earth and burned grass into the air. "You've had it witch! No one is coming to your aid! Just give it up! You can't even hope to harm me!"

Ezrina made no effort to speak to him, she simply uttered another incantation, summoning up a ball of fire between hands held high over her head. Deftly, she lobbed the missile at Malice and, as he moved to bat it away with his magical sword, she called out a fast cantrip that blasted him in the chest with a small arc of lightning from her hands. The electric arc did little to actually harm him, but it distracted him enough that the fireball went unreturned and slammed into him, driving him to the ground in an explosion of heat and light.

Riana cheered as she bounded closer still to the battle. "Go mom!! Get that bastard for what he did to Kat!" She kept up her impossible pace, charging into range of her own spells, certain that between them they could defeat Malice. She and Katrina had nearly beaten him with Jumah's help, but her mother was a much more powerful Wizard than either of them.

Malice stood up out of the small brush fire that had started with the impact of the fireball and at first he looked wounded, even staggered a bit. When he rose to his full height and propped his giant sword on his shoulder, he was clearly laughing. "A valiant attempt, but you have to know in the end that you stand no chance. Give me what I want and it all stops here."

Ezrina offered him nothing but a grim smile as she belted out another incantation and a thick patch of dark clouds began to coalesce over the clearing. Malice shook his head in disappointment. "Somehow I knew you were going to say that."

Riana's eyes flashed as she conjured the crackling black sphere of annihilation in her right hand. Not stopping her charge toward the man, she hurled the sphere at him with all her strength, screaming at him all the while, "Leave her alone!"

As the black sphere careened toward him he turned his head ever so slightly toward Riana, acknowledging her presence for the first time despite her yelling and screaming. With barely perceptible movement, he was suddenly facing her, sword at the ready, and batted the sphere back at her with uncanny accuracy.

It all happened so quickly after that, that Riana didn't even have time to think. Her own deadly sphere of energy was heading straight for her head and she stood no chance of stopping or changing direction quickly enough to keep it from hitting her. Without warning, Ezrina stopped casting her own spell and dove between Riana and the spell-ball, catching it with her left shoulder and falling to the ground in a heap, most of her shoulder missing and the remnants charred, blackened, and smelling of burnt flesh.

Riana skidded to a stop, tripping over her mother's prone form and rolling to a stop at Malice's feet. She looked up into his eyes as he smiled down at her. "You always arrive right in the nick of time don't you? Just in time to see your loved ones succumb to me."

"The *hell* with you!!" Riana shouted through clenched teeth as she lunged up at him, driving her bare fist into his inner thigh.

He doubled over almost instantly, reeling from the pain and shock of the blow. Riana didn't hesitate. She took advantage of the situation, standing up and driving her knee forcefully into his down-turned face. With no small sense of satisfaction she felt his nose break against her knee. Reaching down, she grabbed hold of his head and wrenched him over, flinging his feet haphazardly through the air and driving his back to the ground. Finally, she chambered her right arm back and drove her fist into his bloody face with all of her strength, eliciting another sickening crunch.

His body went slack, whether from unconsciousness or death she did not know, or care. An instant later, she was cradling her mother's body to her chest, sobbing into her dirty platinum hair.

384

"Mom. I'm sorry mom. Why did you do that? Why? What were you thinking?" But she knew what she had been thinking. She had done it to save her daughter. Her foolish, impetuous daughter.

As she cradled her mother's body to her own and cried she slowly began to hear the weak singing emanating from her mother's slackened body. Sitting up a bit and looking down into her mother's face she saw her smiling, golden eyes looking back up at her. She was quietly singing one of Riana's favorite lullabies and smiled weakly as Riana looked down at her.

"I'm sorry mom. I'm so so sorry…"

Ezrina reached up weakly and caressed her daughter's face. Offering her a warm smile. "It's good to see you again."

More tears welled up in Riana's eyes as she clutched her mother's hand to her cheek.

"Don't cry for me daughter. This isn't the end. I still have roads to travel…" She coughed weakly for a moment then looked back up into Riana's eyes and smiled again. "The other keys must be found. They have to be stopped. Everything depends on the keys. You and Kat…"

Riana pulled her even tighter as she coughed again, spitting up some blood. She wiped it away with the heel of her hand and cried more.

"I'm so proud of you… and your sister… The third key… Talanor… Mines…" Her voice was fading quickly as she spoke, causing Riana's sobs to grow louder.

"Mom. Don't go. I need you…" She cried into the hand she still clutched against her cheek.

"Told you… Not the end… Now go… Willhelmina needs you…"

At the mention of Willhelmina's name, Riana opened her tear-filled eyes and looked at her mother. The sound of Malice moving distracted her momentarily and when she looked up at where he had been crumpled on the ground, his body and sword were nowhere to be found. Scanning the clearing, she saw no trace of him, and when she looked down toward where her mother had been clutched in her arms, she was gone as well. Suddenly alone, Riana clenched her fists and screamed her pain into the night sky.

"What the hell?! Are you OK Ree?!" Willhelmina's voice shook Riana out of her howl of pain suddenly.

Riana's eyes snapped open and her world was suddenly black and purple lines again. Willhelmina stood in front of her with a worried expression on her face as she glanced from side to side nervously.

"Kat?" Riana leaned against her, her own knees suddenly weak.

"Ree, what the hell was that?"

"What happened?" Riana stammered as she tried to get her feet under her again.

"We stepped off the train and I walked down to the walk-way before I realized you weren't with me. I turned around and saw you up here. By the time I got back to you, you were screaming."

Riana wiped her face with the back of her hand to check for the tears she knew she had been crying, but her hand came away clean and dry. She looked back up at Willhelmina and blinked. "It was mom again... I was in Kalijor and she was fighting Malice. I think she might have been able to take him but I..." She whimpered at the thought of what she had done but forced herself to say it, "I tried to help, but Malice reflected my attack and mom jumped in front of it... Kat... I think I killed her..."

"Here, this is it." Willhelmina said as she moved toward the blank, unlabeled door on the back of the building.

"Are you sure? It doesn't look like much…" Riana said doubtfully as she looked at the featureless panel.

"This is the address my friends gave me. I trust them, so unless their info was wrong, this is it."

"Fair enough." Riana replied as she moved up to the door herself and searched around its edges. Finally she located the tiny sensor on the edge of the door and moved her hand in front of it, causing a holographic keypad to appear in mid air. "I don't suppose your friend's info included the combination?"

Willhelmina shook her head with a frown.

"I thought not." Riana shrugged as she turned back to the keypad. "Still. I had to ask." Reaching through the keypad she fiddled with the sensor for a moment until it popped free of its mounting point on the wall. Briefly, she poked through the cables between the sensor and the wall, finally deciding on one and disconnecting it from the device and plugging it into the data port on her wrist.

Her eyes glazed over for a moment and a few seconds later, the door chimed quietly and slid open to reveal a pervasive darkness inside the building. Disconnecting herself from the door lock, Riana reassembled the device and reattached it to the wall as though she had done it thousands of times before.

"Have you been sneaking in more classes or something?" Willhelmina looked at her with a quirked eyebrow.

"No." Riana said shortly. "I have been… reading… a lot." She stood up and peered into the blackness, seeing nothing but the wire-frame outlines of the hallway the door opened into.

"Uh huh. Reading." Willhelmina said skeptically.

"We can talk about it later Kat. C'mon, it's all clear." And then she slipped into the darkened corridor leaving Willhelmina no choice but to follow her.

Inside the building, they made a couple of quick turns and were approaching a large door at the end of a hallway when they heard the sound of metal banging on metal and muffled shouting from the other side of the door.

"That doesn't sound good." Willhelmina observed quietly as they crept toward the door.

"Decidedly not." Riana agreed. "Now would be a good time to be able to see through walls though." She tried to add some levity to the situation but didn't think it had come off too well. Finally she settled for, "I don't suppose you brought any guns with you?"

"Nope. But you can bet that will never happen again."

"Me either. But I do have this." She slipped the monowire sword out of her pocket as she whispered, showing it to Willhelmina.

"Great. You go first." Willhelmina offered as she pushed Riana toward the doors.

Riana grunted slightly and waved her hand over the sensor, causing the door to slide open. A large computer room, filled from wall to wall with some of the most advanced computer systems Riana had seen greeted them. There were consoles everywhere, with lights flashing and fans whirring, screens reading out important information about whatever was going on in each system. Had it not been for the spectacle in the center of the room, she might have been duly impressed by the technology present.

In the center of the room, a very large computer console, topped with a holographic emitter projecting an image of Resonance was surrounded by a group of familiar looking soldiers, all wearing black armor and helmets and bearing some impressive looking weaponry. A few of them had large chunks of metal in their hands that they were using to smash and pry open the console beneath the hologram while one of the soldiers was busy interrogating the facsimile.

"Where is it?!" He shouted through the oxygen filter on his sealed combat helmet.

"You'll have to do far worse than this to get me to tell you." The projected elf responded back at him with a smile on her face.

"We know this is your last terminal. If we destroy this one you'll die. Tell us where it is and we will leave in peace." The ominous figure pointed at her as he threatened.

"There are more important things at stake here than my life." The elf replied sweetly without a hint of concern in her voice.

"Fine. Destroy it." The man motioned toward the soldiers bearing metal bars and beams, who eagerly picked up the pace on their banging and prying.

"Mom?" Riana couldn't stop herself as she stood in the doorway staring at the scene.

Instantly, the climate of the room changed. There was a clatter of metal bars and beams hitting the floor and shortly all of the soldiers had turned to face her, weapons drawn and at the ready. The only thing that Riana deemed of importance however, was that the holographic elf turned to look at her, and smiled with recognition.

"Stop there! Get down on your knees!" One of the soldiers shouted. It was the same one that had been yelling at Resonance.

"I'm sorry." Riana said, staring at the soldier with a look that could bore a hole through armored starship hull plates, "you must have me confused with someone else. I'm the one giving orders here now. If you don't like it, then I invite you to come tell me all about it."

Willhelmina put her hands up to show them that she was unarmed and preferred to not be killed by them, but the instant Riana spoke she groaned and dove behind the nearest computer console.

Riana pressed the activation switch on the sword handle and stepped into a fighting stance as she leveled her gaze on each of the soldiers in turn. There was a brief moment of silence, as if they were all considering what they should do, before the air was split open with the sound of gun fire and Riana's mind slipped into high gear.

Everything around her slowed down as she stepped to the side and advanced in a zig-zag pattern on the nearest soldier. Her reflexes and body were so highly tuned that she could anticipate the firing trajectory of each bullet as it left the barrel of the gun and she made sure to be nowhere near the projectiles as she closed the distance to the armored figure.

Two more steps, a flash of metal filament and the soldier found himself holding half of an assault rifle in his hand, the front of the weapon clattering to the ground. The next instant, Riana buried her foot in his chest and sent him flying into another soldier, grinning as they both tumbled to the ground in a heap.

The group adjusted their firing pattern to better pin her down, but were caught off guard when she leapt into the air, vaulting over their crossfire and landing knee first on someone's head, driving them to the ground and splitting open their helmet with a loud cracking noise.

Riana swung her sword in a few short arcs. Lifting the combat webbing from the soldier's body with her free hand, she tossed it back toward the door, where Willhelmina quickly reached out and dragged the equipment back into her cover.

A small burst of bullets tore into Riana's shoulder, causing her to look up at the source of the offending projectiles. The soldier on the other end of the weapon stopped for a moment and seemed to consider what their options were now that she was obviously not dead after having been shot. Finally, they seemed to decide on overkill and laid into their weapon for all it was worth, squeezing the trigger all the way and holding it there.

Riana lunged forward into a somersault, leaping into the air again as she came out of it. she caught a bullet in her right thigh as she passed through the random hail of projectiles. The armored figure seemed completely surprised as she landed lightly beside him. With a few flicks of her wrist, the man found himself devoid of his armor as it fell to the ground at his feet.

"I might be rethinking my strategy right about now if I were you," she said quietly as she ducked under another hail of gunfire and rolled behind a small computer console. The unfortunate man didn't have time to react and his comrades didn't seem too terribly concerned with where their own bullets were heading. Fortunately, he didn't live long enough to experience too much pain from the friendly fire.

Behind the momentary cover of the console, Riana reached into her pocket and pulled out her comm set. Pressing it into her ear she keyed up Willhelmina's set and waited a moment for her sister to pick up the line.

After a moment she was rewarded with, "Jeez Ree, you don't really do subtle do you?"

394

"That's my mom out there." Riana said simply as she peeked around the console and saw the holographic elf looking her direction, concern on her face. Another burst of gun fire forced her back behind the console again an instant later.

"I know Ree. So what can I do for you?"

Riana heard the distinctive sound of a weapon being loaded and cocked over the comm. "Just do what you were about to do anyway sis."

"Ok." Willhelmina said with a grunt. "Right side, be ready in three…"

Riana coiled her feet under her and leaned toward the left side of the console, ready to pounce as soon as Willhelmina made her move. Two seconds later, a burst of gun fire belched out from the right side of the console Willhelmina had been hiding behind. One of the soldiers fell to the ground, clutching their leg, and the rest turned their attention toward Willhelmina's position.

Riana used the distraction to cross the gap between herself and the remaining soldiers with inhuman speed. One deft swipe of her sword and one of them dropped to the ground. Even as he fell, she kicked her booted foot through the face plate of another's helmet, breaking his nose and blurring his vision with his own blood and tears. Another burst of gun fire from Willhelmina's weapon and the last one fell.

"Thanks sis." Riana said softly into the comm as she grinned toward Willhelmina and tapped the device, closing the connection.

"No problem. Thanks for the fire power." Willhelmina said as she stood up, brandishing the weapon. Willhelmina then set about searching the room for any other threats. She found a couple and disarmed them, making a neat pile of weapons in the center of the room and tying up those still living soldiers with whatever computer cables she could find on hand.

While Willhelmina searched, Riana switched off her sword and slipped it into her pocket. She approached the console with the holographic image of her mother floating above it cautiously.

"Mom?"

The platinum haired elf crouched down a bit and looked directly into Riana's violet eyes with her own semitransparent golden orbs. "I'm sorry Riana, there isn't time for a reunion. They severed my net connection so I can't escape this terminal. Can you reconnect it please?"

She pointed toward a thick rope of cables snaking across the floor from the central computer terminal. Riana saw that the cables had been pulled free from a socket in the wall at the other end.

"Mom is it really you?" She looked back toward the elf hopefully with her ears drooping down.

"Riana. I know it has been a long time, but we both have a mission, and right now I need your help to accomplish mine. Can you please reconnect my terminal?"

"You'll leave if I do. Won't you?" She would have cried if she could.

The holographic elf's features softened a bit and she reached out, caressing Riana's cheek with a photonic hand. "I'm sorry my daughter. I wish that there were more time. You have been through so much, and even now we are worlds away."

Riana's hand moved to her mother's but passed through it and landed on her own cheek. She barely stifled a dry sob as she looked down at the floor, unsure what to say. She had so many questions, so many things she wanted to share.

Suddenly Willhelmina was beside her, one hand on her shoulder in support and an understanding look on her face.

"Kat." The hologram spoke, turning to look at Willhelmina. "Thank you. For taking care of her and for always being there for her."

"What are sisters for?" Willhelmina smiled as she squeezed Riana's shoulder lovingly.

"Mom. I just had… a vision… or a daydream… or something… You were in it. You were fighting someone, and you… I…"

The hologram turned back toward Riana and smiled sweetly. "I know Ree. It's ok. You are still learning to control it. It is bound to be disconcerting but it will get better."

"Control what?" Riana looked at her mother questioningly.

"I'm not allowed to say." Ezrina frowned and looked over her shoulder as if she were looking at someone standing right behind her.

"What is going on mom?"

"Riana. I know it is difficult, but you are on the right path. Stay your course and keep the wind at your back. Kat, will you please go plug my terminal back into the net connection?"

Willhelmina looked from Ezrina to Riana and frowned. Reluctantly, she released Riana's shoulder and moved across the room where she crouched down and began plugging the cables one-by-one back into their appropriate ports.

"Don't go mom." Riana pleaded with the image of her mother. "I have so many questions and no one will give me answers."

"I know." Ezrina reached out to caress her daughter's cheek once more, causing Riana to lean into the intangible fingers in anticipation of the touch that she knew would not come. "All will become clear in time, but there are rules my daughter, even for those of us who have broken the bonds of the system. Now, listen to your mother Riana Thorindal. You and your sister stick together. Keep your ears to the ground and your noses to the air. It's going to get worse before it gets better, but it *will* get better, I promise."

"Done… mom." Willhelmina returned to the terminal, adjusting the strap on her procured weapon so that it hung more comfortably off her shoulder. She brushed a lock of raven hair out of her face and looked at the holographic image with a quirky grin. "This is odd uh?"

Ezrina only smiled at her, then turned to Riana once more. "Be strong Riana and remember, it is you. It always has been, and it always will be. I love you, daughters."

The image of Ezrina flickered a few times and then winked out, leaving the room only slightly darker than it had been, but Riana felt as though all of the lights in her world had been extinguished all at once.

-50-

'The rising star known as Resonance was assaulted in her hotel this evening. A group of juveniles forced their way into her accommodations and were in the midst of destroying some of her equipment when two anonymous citizens happened by the scene and aided the young singer. Reports say that Resonance was unharmed during the assault on her temporary home and there is, as yet, no indication as to what the assailants were after, or who the friendly citizens were. Resonance is a fresh new vocalist who has made an overnight name for herself by singing powerful ballads, love songs, and folk songs, all in the the language of the elves from the MMO world of Kalijor. Her first album...'

"Ok, turn it off..." Willhelmina groaned at the entertainment console from the couch where she was cleaning the handguns they had taken with them from the scene of the attack.

"I can't believe they are not being truthful about this." Riana complained as she keyed off the screen and started up Resonance's newest album that had been mysteriously delivered to her netmail box since the attack.

The album had been delivered from an anonymous address, which Willhelmina had assured was next to impossible to do, along with a message that simply read, 'Remember your vision.'

They had mulled over the message for half an hour before turning on the news and seeing the incident all over the headlines. It hadn't even been two hours since it had happened. The media seemed to have changed a few details here and there, but they had also left out any description of them, which was a good thing.

Riana sighed a bit as she listened to her mother's voice on the sound system, moving through the full range of notes and tones as she sang about a powerful love, lost and found again over the centuries.

Willhelmina clicked together another handgun and cocked it forcefully, causing Riana to look over at her with a raised eyebrow. "What's the matter Kat?"

"It just doesn't make sense." Willhelmina said, half to herself as she set the weapon aside and picked up another, stripping it down in seconds and attacking it with the cleaning gear she had procured from some unknown source.

"Which part?"

"The part about how these idiots are all using thirty year old guns. They are barely even caseless, and it looks like they have been pretty poorly maintained in that thirty years."

Riana sighed as she adjusted her position in her chair, eliciting a protest from the furniture at her awkward angle and deceptive weight.

"What?" Willhelmina gave an offended retort.

"Nothing. I was just thinking about how the news got the story all wrong, that's all." Riana spoke to the ceiling as she closed her eyes and focused on the music.

"Well what are they going to say Ree? 'Resonance was nearly killed by an unknown paramilitary group this evening in a warehouse in D sector, and oh-by-the-way she is actually a holographic representation of a virtual person projected from Kalijor. I mean it isn't as though that sort of thing happens so often that it is common place you know."

Riana huffed a bit, offering no other response for a moment until she finally hung her head over the chair's armrest and looked at Willhelmina, who was upside-down in her vision. "She isn't a virtual person Kat. She's my mother. And may as well be yours too."

"I know Ree." Willhelmina sighed as she pulled a stiff wire brush through the poorly maintained rifling of a pistol barrel. "But we don't even really know what is going on with her, so we can't very well expect the media to get the story straight. Any ideas on the message at all?"

Riana sighed again as she slumped back into her chair and closed her eyes once more. "No. Except that in the vision she said something about the third key… She said it was in Talanor. In the mines."

"Do you think we should go after it?"

"I think she wants us to. But I can't help thinking that the more of these things we uncover, the more complicated our lives are going to get."

"That seems a logical assumption at this point." Willhelmina blew through the barrel and then held it up to the light, peering through it to check her work. Nodding satisfactorily she set the barrel down and picked up the breech, inspecting it with another deep sigh of disappointment.

"We need to get more information Kat. I mean, we don't even know what these items are really for. I can see into this world from Kalijor with that circlet on. What if the other items give similar, or even more power over the real world from within Kalijor?"

"I don't see how that's really possible Ree. Seeing stuff is one thing, especially in your case. The object may not even be the source of that ability as far as we know. It may be just you… doing what you seem to do." She set the part down on the table next to its mates and picked up another piece.

"Doing what I do?" Riana rolled over in the chair again and glared at Willhelmina over the top of the puffy arm rest.

"Yeah, nothing personal Ree, I mean I love you and all. But some of the stuff going on with you is a bit odd wouldn't you say?"

"Yes I would. But that doesn't mean you have to talk about me like I am some sort of weird-o or something." She frowned, ears drooping low.

"You *are* a weird-o sis. But no more so than myself. I think that's why we get along so well. So what are you thinking about this key thing?"

"I think we need to look a little deeper into the ancient Obscuri artifacts. Find out what powers they actually are reported to have. I hate flying blind and this is pretty blind, even for us."

Willhelmina chuckled a bit as she reassembled the final handgun and cocked it with a smile. "These are ready to go. I can't believe it took me an hour. These guys should have been arrested simply on the basis of how they were treating their gear. I'm glad we didn't take any of the big stuff now."

"We couldn't have. Can you imagine walking though the streets with all of that hardware? It was odd enough walking through the streets with a bunch of bullet holes in me."

"Yeah but you have to admit, the way that couple crossed the street to steer away from us was pretty funny." Willhelmina grinned at Riana and Riana giggled a bit herself at the thought. "OK, so what's the plan here? Who are we going to shake down for information?"

"Well I know he hasn't been totally helpful in the past when asked point blank questions, but I think we should start with Gornin. The only other thought would be the guardian in the Ziggurat but I'm not sure we can even see him without one of the keys."

"Alright. Gornin it is…" Willhelmina said as she leaned over and began rummaging through her small bag.

"What are you looking for?" Riana asked, ears perking up again.

"Just this…" Willhelmina replied as she pulled a tangle of cables from her bag. She set the knot of wires on the table next to the four handguns and began pushing and pulling at the wires until Riana was finally able to recognize the almost insect-like shape of the Encephalographic Induction Harness and a separate ODN patch cable. With a wry grin she offered the ends of the cables to Riana and pointed toward the entertainment console next to her.

Riana took the cables with a smile and a nod and then rolled over again in the chair and plugged the two cables in. Less than five minutes later, they were both hooked up and logging in.

-51-

"No one knows what effect the artifacts have in your world. They were used to destroy the Lich King and then they were sequestered away in the Ziggurats for safe keeping. Until now..." Gornin's gravelly voice trailed off as he eyed the circlet on Riana's head suspiciously.

Riana touched the metal band reflexively. She had tried to take it off again as soon as they had logged in but it still held fast to her, unwilling, or unable to let go. "We had no choice Master Gornin, they were holding all of Avian hostage." She mounted the best defense she could think of, but somehow knew that it would not be up to par with his line of thinking.

"There is always a choice Riana. Our lives are nothing more than a series of choices that bring us all to our own inevitable ends. If you seek my approval, then you still have much to learn."

"Master Gornin, we are here to find out what we can about the artifacts. We need to know why people are so willing to destroy lives for them." Katrina piped in from her perch sitting on top of a large boulder in the Cohai courtyard.

The troll turned his deep blue eyes on her and offered her a wan smile. "It is an unfortunate truth that most people with power are driven to acquire more power. It rarely matters what form that power takes. You are starting down a dangerous road if you are planning to quest for the rest of the artifacts. You have already marked yourself as a target." He pointed to Riana then as he finished speaking.

"Our mother asked us to go after them." Riana said matter-of-factly.

"Yes. Ezrina always was a bit brash. And I suppose she has offered you a bread crumb as well?"

"She told us the next key is in…"

"I *know* where the next key is. Such things should not be spoken aloud. This conversation is already dangerous enough."

"Master Gornin, we didn't come here to cause you any trouble, we just came to see if you could help us figure out why people are killing one another and blatantly hacking the system in order to get them." Katrina kept trying to put a logical spin on things, to see if she could get him to offer some kind of information.

"I can not give you that which you seek. However, I can tell you the shape of things to come if you pursue this fracas to its final, dying breath. The circlet you have was locked up by the Rune of Knowledge.

There is also the bracelet bound by the Rune of Justice, and its counterpart bound by the Rune of Balance. The pendant is held fast by the Rune of Secrecy and finally, a belt bound to the Rune of Power. No one knows for sure what each of these items does, although guesses can be made based upon the runes that bind them."

"Well, it's something at least." Riana nodded at the Troll. "I don't know what keeps you from being straight with us Master Gornin, but we do appreciate your efforts. As frustrating as they can be sometimes."

Gornin looked at her without malice or hurt, still just as passive as ever. "My place is as a guide and as such I can not tell you your path, merely help you to see the route you have chosen to follow. You said you have seen your mother recently. How is she?"

Riana looked at her feet, kicking some pebbles around with the toe of her boot. "I'm not sure. She is posing as a singer in our world somehow. She didn't give us much time to talk before she disappeared. I don't even know what is going on with her really. It's like she wasn't really in our world, just in the computer or something."

Suddenly Katrina was off her rock and standing next to Riana with an excited look on her face. "That's it Ree! She *isn't* in the real world! Not really. Somehow she is getting past the Kalijor server's firewalls and moving from computer to computer in the real world. That's why she asked me to reconnect her net connection, and why she was really in danger of being killed by those thugs. If she was in that computer and they destroyed it while the net connection was severed then she would have died with the computer. As it is though, she should be able to move from system to system almost at will, as long as she can defeat the countermeasures protecting it."

Gornin smiled faintly as Katrina spoke. "You always did take after Ezrina in that regard. Very quick to figure things out. Although, she too was usually slow to find the reasons once she knew the methods. Have you discerned the reason?"

Katrina looked at him thoughtfully for a moment then turned around and clambered back up on top of her boulder, sitting down and resting her chin in her hand.

"I thought as much. But now you have a new puzzle to solve." He raised a knobby eyebrow at Riana. "Riana, did she speak with you? Did she have anything to say?"

"You mean aside from telling us where the next key is?"

"Yes."

"No, she didn't say anything else. There wasn't time before she dashed off to wherever." Her ears drooped as she spoke.

"Really? She said nothing else?"

Riana thought back to the events in the building, trying to remember what exactly was said. Eventually, she looked up at the troll again. "She also said something about remembering the visions I've been having and about 'it' being me."

"Indeed. I would caution you against paraphrasing her words. Oft times people like her say *exactly* what they mean to."

Riana just looked at him dumbly for a moment, trying to remember the exact phrasing that her mother had used. She wasn't sure what exactly was said and finally looked over toward Katrina for help. Her sister just shrugged at her and went back to thinking about her new puzzle.

"Why is it that whenever we see you, we leave with more questions than we have when we arrive?" Riana arched an eyebrow at Gornin as her ears perked up.

"That is often the course of those who seek true enlightenment. Every question leading to another question, or more often than not, several more questions."

"Uh huh. And I suppose you have found true enlightenment by now?"

"Of course not. Although I long ago realized the truth of it."

"And what is the truth of true enlightenment?" Riana placed her hands on her hips, challenging Gornin to tell her. Katrina even looked up, expectant for some deep, meaningful prose to escape the troll's lumpy lips.

"I can not tell you."

"Rules of the system again?" Riana was less than surprised by his answer.

"Not at all. I just think that this is one realization best found out for oneself. Now, if you two will excuse me, I have other pupils to attend to yet this day." He bowed so low that his spindly nose nearly touched the ground, turned on his heels and moved off into the courtyard to confound some other unsuspecting individual.

"Well that was slightly less helpful than usual." Riana commented as she moved over toward Katrina's seat.

"Not entirely so." Katrina smiled. "At least now we have some idea what we are looking for."

"I suppose. But that still doesn't tell us where these things are, or what they are capable of. She focused on Gornin's figure for a moment, willing her mind to seek out his source as she had been able to do with the people in Avian before. She was very surprised when his image did not change at all. "Now *that* is odd."

"What's that?" Katrina looked toward the Troll's back curiously.

"Well this circlet thing gives me the ability to see what people in Kalijor are connected to. If they are PC's then I usually see the person in their game pod or chair or whatever, with an EIH on. If they are NPC's then I see something else. Kids playing, folks sitting at work, stuff like that."

"Yeah OK… Wait a minute. Just random people somewhere?"

"Yeah. Like kids, old people, folks not in the system."

Katrina gaped at her sister, clearly shocked.

"What's the matter Kat?" Riana was starting to feel like she was not noticing a very large creature standing behind her with razor sharp claws poised to strike her down in an instant.

"Ree, if NPC's are connected to anything it should be equipment inside the Tyconderoga, specifically the mainframes that run Kalijor. All of

412

the code is supposed to be resident there. If the NPC AI is not there, then it means what Ezrina is doing is not an isolated incident. It means that lots of programs are getting off the server and into the real world." She looked as though she had just had a revelation. She was almost panting as she spoke, and had to brace an arm on the top of the boulder to keep herself steady.

"So that is a bad thing then?" Riana still wasn't quite clear on the issue, she had thought she was seeing things as they had been designed.

"You have no idea Ree. Look. This world was designed as a closed system. There is supposed to be no way for any software to get in or out. Especially without SO's explicit knowledge." Kat shook her head absently. "But if what you are seeing is true then there isn't just a small leak somewhere. Instead, it turns out there is some kind of major highway allowing two-way travel between the Kalijor servers and the rest of the net. We should go talk to someone about this immediately."

"Alright so if I am seeing these connections, and the PC's link to their players, and the NPC's link to random people who don't play the game, on the station or off, what does it mean when there is no connection to anything?"

"What?" Katrina twisted back around to look at Riana, who was still watching Gornin with interest.

"Master Gornin. He has no connection to anything at all. It's like he is nothing at all, just... him..." She motioned to the troll who suddenly looked over his shoulder at them and smiled a tiny, knowing smile.

-52-

"What do you mean the firewalls are all OK?" Willhelmina almost screamed at the technician.

"I'm sorry Miss Orlova, but I am not seeing anything to indicate what you are talking about. All of the firewalls and countermeasures are performing up to specs. I just don't see any evidence that programs are moving in and out of the system." The technician was obviously reaching the end of his rope with the conversation. His brown hair had become frazzled from running his hands through it so frequently in trying to explain things to Riana and Willhelmina.

"Fine. If you won't help me then I'll go talk to Xavier about it and we'll see what happens then." She spun on her heels and stomped past Riana who stood there, mouth agape, watching her sister abuse the poor man. As she reached the door she spun around again and eyed him coldly, "What is your name?"

"Err. Jax ma'am, Jax Palan." He adjusted his collar nervously.

"Fine Jax. We'll see just how secure things are around here. C'mon Ree." She was through the door before anyone had a chance to breathe.

Riana turned from the hallway door back to Jax and offered him a sympathetic frown. "I'm sorry. I'm not sure what she's so upset about."

"It's OK. You get used to it around here. We tend to take security pretty seriously." He seemed to be calming down quickly.

"Still though. She's pretty upset. Look, I'll go calm her down, is there any way you can do a more in-depth diagnostic of the security systems and get back to me?"

"Of course Miss Thorindal. It takes a few hours to do deep diagnostics, I'll send you a message when it's done."

"Thank you, Jax. Now, I better go catch up to her before she finds someone else to abuse in the halls." Jax smiled at her impishly as she dashed out of the room behind Willhelmina.

They had left Tranquility almost as soon as they had finished speaking with Gornin. Willhelmina had taken the helm of the Kestrel and pushed the ion drives to maximum, almost causing the engines to melt down before they reached the Tyconderoga. They hadn't been on the station more than ten minutes before they had ended up at Jax's computer station. Now, Riana moved up beside Willhelmina and slowed her pace to keep even with her. They walked silently for a few minutes before she finally cleared her throat to get her sister's attention, "So uh… why the uproar over this all of the sudden?"

Willhelmina stopped suddenly and turned to Riana seriously. "Ree if there is a problem with the security systems on Kalijor, it means that people will be able to hack the system. We've seen someone doing just that, but this is much bigger than a single hacker. There is a very real link between Kalijor's economy and our own. If people are hacking the system, it is tantamount to counterfeiting currency. We need to find the leaks and plug them, and Xavier has to know!"

Riana shrank back a bit as Willhelmina moved in on her as she spoke, obviously very serious about what was going on. "Alright, but he said there was no problem with the system. I asked him to run a more detailed diagnostic, he said it would take a few hours and he would let us know. Can you wait until then before we go see Xavier? That way we can present some more detailed information to him."

Willhelmina sighed heavily, her hands perched on her hips. "Alright. But only until we hear back from him."

"Right. So. Dinner?" Riana moved off toward the nearest lift, confident that Willhelmina would fall in step with her.

"Yeah, ok. Your place or mine?"

"How about the promenade? My treat."

"Sounds good. What's the occasion?"

"No occasion. Just in the mood for something I probably don't have in the pantry."

"Like what?"

"No idea. So… he was pretty good looking uh?" Riana jabbed the call button for the lift and turned to raise an eyebrow at Willhelmina.

"Who was?" Willhelmina looked back at her with a confused look.

"Jax, silly."

"Was he? I didn't notice." She looked away quickly, cheeks reddening.

"Really? Because I could have sworn you were checking him out. And I've never seen you unload on someone like that before. So either you like him, or you've gone completely insane."

"I think *you're* the one who has gone completely insane Ree." Willhelmina spoke to her feet and refused to continue. A moment of awkward silence and the lift door slid open, permitting them access.

As they were finishing up their meal under the stars, Riana's comm chimed. When she checked it, she saw a message from Jax saying he would like to see them, so they settled their bill and made their way down to the Network Operations Center. Jax was waiting for them with a slight smile on his face.

"You found something?" Riana asked as they came to a stop near his station.

"Yes, but nothing that would have been uncovered by any regular sort of checking." He said as he looked up at Willhelmina with an expectant look in his steel grey eyes.

Willhelmina was busy looking over his shoulder at his terminal display. "So what have you found then?"

He looked at her for another moment before turning his attention back to the display. "Alright, while the system was running deep diagnostics on the firewalls and security apps, I took the opportunity to start playing around with some theories of mine." He tapped his controls a few times then touched the display floating in mid-air, causing it to stop scrolling and zoom in on a series of port scan results for the firewalls. "As you can see the diagnostics came back negative, with the exception of the occurrence in Avian. We are still back-hacking and there hasn't been so much as a hiccup in the system from inside or out."

Willhelmina stared at the results, dragging the information up and down the display with her finger. "Are you sure about this? How many times did you check it?"

"The standard deep diagnostic cycle includes four iterations of the scan for redundancy and parity, but that's not the point. The interesting stuff happened when I started looking here." At that, he tapped his controls a few more times and the display changed to show another series of figures that looked to be even more complex than the firewall information by a good margin.

"What is that?" Willhelmina asked with no small degree of skepticism.

"That." Jax replied with a tone of pride in his voice. "Is an analysis of the station's sub-space activity."

"Sub-space?" Riana asked, her ears perking up in interest.

"Sub-space is an infinite realm that is contained within a finite border, at least mathematically. It's difficult for most people to conceptualize, but the short version is that basically there is a realm of space that is infinite, yet contained within our own space. The reason Kalijor works as well as it does is because we use sub-space as our transport medium. Basically, we can move signals across whole parsecs of space almost instantaneously simply by moving them through sub-space."

"Ok, so if sub-space is infinite then why does the signal get anywhere any faster?" She raised an eyebrow at him.

"Because even though it is an infinite space, it is still measured on a different scale. Basically every point in sub-space corresponds with a point in real-space. We broadcast the Kalijor signal into sub-space and because of the relative difference in scale, we basically fill the entire space at once, thereby hitting every point in sub-space at nearly the same time. The far end simply needs to tap into the same sub-space and pick up the signal."

"And then they can return their own broadcasts the same way. And as long as everyone uses the same sub-space then everyone communicates instantaneously." Riana finished with a widening smile.

Jax grinned at her a moment before carrying on. "Exactly. Now, here is a visual representation of our normal sub-space activity, averaged over the previous twenty years."

He pressed a few controls and the display changed to show a graph with several jagged lines moving across it in a fairly tame progression from left to right.

"Ok…" Willhelmina was getting testy with the whole situation.

"And here." He said as he pressed another control and the graph changed to display a severely jagged line wandering across a similar graph. This one bore peaks and valleys easily ten times the size of the previous graph. "Here is what it looks like over the last four years or so."

Riana and Willhelmina looked at the graphs for a moment, inspecting the steady increase in activity with interest.

"But this increase in transmission density doesn't seem to have any point of origin." Riana finally pointed out, looking at a secondary display for correlation.

"Exactly!" Jax replied.

"What do you mean?" Willhelmina asked, looking over at the other display.

"See here?" Riana pointed at the figures. "This is the Tyconderoga's activity, and here are the other stations and colonies, all the way out to Barnard's Star. But none of them are showing any increase in activity at all over the last four years." She poked at the holographic display a few times to pan it around to the various figures.

"So what the hell is going on in there?" Willhelmina wondered aloud.

"That is a very good question." Jax replied with a shrug. "But whatever it is, it isn't coming through the firewalls, or even through our systems at all. The only thing we can say for sure is it seems to tie in with a certain event that happened about four years ago, and that the increased traffic occupies the same sub-space domain as our normal Kalijor operations."

"So." Willhelmina began as she lunged at Riana with a quick front punch and followed it up with a front kick and a reverse punch. "We know that all of these programs from Kalijor are connecting to miscellaneous people in the real world."

"Right." Riana agreed as she stepped out of the path of Willhelmina's combination and stuck her own foot out, causing Willhelmina to trip and stumble for a moment before catching her balance.

"And we know that the firewalls and other security measures are still secure, save for the one breech we ran into and took care of." She leapt at Riana with a jump kick.

"Correct." Riana agreed as she grabbed Willhelmina's leg and twisted her around mid-flight, forcing her face first into the ground.

Willhelmina extended her arms and caught herself before her face hit the mat, forcing her legs over into a hand spring and landing on her feet again. As she turned to face Riana, she threw her leg out into an arcing round kick aiming for her friend's head. "And we know that there is an increase in activity, to the tune of ten-fold more than normal, in the same sub-space domain that Kalijor uses for its backbone."

"Yes." Riana said as she stepped inside Willhelmina's stance and pushed hard on her hips before the kick was even fully extended.

Willhelmina rolled off of Riana's hands, coming to her feet again and driving forward with a series of kicks and punches. "But there is no evidence at all that the increase in activity is in any way related to Kalijor since it doesn't actually seem to be coming from anywhere at all."

"Sounds about right." Riana replied calmly as she batted away Willhelmina's attacks, catching her arm on the last punch. She twisted it around behind Willhelmina's back, locking the joints of her wrist and elbow up and resting a hand on her other elbow.

Willhelmina went limp suddenly, rolling forward out of Riana's arm lock and throwing her foot up toward Riana's face. "So the only thing we have to go on is the time frame. What happened around four years ago that could have set all of this in motion?"

Willhelmina felt the unexpected sensation of her foot hitting something solid then and was simply too stunned by it to pull her punch any at all. The impact was followed shortly by the sound of Riana hitting the ground solidly. The whole gym fell silent. Willhelmina stood up slowly and looked down at the floor where Riana lay, staring at the ceiling and not moving a muscle.

"Ree? Are you OK?" She crouched down next to Riana's prone form and touched her shoulder gently.

Riana's mouth slowly broke into a slight smile, which widened into a wide grin. Her eyes shifted and focused on Willhelmina's concerned face, but still she said nothing.

Willhelmina smiled back at Riana, although she still had no idea why they were smiling. Tentatively she squeezed Riana's shoulder again. "Ree?"

"Kat. I remember what she said." Riana said calmly.

"What who said Ree? Are you alright?"

"Oh yes. I'm alright. Mom, Kat. I remember what mom said in that warehouse. She told me to remember my vision. Not remember my visions."

"Remember your…" She looked down at her friend doubtfully. "Ree, what's going on?"

"It's OK Kat. I figured it out. My vision was never gone. I blinded myself because I felt blinded by events. I felt lost and alone and my own feelings got the better of me."

Willhelmina offered Riana a sour look and perched herself on the balls of her feet, crouching over her sister with her elbows on her knees. "And this has what to do with the topic of conversation? Not that I am in any way trying to lessen the value of your realization or anything…"

"You don't get it Kat. It's me. It always was…"

"What's you? Are you sure I didn't just jar your titanium skull or something?"

"Think about the time frame Kat. What happened in Kalijor four years ago? What turned the entire system on end four years ago?"

Willhelmina straightened her back up a bit and looked up at the view ports in the ceiling as she thought. Finally, it hit her and she dropped to a sitting position on the mat. "Oh my god."

"Now you know why you got that kick in." Riana said, her grin still splitting her face from ear to ear.

"Ok so you are the common denominator. That still doesn't explain what is going on in sub-space Ree. And why is all of this making you so happy?"

"Because Kat. I remembered my vision, and the stars have never looked better than they do right now."

Suddenly Willhelmina was on her knees, perched over her friend again, eyes glowing happily. "Ree! Do you mean it? You can see again?"

"Oh yeah." Riana's smile widened even further if such a thing was possible. "I can see. And more than just the stars."

"What does that mean Ree? What the hell are you talking about?"

"Don't you get it Kat? The power surge that caused me to become sentient. The one that tore through your compartment and electrocuted you at the same time. Its effects were more far-reaching than anyone has even thought possible. It didn't affect only me."

"What are you saying Ree? You think something else was changed by that surge?"

Suddenly Riana sat up and looked Willhelmina right in her sparkling green eyes. "I am saying that it wasn't just me that was changed. It was everything."

"Everything?"

"Everything Kat. All of Kalijor was changed by that event. It wasn't just me that came alive, it was the whole damn thing."

"What? What whole thing?" Willhelmina looked more confused than ever, and Riana just smiled wider, happy to be seeing her face in full, colored detail again.

"All of it Kat. All of Kalijor and everything in it was changed. And it's all alive. Just like me."

www.ingramcontent.com/pod-product-compliance
Lightning Source LLC
Chambersburg PA
CBHW030349030726
47497CB00002B/252